## "WHAT ARE OUR ORDERS, COMMANDANT?"

"It's your discretion, Fraser," Commandant Isayev replied. "If you think you can hold out until we can get you relief, do so . . . But I can't tell you how long that will be. Otherwise . . . you know the score better than I do, son."

"Yes, sir," Fraser swallowed. "I understand."

"Just remember that you're in the Legion, Fraser."

"Are you telling me to hold on here to the last man, Commandant?"

Isayev coughed. "What you do with those men is your decision, Fraser. Just make sure whatever they do brings credit to the Legion. If you stand, then stand with courage. If you die, do it with honor."

"We'll do our best, Commandant," Fraser said slowly.

"I know you will, Fraser. Lancelot out."

Fraser's hand was shaking as he replaced the handset. He and his troops had been abandoned!

# THE FIFTH FOREIGN LEGION #1:
## *March or Die*

---

**Andrew and William H. Keith, Jr.**

---

A ROC BOOK

ROC
Published by the Penguin Group
Penguin Books USA Inc., 375 Hudson Street,
New York, New York 10014, U.S.A.
Penguin Books Ltd, 27 Wrights Lane,
London W8 5TZ, England
Penguin Books Australia Ltd, Ringwood,
Victoria, Australia
Penguin Books Canada Ltd, 10 Alcorn Avenue,
Toronto, Ontario, Canada M4V 3B2
Penguin Books (N.Z.) Ltd, 182-190 Wairau Road,
Auckland 10, New Zealand

Penguin Books Ltd, Registered Offices:
Harmondsworth, Middlesex, England

First published by Roc,
an imprint of New American Library,
a division of Penguin Books USA Inc.

First Printing, January, 1992
    10  9  8  7  6  5  4  3  2  1

Roc is a trademark of New American Library,
a division of Penguin Books USA Inc.

Printed in the United States of America

To the soldiers of the
Foreign Legion—past,
present, and future.

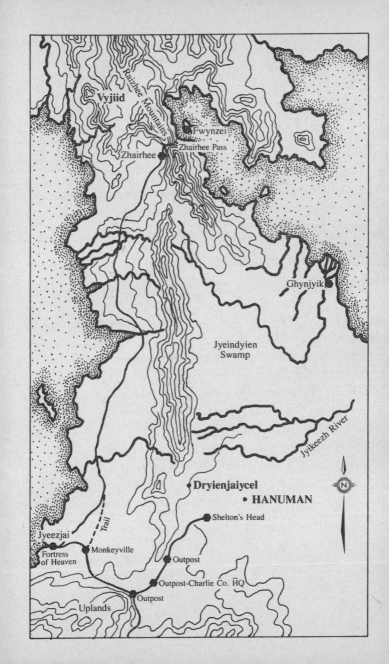

# Prologue

[Morrison's Star]: Distance from Sol 112 light years . . . Spectral class F7V; radius 1.252 Sol; mass 1.196 Sol; luminosity 2.548 Sol. Stellar Effective Temperature 6420°K . . . Eight planets, one planetoid belt. The sole habitable world is the fourth planet, known as Hanuman . . .

[IV Hanuman]: Orbital radius 1.25 AUs; eccentricity .0102; period 1.28 solar years (466.76 std. days) . . . No natural satellites . . .

Planetary mass 0.8 Terra; density 1.15 Terra (6.33 g/cc); surface gravity 1.02 G. Radius 5658.14 kilometers; circumference 35,551.1 kilometers . . . Total surface area 402,306,340 square kilometers . . .

Hydrographic percentage 87% . . . Atmospheric pressure 1.10 atm; composition oxygen/nitrogen. Oxygen content 24% . . .

Planetary axial tilt 9°19′42.8″. Rotation period 33 hours, 48 minutes, 7.8 seconds . . .

[Planetography]: Hanuman is somewhat less active geologically than Terra . . . The planetary terrain, however, is fairly rugged. Just over half the land surface is hill or mountain, with broad, level tracts of ground—coastal or upland plains—comprising the rest of the land area. There is one major continent dominating the northern hemisphere, plus five smaller continents and scattered islands . . . Tidal effects are minimal . . .

Equatorial temperatures average near 55°C, while polar temperatures rarely drop below freezing. Warm ocean currents keep coastal areas pleasant even above the Arctic Circle. Humans can live in regions north or south of the 55° latitude lines (particularly in the cooler uplands) . . . High mountain elevations are dangerous due to the high ultraviolet output of Morrison's Star . . .

Temperature and humidity produce wide jungles in the equatorial regions, extending as far as the 60° latitude lines. Beyond these the climate moderates, with temperate forests, upland steppes, deserts . . .

[Biology]: Intelligent life first arose in the mid-latitude jungles, evolving originally from brachiating omnivore/gatherer stock in a niche closely paralleling Terrestrial mangrove swamps . . . Intelligence arose as a defense mechanism to counter a variety of predators . . . The sophonts of Hanuman (they call themselves *kyendyp* in the language of the primary human-contacted nations) are bilaterally symmetrical, upright bipeds, basically humanoid in gross appearance but differing significantly in detail. They are homeothermic, with leathery olive-green skin . . . The average local stands roughly 1.25 meters in height. They are hairless but possess a ruff of short, quill-like spines around the neck. These normally lie flat against the skin but may stiffen in response to certain emotional stimuli (fear, anger, etc.). The movement of the ruff can be used as a gauge to their reactions . . .

The *kyendyp* are full hermaphrodites, simultaneously possessing fully developed male and female sexual organs. Either partner in a sexual union can become pregnant, and any individual can bear and rear young. Children are born live and drink an analogue to milk secreted by the parent. Kyendyp languages have no terms or cases involving gender; the word adopted by humans to replace "he" or "she" is "ky" . . .

[Civilization]: The *kyendyp* of the mid-latitude jungles never advanced out of the Stone Age. Those who left the jungles for the cooler uplands of the northern latitudes, however, found that their simple hunter-gatherer life-style was inappropriate . . .

At the time of the Semti Conclave's surrender to the Terran Commonwealth a hundred years ago, the civilized *kyendyp* were still roughly equivalent to nineteenth-century Europe in technological achievement, though once the Semti influence was gone their development accelerated dramatically . . . There are still large numbers of Stone-Age savages in the jungles, however, who are often exploited by more civilized groups as cheap labor . . .

[Commonwealth Contact]: The first Terran settlement

was at Fwynzei, an island leased to the Terrans by Vyu-jiid, which remains the largest and most civilized of all *kyendyp* nations . . . Penetration of Vyujiid was achieved with little difficulty, thanks to the relatively enlightened views of the local leaders . . . The medicinal value of zyglyn vines spurred commercial development, strongly sponsored by StelPhar Industries, which uses processed zyglyn from Hanuman as a base for a line of full-spectrum antivirals . . .

*Excerpted from Leclerc's Guide to the Commonwealth*
*Volume V: The Devereaux/Neusachsen Region*
*34th Edition, published 2848* A.D.

# Chapter 1

We shall all know how to perish,
Following tradition.

from *"Le Boudin"*
Marching Song of the French Foreign Legion

"I can't really explain it." Captain Armand LaSalle made a gesture to encompass the banquet hall. "I just don't think we should trust these monkeys."

Howard Rayburn shrugged. "One hannie's pretty much like another," he said. His languid tone seemed out of character for a captain of the Fifth Foreign Legion. It reminded LaSalle of the pampered young officers of the regular Terran Army. "Why should this bunch be any different?"

LaSalle frowned. "That's just it. This bunch *is* different. When the Semti pulled out a hundred years ago, these little bastards were still primitives. Up to now we've been dealing with civilized hannies, but we can't just assume the same rules apply here."

*"Iy-jai wei sykai?"* A hannie—one of the short, olive-skinned humanoid sophonts native to Hanuman—held a tray before the two Legion officers. "What will you drink, masters?"

*"Jyuniy."* LaSalle crossed his arms in the local gesture of negation to emphasize the refusal.

"Damn monkey gibberish," Rayburn said irritably. Touching a stud on his wristpiece computer, he said "Gimme wine, junior." The computer echoed his words in the kyendyp tongue of the locals. *"J'iyyi diiegyi kytujjai."*

The ruff of quills around the hannie's neck stiffened. LaSalle wasn't sure if they were expressing fear or anger. Adchip orientation had left him with a good working knowledge of the languages and customs of the human-contacted regions of Hanuman, but translating the subtle nuances of a local's ruff movements was something few humans ever mastered. The alien might have been in awe of the human-sounding voice speaking from Rayburn's 'piece, or angry at the man's arrogance and disdain. Terran officers who let their computers translate for them instead of taking the trouble to learn local dialects or mores were all too common in the Commonwealth, though.

As Rayburn accepted a slender glass filled with the vile yellowish liquid that passed for wine on Hanuman and sipped it gingerly, LaSalle made a face, looking away. *Diiegyi* contained enough alcohol to satisfy any hard-drinking legionnaire, but its sour flavor was a taste LaSalle didn't like to think about.

The banquet hall was the largest reception room in the sprawling palace the locals called the Fortress of Heaven, the ceremonial capital of the realm of Dryienjaiyeel and the seat of power of the hereditary monarch, the *yzyeel* Jiraiy XII. Most of the throng of guests were members of the nobility of Dryienjaiyeel, the court, military leadership, and clergy of the realm. A few lighter-skinned natives moved among them with an air of confident superiority, merchants and diplomats visiting Dryienjaiyeel from Vyujiid, its more civilized neighbor to the north. The handful of humans from the Commonwealth mission to Dryienjaiyeel stood out from the crowd like trees towering over the barren steppes of LaSalle's homeworld, Saint Pierre.

Hairless, with dry, wrinkled, leathery skin, the natives didn't look that much like Terran monkeys, but there were just enough similarities to make the epithet appropriate. The hannies were short and dark, with long arms and barrel chests, wearing colorful but scanty garb. It was hard to think of them as an industrialized civilization here in the barbaric splendor of their ancient royal city. Men like Rayburn came by their bigotry naturally. *We conquered the Semti; we made the Ubrenfars back down. The Terran Commonwealth stands head and shoulders over the rest . . .*

That kind of arrogance had killed a lot of good soldiers.

"Captain Rayburn?" The voice came from behind, speaking Terranglic with a soft, lilting accent. "Captain LaSalle?"

LaSalle turned to meet the new arrival, a lieutenant dressed like the other officers in the formal full-dress uniform of the Fifth Foreign Legion. The khaki jacket and trousers, blue cummerbund, archaic red and green epaulets, and black kepi were part of a tradition that stretched back over the centuries. Since the days before Mankind had left Mother Terra, legionnaires in similar garb had kept the peace in far-flung colonies. Five different legions serving different masters, different ends . . . but always the same tradition of service, honor, and glory.

"What is it, Chiang?" Rayburn was asking.

"Sir, Mr. Leighton wanted me to remind you that it is almost time for the reception ceremony." Chiang blinked owlishly behind thick glasses. Rayburn's Executive Officer didn't look much like a soldier. He was typical of the officers Rayburn preferred for his company: Terran-born, gentlemanly, well-educated. For the officers, at least, Charlie Company was like a miniature Regular Army unit, a far cry from the typical mixed bag of the Legion. Whatever Rayburn, Chiang, and their platoon leaders might have done to warrant assignment to the frontiers, they seemed determined to maintain their own standards regardless of their surroundings.

LaSalle smiled faintly. He wondered if Charlie Company's fastidious officers liked outpost duty here in Dryienjaiyeel, in Hanuman's mid-latitude jungles where temperatures rarely dropped below 30°C and humidity, rain, and mud were worse enemies than any native.

"I guess we'd better go line up so the head monkey can play king," Rayburn said. He set his glass carelessly on a passing waiter's platter and straightened his tie. "Then maybe we can get out of this goddamned hothouse and back into cli-control. Coming, LaSalle?" Though Rayburn was nominally the junior captain, he managed to sound like an aristocrat ordering a servant.

That was inevitable any time you mixed Terran-born officers with men like LaSalle, colonials whose fathers and grandfathers had won their Citizenship the hard way, earning it in service to the Commonwealth. Anyone born on Terra or one of the other Member-worlds was a Citizen automatically, part of a long line of Citizens, and was apt to regard himself as superior to any mere colonial. LaSalle had suffered under the system since the first day he'd entered the army.

The two officers pushed their way through the throng, past native courtiers in elaborate ceremonial headdresses, minor functionaries whose clipped neck ruffs were tokens of their complete identification with their *yzyeel*, and soldiers whose trappings were an odd cross between the traditional and the starkly functional. LaSalle's eyes narrowed as he studied one such, a senior NCO in the Dryien army according to the facial dye that marked unit and rank around the soldier's muzzle. The native's complex harness and ornate daggers were traditional enough, but the short assault rifle and the pistol holster both showed signs of long, hard service. That was unusual; Dryienjaiyeel court troops were hardly ever employed in the field . . .

The NCO had the look of a trained soldier, too. LaSalle had seen enough nonhuman troops in his service with the Legion to recognize the universals that transcended species lines. Ky was a veteran, no mere ornamental court guard. Transferred for meritorious service in the *yzyeel's* ongoing war with the savages of the southern jungles? Maybe. But the sight brought back LaSalle's concern in full force.

"Ah, LaSalle, Rayburn. 'Bout time." Geoffrey T. Leighton, Commonwealth Envoy to the *yzyeel* of Dryienjaiyeel, was a big man with a booming, jovial voice. "It wouldn't do for the senior garrison officers to be out of place when The Excellent makes kys appearance, y'know."

"Yes, sir," LaSalle responded, but Leighton didn't seem to notice the answer. The diplomat's eyes had taken on a glassy, far-away look.

*Listening to his implant,* LaSalle thought with a twinge of jealousy. Back on Terra, tiny computer implants were all the rage among aristocrats and government functionaries. They filled the same role as LaSalle's wristpiece, but they were lodged directly in the user's brain. Implants gave their owners what amounted to instant access to any computer records or programs, total recall, automatic translation, near-telepathic communication with others wearing implant chips—a full range of functions without the bother of operating a primitive wristpiece.

"Ah, very good. Very good indeed." Leighton smiled as his eyes focused again on the two officers. "We've just received word from the harbor, gentlemen. Transport just set down in the bay with StelPhar's first consignment of equipment and technicians aboard. They'll hold meetings here before going out to the Enclave."

StelPhar Industries, Terra's largest importer of exotic pharmaceuticals, was the main reason for the Colonial Administration's interest in Dryienjaiyeel. For over thirty years the Commonwealth base at Fwynzei had been sufficient as Hanuman's main port and administrative center, handling a steady traffic in the planet's one valuable export commodity, the zyglyn vine. Processed zyglyn was a useful base for StelPhar's line of full-spectrum antiviral agents and commanded a high price Earthside. But zyglyn grew only in the hot, inhospitable mid-latitude jungles of Hanuman, and for just under a century StelPhar had been forced to depend on native traders to bring the vines from Dryienjaiyeel to Fwynzei.

Now, though, Leighton's patient months of negotiation with the *yzyeel* had yielded a new off-world enclave on Hanuman where Terran colonists would soon be settling to establish direct Commonwealth control over the harvest and shipment of zyglyn vines in much larger quantities than the native traders could hope to supply.

"So soon, sir?" LaSalle asked. "I thought we'd have at least another month before civilians settled in Monkeyville."

Leighton pursed his lips in disapproval. "The Enclave, Captain LaSalle, or Outpost D-2," he said irritably. "How many times do I have to tell you not to use that pejorative name in dealing with the kyen?"

"Sorry, sir," LaSalle answered. Everyone in the two companies of legionnaires employed in constructing and garrisoning the new Terran enclave referred to the complex as "Monkeyville," and to the Legion fort protecting it as "Fort Monkey." The diplomats, of course, were never happy at any hint of bigotry toward the natives and tended to become disdainful at the use of epithets like "hannie" or "monkey," or even the generic "loke" or "ale" in referring to the nonhuman inhabitants of Hanuman.

"As far as the schedule goes," Leighton continued as if LaSalle hadn't spoken, "I believe you reported last week that the Enclave is ready, didn't you?"

"The fort, the landing field, and the settlement buildings are, yes, sir," LaSalle replied. "But we've got more work to do on the inland roads, and I'm still not happy with the outer defenses."

"That work can continue after the StelPhar people settle in," Leighton told him. "After all, your legionnaires will need to find things to keep them employed while they maintain the garrison." Like most of his ilk, Leighton managed to convey massive disapproval in that simple word "legionnaires." The Colonial Administration needed the Legion to do the dirty jobs no one else would do, but that didn't mean they accepted the unit of misfits . . .

LaSalle pulled his chin thoughtfully. "Mr. Leighton, I don't think it's a good idea to bring in civilians this early," he said at last. All his misgivings seemed to surface at once. "We've had reports of Dryien troop movements into the area around Mon . . . the Enclave for over a week now. Not to mention the reports we've been getting of military maneuvers on the northern frontier. And our native contacts have been hinting at some kind of trouble with the government. Not the *yzyeel*, but lower levels. Bureaucrats and military officials, those sorts."

"Unsubstantiated rumors," Leighton huffed.

"Maybe so, sir. But if they're not . . ." LaSalle paused. "A lot of the locals out in the jungles are afraid of us. They think Terrans are some kind of demon come to rape the planet after casting out the Gods. I've even picked up stuff like that from the civilized ones here on the coast. Two companies aren't enough to garrison the Enclave against a heavy attack. More than a quarter of my men are brand-new recruits, and my Exec's just out of a Regular Army intel unit, with no combat experience." He glanced at Rayburn. "I'm sure Charlie

Company's got the same sort of problems. If there's trouble, my men might not be able to protect civilians."

Leighton turned to Rayburn. "Do you agree with Captain LaSalle on this?"

The other captain grinned. "Hell, no, sir. Ain't no loke—er, native, sir—able to beat the Legion."

LaSalle interrupted. "All I'm asking for is more time, Mr. Leighton. Time to get the recruits shaped up and my Exec broke in . . . time to firm up the outer perimeter of the Enclave. And time to find out if there's anything behind those rumors."

The envoy shook his head. "Nonsense. Captain. I can assure you that the *yzyeel's* government is entirely behind us. I'm certainly not going to put off StelPhar just because your legionnaires aren't spit-and-polish soldiers. If I waited for that, the Enclave would never be ready, y'know." He smiled, but there was steel in his eye.

*Maybe the* yzyeel *is behind us,* LaSalle thought. *Ky's happy as long as the offworlders keep sending pretty new toys to play with. But what about the plantation owners and merchants StelPhar's putting out of business? And what about the bureaucrats who won't be getting the tax revenues from the zyglyn trade any more?*

"If you're concerned about getting the construction work for your perimeter finished, I suggest you see Lieutenant Winters when you get back," Leighton went on. "Schedule your work through her office. Otherwise, I expect you to deal with your problems yourself, Captain." The diplomat turned away, cutting off further discussion.

LaSalle seethed inwardly. As usual, it looked like the Legion was getting the short end of the stick. *That's the way it always is,* he thought bitterly.

Around the banquet hall Terrans and hannies were jostling for position for the entrance of the *yzyeel.* LaSalle watched the courtiers as they argued over precedence. The Terran diplomats remained aloof; they *knew* they were superior to the natives. They moved among the native servants and guards as if the locals didn't exist.

There were quite a few guards in the hall—more than there had been a few minutes ago. Or was it just his imagination finding danger where none existed?

Movement near The Excellent's dais caught LaSalle's eye. A hannie in a particularly ornate harness was just entering the room, not the *yzyeel* but a high-ranking officer. LaSalle recognized ky: Zyzytig, the Dryien general whose office roughly corresponded to chief of staff. The general was in deep conversation with a taller figure swathed in a dark cloak. That angular, gaunt shape filled LaSalle with an instinctive loathing. *Semti! What's one of those ghouls doing here?*

A hundred years ago, the Semti had owned this part of space, before their defeat at the hands of the fledgling Terran Commonwealth and the destruction of their capital. Now the Commonwealth was expanding into the old Semti Conclave while the surviving Semti, their central government gone, submitted meekly to the conquerors. They were superb governors and xenopyschologists, useful mandarins in the Terran administration of the newly acquired territories, apparently eager to continue their work under their new masters without a thought for the war.

But a lot of people found it hard to trust them, LaSalle included. Maybe it was their scavenger ancestry, the foul breath and the hairless vulture skulls. Or perhaps it was their ancient culture and unfathomable philosophy, which seemed to mock everything human under a mask of helpful service. Not *all* the Semti were friendly; stories of plots against the Commonwealth fomented by discontented Semti schemers surfaced time and again. They were too useful to dispense with, too dangerous to trust . . .

And one of them was here, in the court of The Excellent. When the Semti ruled Hanuman, they had been worshipped as gods in Dryienjaiyeel, while the Terrans who replaced them were cast as devils who had overthrown the natural order. A Semti agent could do a lot of mischief playing on old superstitions . . .

"Leighton," LaSalle began. "What's a—"

"Shh! The Excellent is coming." Leighton's voice was a reproving hiss.

Wide doors behind the dais swung slowly open to ad-

mit The Excellent, the *yzyeel* of Dryienjaiyeel, Brother
of Heaven, Lord of the Eternal Mists, Champion of the
Gods. Not quite a king, not quite a pope, the *yzyeel*'s
power was little short of absolute, but kys authority in
the ordinary government was almost nonexistent.

Barely a meter tall, with a soft, innocent face, ky would
not reach the age of maturity for another four standard
years, but as *yzyeel* the young ruler commanded near-
total obedience throughout Dryienjaiyeel. There had been
other claimants, of course, when kys parent had died two
years ago, and LaSalle had heard mutterings among the
common hannies that the selection of Jiraiy XII had been
a mistake, that the child-*yzyeel* was too enamored of the
offworlders, too easily manipulated, tainted with the
curse of the old gods . . .

The *yzyeel* paused at the front of the dais and Leighton, flanked by LaSalle and Rayburn, stepped forward to
honor the young ruler. Each bowed in turn, rendering
the ceremonial greeting: fingers clasped, thumbs crossed,
palms outward, touching forehead, mouth, and throat. It
was all correct, proper, but LaSalle thought he heard a
stir in the crowd. Perhaps they resented the fact that the
Terran envoy and his military leaders now took precedence over their native counterparts. Or was it something
else, some ceremony or gesture Terran chip-training had
left out?

A whipcrack sound filled the hall, a thunder LaSalle
recognized instantly. *Gunshot!* Dark blood bubbled from
the *yzyeel's* throat, oozing through kys ruff. The ruler
swayed, staggered, fell. Gunfire erupted throughout the
room.

LaSalle threw himself sideways, seeking the cover of
a pillar. Leighton and Rayburn went down together as
one of the heavy native assault guns sprayed the foot of
the dais with full-auto fire. Another Terran, an economic
attaché on Leighton's staff, fell to a savage hannie bayonet thrust. Someone was screaming. He wasn't sure if
it was a Terran voice, or a native.

Clawing at the holster of his 10mm rocket pistol,
LaSalle peered around the pillar at the chaos of the
hall. Two hannie guards burst through a door a few
meters to his left and opened fire at a trio of native

soldiers running toward them, only to fall as autofire hammered from across the room. Two more Terrans fell beyond them, Lieutenant Chiang and Rowlands, the mission's linguistics expert. Near the rear of the hall a man in a Terran Army lieutenant's uniform urged one of the diplomats toward another door. A hannie raised kys gun . . .

LaSalle squeezed off a round, aiming at the soldier. The tiny 10mm rocket projectile left the barrel with a soft *swoosh* that grew louder as it gathered speed. His target went down in a bloody heap, and the two Terrans dived for safety. The lieutenant fired twice with a laser pistol, the shots making a crackle in the air that left a tang of ozone, but no visible flash. Behind the officer, the diplomat crouched low, eyes darting wildly from side to side.

The captain tried to cover the two, but answering fire from a dozen native rifles *pinged* off the pillar and the wall behind LaSalle. *If I had combat battledress I might have a chance,* he thought grimly. His dress uniform wasn't intended to stop bullets, even the primitive rounds they used on Hanuman.

He snapped off four quick shots and rolled to his left. If he could just reach the other two survivors, they might make it out together.

A piledriver blow to his chest staggered him, spinning him around. He coughed and gasped, feeling pain lance through his body. Then a second bullet hit him, and a third. His hand went numb and he dropped the rocket pistol with a clatter. LaSalle felt himself spinning, falling, hitting the unyielding tile floor. He tried to rise, but another shot slammed into his back.

LaSalle raised his head from the round, squinting through the red haze of pain. Across the room the Terran lieutenant fired again, then spun backwards as autofire slammed into his chest. Then the civilian was kneeling over the fallen officer, scooping up the laser pistol and firing wildly.

Struggling to rise again, LaSalle felt his strength ebbing fast. A shadow fell across him. He rolled onto his back and found himself looking up at the stooped, gaunt, black-robed form of the Semti. The alien raised one arm slowly, and the tiny weapon concealed in his hand flared.

Agony seared deep in LaSalle's chest. Blackness closed around him, and he felt his life slipping away.

His last thought was of his home . . . the Legion.

# Chapter 2

You legionnaires are soldiers in order to die,
and I am sending you where you can die.
—General François de Negrier
French Foreign Legion, 1883

"Keep firing, dammit! Maintain your fire!" Lieutenant Colin Fraser staggered and swore silently as a bullet slammed into the plasteel chest plate of his battledress. He dropped to one knee behind an improvised barricade. "Trent! Where the hell is Dmowski with the heavy weapons?"

Gunnery Sergeant John Trent fired a burst from his FE-FEK kinetic energy assault rifle before answering. "He's on the way, L-T." He sounded strangely calm and unemotional, as if oblivious to the firefight raging around them. "Five more minutes." Trent raised his voice abruptly but lost none of his detached, professional manner. "Come on, Krueger, get with it! You've got grenades—use 'em!"

Fraser flipped down the light intensifier display on his helmet. Chaos reigned within Fort Monkey. Panic gripped him with icy fingers, but Fraser forced himself to follow Sergeant Trent's example and remain outwardly calm, in control. *The men are looking to you,* a stubborn inner voice reminded him. *You're in charge until Captain LaSalle gets back.*

If LaSalle was coming back. In the ten minutes since the first attack by Dryien troops, every effort to raise LaSalle and the diplomatic mission in the Fortress of Heaven had been answered by crackling static. And even if the captain was all right now, how was he supposed to reach Monkeyville in an unarmored staff car when what looked like half the *yzyeel's* army was trying to overrun the Legion garrison?

A native machine gun hammered from the top of the north wall, its muzzle flashes showing on LI as a strobing beacon in the gloom. Legionnaire Krueger raised his FEK and triggered a three-round burst of 1cm rocket grenades. They arrowed toward the target with a hiss, impacting in a neat pattern just below the stuttering MG. With a scream, the hannie soldier spun backwards over the parapet and out of sight, kys weapon tumbling to the ground inside the compound.

Two more bullets flattened themselves against Fraser's battledress in quick succession, one against his chest plate, the other on the duraweave material covering his left arm. The second one stung, and Fraser's heart beat faster.

The hannies were primitive by Legion standards. Their technology was roughly equivalent to mid-twentieth century Terrestrial standards, with weapons that would not have been out of place in either of the first two World Wars. Their equipment was eight centuries out of date even measured against the cast-offs that made up the bulk of Legion gear. It would take a lucky hit for conventional munitions to penetrate issue battledress, with or without plasteel armor plates augmenting the protection of the tough fatigue uniform. But sooner or later one of the hannies occupying the northeast tower was going to score that lucky hit—if not on Fraser, then on one of his men.

Even if the hannies were primitive, they outnumbered Bravo Company by at least ten to one. The legionnaires just couldn't afford to take casualties . . . *any* casualties.

"Sergeant!" Fraser tried without much success to make his orders sharp and crisp. "I want that tower cleared *now.* Those snipers are getting too good a view."

"On it, L-T," Trent responded. He sprinted down the defensive line in a half-crouch, bawling orders as he ran. "Recon lances! Time to earn your pay, you lazy buggers!"

Fraser's FEK whined on full auto, sending a stream of needle-thin slivers hurtling from the muzzle at over 10,000 meters per second with scarcely any recoil. He swung the rifle in a smooth arc, laying down fire across the ragged line of hannies at the foot of the north wall.

This fight wasn't so much a battle as a slaughter, but there were a lot more native soldiers out there to replace the ones who fell.

The first attackers had burst in through the north gate, apparently admitted by one of the company's hannie servants or auxiliaries without raising an alarm. If Sergeant Trent had not been making the rounds of the barracks area when the first shots were fired . . . Fraser didn't want to think about that. Alerted, with high-tech weaponry and uniforms virtually impervious to small arms, the legionnaires could beat the monkeys easily.

But the natives had the advantage of numbers . . . and they were on their home turf, with supplies and reinforcements close at hand. The legionnaires couldn't even raise their captain. Or Charlie Company, scattered in outposts deeper in the Dryien jungles to the west. He glanced at his command/control/communications technician. *If only she would get through to someone . . .*

As if in answer to Frazer's unvoiced thoughts, the C³ operator looked up from her field communications pack and grinned at Fraser. "I've got something, Lieutenant!"

"What is it, Garcia?" Fraser ducked down behind the barricade. Around them the other legionnaires kept firing.

"A transport lighter . . . *Ganymede.*" Angela Garcia made a quick adjustment to the console and handed Fraser a patch cord. "They're in the capital harbor."

He plugged the cord into a terminal on the side of his helmet, switched on his commlink, and spoke aloud. His throat mike picked up his words. *"Ganymede,* this is Alice One. Do you copy? Over."

"Alice One, *Ganymede.* Reading you five by five. Hold for Captain Garrett."

Static crackled on the line before a new voice cut in. "Alice One? What's your situation?"

Fraser winced as machine-gun fire rattled off the barricade. *"Ganymede,* we're under attack by an unknown number of native regulars. Nothing but infantry so far, no armor, air support, or heavy arty. At least not yet. We're holding our own, but . . ." He trailed off.

"Roger that, Alice One," Garrett responded. "We've had trouble here, too. Native troops attacked our shore party about half an hour after we set down. We've also had reports from the Fortress of Heaven of a massacre of Terrans at the diplomatic reception. Those are unconfirmed, repeat, unconfirmed.''

Fraser bit off a curse. A massacre . . .

If it was true, then Captain LaSalle wouldn't be coming back. Fraser recoiled from the thought. For a long moment everything—the Legion, the battle, the bullets slamming into the barricade in front of him—all seemed remote. He fought to get his whirling feelings back under control.

''Acknowledged, *Ganymede,*'' he said at last. ''Have you had any orders from HQ?''

Garrett sounded grim. ''They're ordering an evac, Alice One. We're checking for Terrans in town now. Then we're coming to pull you people out.''

''Sounds good to me, *Ganymede,*'' Fraser said. ''You have a timetable on that yet?''

''We've got a couple of hundred civilians to pull out here, Lieutenant,'' Garrett replied. ''I'd say we'll be stuck here 'til morning, unless the lokes bring in artillery our hull can't handle. We'll keep you apprised.'' There was a pause, *''Ganymede,* out.''

Evacuation. The word echoed in his mind.

Unless they drove back the hannie attack, though, an evac was going to be tough to manage. And the heavy weapons and the Legion's fire support vehicles still hadn't come up. *Damn it! Where the hell are they?*

Colin Fraser braced his FEK on the barricade and opened fire again. Right now, the legionnaires needed every rifle they could muster if they were going to hold off the hannie attack . . .

''Keep down, Honored,'' the native hissed. ''Down!''

Lieutenant Kelly Ann Winters, Commonwealth Space Navy, nodded and hunkered lower behind the rocks, her fingers tightening around her LP-24 laser pistol. Hardly daring to breathe, she waited. Seconds dragged by.

The cluster of buildings that made up the Enclave Rezplex were lost in the darkness less than a kilometer behind her, but they remained a looming, half-felt presence, a grim reminder of danger. It was hard to keep

memory at bay, to hold back the terror of the massacre
there. All those people slaughtered . . .

Kelly gripped the pistol harder, forcing the picture out
of her mind. She couldn't give in now, or she'd end up
like the others. Somehow she'd won free of the rezplex
and onto the rugged slopes of the plateau. Above her, on
the highest hill of the Enclave Heights, lay Fort Monkey.
Safety . . . she hoped.

*"Azjai-kyir zheein sykai,"* the native said at last.
"They are gone, Honored. We must move before another
patrol comes."

Nodding reluctantly, Kelly rose to a half-crouch and
followed the native. Ky was right; they had to keep moving. But every instinct rebelled at leaving cover. That
rocky outcropping hadn't offered much protection for a
human, but it was better than nothing.

The native moved rapidly, barely pausing to check for
signs of Dryien troops. *Can I really trust one of them?*
After the horror of the native attack, it was hard to see
the hannie as a friend. *But ky did save me from the soldiers. Why?*

Maybe it was safest to accept the native as an ally. If
ky hadn't been friendly, ky wouldn't have helped Kelly
in the first place. The local, a native servant working for
a Terran xenobotonist, had spotted the native troops as
they crept into the rezplex, overheard their officer ordering the Terran demons slaughtered. Kys employer was in
the capital tonight, at the banquet being thrown in the
Fortress of Heaven. It had taken time for the servant to
locate another Terran to warn—Kelly . . . and by that
time the shooting had started.

She'd been able to escape in the first moments of the
attack. With the native's help, she'd evaded the soldiers
in the streets of Monkeyville and the patrols beyond. Ky
seemed to like the Terrans . . . or perhaps ky hated the
soldiers more.

The little servant made an unlikely ally. She didn't
even know kys name.

*"Hykwai! Hykwai!"*

Kelly dropped and rolled as the shouts echoed behind
her. Autofire rattled, the bullets passing over her head.
Acting more by instinct than training, Kelly opened fire.
The LP-24 pulsed once, the invisible shot burning a hole

through the throat of the closest hannie soldier. Three more were still on their feet, shooting wildly.

The natives, their eyes adapted to Hanuman's bright F7V star, were ill-suited for night fighting. *I'm not much better,* Kelly thought, firing twice more and rolling to one side so the natives wouldn't locate her position. *I'm supposed to be an engineer, not a combat soldier!*

Her next two shots missed, but the sixth caught another hannie in the leg. The soldier screamed, firing a long burst as ky fell. Behind Kelly there was another cry. The two remaining soldiers rushed forward, sweeping the ground with autofire. A bullet plucked at her uniform as she rolled to the left and fired again, catching one of the attackers square in the chest. An unpleasant smell of burning flesh stung her nostrils.

She fought down her nausea and squeezed off another shot. The laser pulsed again, then died. Empty . . . and she didn't have a fresh cell.

And the native soldier was still on kys feet still firing randomly. If she didn't act fast, the whole Dryien army would be here soon, and she'd never escape.

Kelly screamed as autofire probed toward her. Then she lay still, moaning softly.

The soldier advanced slowly. She watched as the hannie's figure emerged from the gloom, kys weapon pointed straight at her. Her heart beat faster. If the native decided to be thorough, she was dead . . .

She stopped moaning and tried to keep still. What would the native do?

The soldier stood over her, prodded her once with the barrel of kys autorifle. With a quick motion she grabbed the rifle with both hands, pulling the soldier down on top of her. The rifle rolled free. Kelly lashed out with her forearm, trying to crush the native's windpipe. Pain lanced through her arm.

The neck ruff! Those sharp quills were like dozens of tiny knives. The soldier sprang back as she cried out, drawing a long knife with a lightning motion. Ky leapt to the attack again, but her foot arced sideways and caught the soldier in the back of the leg. Kelly rolled as the native fell, still trying to slash at her with the heavy blade.

Something hard and metallic tripped her as she tried

to scramble to her feet. The hannie rose slowly, deliberately, weighing the knife in one hand as ky stalked her. Kelly's hands groped on the wet ground, closed on the rifle . . .

With a screech, the hannie charged. The alien weapon was heavy, awkward. She fumbled for the trigger, but the unfamiliar design balked her. Kelly swung the rifle wildly and caught the hannie's knife arm. There was a sickening crack of breaking bone, and the native screeched as ky dropped the knife. Kelly swung again . . . again . . .

The native fell, blood oozing from kys head. She backed away, feeling sick.

There was a moan in the darkness. "Honored . . . Honored . . ."

Kelly rushed to help. Her native ally was huddled in the grass, clutching a wounded leg in both hands. She shied away at the sight of more blood, then forced herself to act. Dropping to one knee, she tore a strip of cloth from the sleeve of her uniform jacket and bound the wound.

"Leave me, Honored . . ." the native gasped, weak.

"Forget it," Kelly answered in Terranglic. She glanced away, straining all her senses to detect signs of more hannie soldiers approaching. There wasn't much time. "I'll carry you," she told the native in kyendyp. "But you'll have to guide me."

Her arm still hurt from the soldier's quills, but Kelly ignored the pain. *I have to work fast. We can't stay here.*

Gunnery Sergeant Trent peered over the top of the low drainage ditch and pointed. "Braxton, your lance on the left. Clear the top of the wall and *keep* it clear. Got it?" He didn't wait for Corporal Braxton's nod. "Strauss, your boys'll go up to the ladder under Braxton's cover fire. Secure the tower. Pascali's lance stays at the bottom of the ladder to keep the hannies busy. Any questions?"

The three corporals shook their heads.

"Right. Get your boys and girls together and get ready to move." Trent continued to scan the north wall as they crawled off to join their lances. The eerie green images on his IR readout seemed oblivious to the legionnaires in the trench. They'd worked their way along it from the barricade in silence and were now poised less than twenty meters from the ladder that led to the northwest observation tower . . . and the hannie snipers.

He had fifteen legionnaires against . . . how many? It looked like there were fifty or sixty hannies fanning out along this stretch of the wall, and probably more coming fast. *Pretty good odds,* Trent thought. With surprise, and with their high-tech weapons, the three recon lances would cut through the locals easily. *As long as they don't start bringing up the heavy stuff,* he added grimly.

As if in response, a deep-throated *wham-WHAM* shook the compound. A two-meter section of the wall collapsed inward in a shower of loose masonry. One hannie soldier was buried in the tumbling debris; another, dodging the danger behind, ran directly into a stream of FEK fire and was flung back against the rubble, screaming. The explosions showered dust and debris over Trent.

Behind the dying native, a squat shape clanked slowly forward on broad treads, the barrel of its fixed-mount 8cm cannon poking through the hole, questing, searching. The self-propelled gun was primitive and ungainly by Legion standards, but its shells could turn the tide against Bravo Company.

*Tanks breaking through the wall,* he thought. *Hell, that's* all *we need.*

But the noise and confusion could be turned to good advantage. "Go! Go! Go!" he yelled, waving the legionnaires forward. They rose from the ditch with a yell and rushed forward. Trent fired his FEK as he ran, sending needle-sharp slivers slicing into the natives on full-auto. Nearby, Legionnaire Rydell dropped to one knee and raised his Whitney-Sykes HPLR-55. The laser rifle pulsed invisibly, but a hannie at the top of the wall screamed and toppled over backwards. Laser rifles weren't as common in the Legion as they were in regular Commonwealth Army units, but Legion snipers like Rydell made every one count.

Trent reached the ladder first and fired upward, catching a native soldier who was having trouble with rungs spaced too far apart for kys compact body. The hannie lost kys grip and fell in an untidy heap near Trent's feet. He ignored the twisted body and sought out new targets among the natives swarming through the opening behind the lumbering SPG thirty meters away. More soldiers from Pascali's and Strauss's lances joined him under the looming shadow of the tower.

"Get your people moving, Strauss!" Trent shouted. "The rest of you spread out and cause trouble. You boys know how to do that, don't you?"

Corporal Helmut Strauss, a burly native of Neusachsen with a bushy blonde mustache, grunted acknowledgement. "Ve climb," he said harshly. He spoke Terranglic, like every soldier in the Legion, but eight years in the service hadn't softened his accent much. "You, nube, first."

Trent hid a smile. As long as there were NCOs in the Legion, the nubes—the raw recruits—would always get ridden the hardest. Strauss's victim, a kid who looked no older than sixteen, slung his FEK and started climbing the ladder. Darkness quickly swallowed his black, chameleon fatigues.

The sergeant turned his attention back to the problem at hand. While Strauss and his lance climbed, the rest of Trent's men had to occupy the hannies . . . without drawing too much attention from the self-propelled gun that was slowly forcing its way into the compound. Trent switched from infra-red to light-intensification vision and signalled to Corporal Pascali. *Move out.*

Pascali's lance fanned out in a loose arc around the base of the tower, weapons probing the darkness. Trent caught movement on the wall to the left on his LI display, dropped sideways and rolled, triggering a short burst on his FEK as the barrel came into line. Behind him, he heard the whine of Legionnaire Cole's weapon. A chorus of shouts and screams answered, then the stutter of native autoweapons returning fire.

Bullets ricocheted off the base of the tower and raised gouts of dust around Trent's feet. He fired again, a long burst this time, then shifted to a quick spread of grenades. The ripple of explosions along the top of the wall illuminated the hannies better, and he fired again.

"Look out, Sarge!" Cole yelled. The legionnaire knocked the sergeant down, sending him sprawling in the dirt. As he fell, Trent saw a hannie stepping from the shadows behind the vehicle. The native was balancing a heavy tube on one shoulder, one of the primitive rocket launchers the Legion referred to as blunderbusses. Flame spat from both ends of the tube and the rocket leapt across the compound. Too late, Cole tried to roll aside. The rocket caught him in the back, tearing through plasteel and duraweave cloth before it exploded. Sickened, Trent turned away from the bloody remains and flipped his FEK to full-auto. The launch tube rolled under the treads of the tank as the local's face and throat were shredded by dozens of needle-thin metal shards.

Trent crawled to where Cole had fallen. There wasn't much left of the legionnaire who had saved the sergeant's life. *You are soldiers in order to die.* The saying had been part of Legion tradition for centuries. It seemed grimly appropriate now, an epitaph for Legionnaire First Class Arthur Cole . . . or whatever his *real* name had been, before he'd sought the anonymity of the Legion.

The sergeant reloaded his FEK and fired again, smiling grimly as hannie soldiers took refuge behind the bulk of their big vehicle.

Then the smile faded as the clash of changing gears and clattering treads deepened, and the vehicle began to turn. The cannon barrel was swinging slowly, relentlessly toward Trent . . .

# Chapter 3

Don't trust any legionnaire who tells you he has
no fear.

—Colonel Fernand Maire
French Foreign Legion, 1918

Legionnaire Third Class John Grant paused three meters
from the top of the ladder and took a deep, careful
breath—"tasting the air," his brother might have called
it, back in the days when they ran together in the back
streets of Old London.

"John Grant" wasn't his real name, of course. He no
longer answered to his real name, and Old London was
no longer his home. The memories of the good times,
before Billy was killed, seemed distant now, but as he
clung to the ladder and steeled himself for his next move
he could almost see himself back on Terra. The long
climb, the need for absolute silence and perfect timing,
all brought back that last caper where Billy had died. For
a moment, it was as if the trial, the sentence condemning
him to lose his citizenship and serve five years in the
Legion to get it back, the long hours of tortuous training
on Devereaux, all were part of some dream. He almost
expected to look down and see Billy's cheerful grin
gleaming in the darkness below his feet.

But below him was Vrurrth, the hulking Second Class
Legionnaire from Gwyrr. *What's that stupid SOB Strauss
doing sending the Gwyrran up here? Silence, finesse . . .
that's what we need. Not brute strength.*

Carefully, he drew his combat dagger from its leg
sheath and tested its weight in his hand. In the old days,
he'd knocked over some fancy rezplexes, but though he
might have been a criminal he had never been a killer.
Now he had to use his old skills for a new, grisly pur-

pose. *Well, Slick,* he told himself, using the nickname Billy had given him so long ago. *This is it!*

Keeping the knife firmly gripped in his left hand, Slick started climbing again, every move smooth, silent. The ladder came up to an open trap door on the bottom of the tower floor, and there was no one in sight above it. Cautiously, Slick raised his head above the level of the floor and scanned his surroundings. One ale soldier . . . two . . . three. All of them were at the parapet, firing down into the compound below. Slick allowed himself a smile. *A kid could pull this one off.*

There was a metal-on-metal clatter just below, and the nearest hannie soldier cocked kys head and started to turn. *Damn Gwyrran monster!* Slick thought angrily. He gathered his strength and sprang through the opening, his knife blade flashing in the dark. The hannie gurgled and slumped, lifeless. The *clang* of kys rifle on the floor made the other two natives swing around. One of them loosed a shot that skimmed above Slick's helmet.

He rolled to one side, fumbling with the sling of his FEK. Adrenaline pumped through his veins. At this range, those native rifles could penetrate duraweave, and Slick wasn't wearing any plasteel armor over his fatigues. *Speed over protection, that's what you wanted . . .* The hannie fired again, and Slick reeled backward. Blood flowed freely from a ragged gash in his shoulder, and raw pain throbbed down his left arm.

The other hannie thumbed the selector switch on kys weapon, brought it up . . .

. . . and reeled, a dozen dark blossoms of blood opening in kys chest and stomach. The second soldier collapsed over the body of the first. The high-pitched *whir* of Vrurrth's FEK died away.

"Nube fights, does not ready." The Gwyrran's grin revealed his sharp-pointed carnivore teeth. "The haste is danger. Death." He clambered slowly through the trap door, eyes roving warily around the platform.

"Dammit, I could've taken 'em all if you hadn't made a noise!" Slick exploded. "You almost got me killed!"

Legionnaire Dmitri Rostov, the lance's demo expert, was next up the ladder. "Save the fighting for the bad guys, nube," he advised. "We're supposed to be a team."

Slick turned away, unslinging his FEK and surveying the compound. *Yeah, a team,* he thought bitterly. *I can take care of myself, as long as my so-called team leaves me alone.* He fought back anger. *I can take care of myself!*

Trent scrambled to his feet, eyes darting left and right. The self-propelled gun was lumbering toward him now. The main gun remained silent, but the heavy machine guns mounted on each side of the sloping hull chattered as the vehicle slowly advanced. The sergeant dived for the cover of a man-sized chunk of rubble as the 15mm bullets tracked across the ground.

Corporal Pascali dropped into a crouch beside him, raising her FEK and triggering the grenade launcher. The rocket grenade exploded just above the right-hand tread but did not penetrate. Pascali fired again, with the same result.

*Damn! We need something heavier . . .*

Hannie soldiers swarmed through the opening the tank had made, and more natives were rising from cover where they had been pinned down by fire from the main perimeter. Trent scanned the improvised barricade where the company had dug in. Their firing was slacking off now. What was the lieutenant doing over there?

"Fall back, Pascali!" he ordered sharply. "I'll cover you!"

She seemed about to argue, then nodded grimly. As Trent fired, the corporal sprinted back toward the base of the tower, shouting orders to the rest of her lance.

The SPG roared, and a fireball erupted near the west wall. Still firing, Trent lurched to his feet and followed Pascali. Machine-gun fire probed toward him. Something slammed into his leg, knocking him off balance. He fell and rolled, then crawled desperately for cover. The enemy cannon roared again. The explosion burst barely ten meters away from Trent, and dirt showered over him from the blast. Someone—a legionnaire, from the sound of the voice—was screaming now.

*If the lieutenant doesn't get it together, we've all had it!*

Trent slid into a drainage ditch and checked his throbbing leg. No blood, no signs of a serious wound. His duraweave fatigues had stopped the hannie bullet, but he'd have a bruise and a limp for a while . . . assuming he lived through the battle.

He pulled himself up against the side of the ditch and braced his FEK against his shoulder. Death rumbled toward him on broad, clattering tracks.

Colin Fraser slapped a fresh clip into his FEK as he listened to the tinny voice in his earphones. "Repeat that last, Sergeant," he ordered sharply.

Platoon Sergeant Persson was breathing hard. "Don't know how many there are, Lieutenant, but they've got us pinned!" he answered. "And there're booby traps everywhere! I lost ten men in the motor pool alone, and Dmowski says he lost a couple when the armory door blew up in their faces!"

"God *damn!*" Fraser ground his teeth in helpless rage. "Can't you do anything, Sarge?"

"Lieutenant, half my people aren't even armed!" Persson said. He sounded angry. "We can't get past those booby traps while we're dodging snipers, and I can't clear the snipers with a handful of pistols and a couple of FEKs!"

Fraser looked up, over the barricade. There was another self-propelled gun starting through the hole in the north wall. Without heavy weapons or the fire support vehicles in the motor pool building, Bravo Company didn't stand a chance against those hannie tanks. If Persson couldn't handle it alone . . .

"All right, Sergeant. Hang tight. I'm sending help." He cut the comm channel and looked around him. "Bartlow!"

"Here, sir." Subaltern Vincent Bartlow looked terrified. He was the youngest of Bravo Company's platoon leaders, Fraser remembered, and this was his first time in action. *Welcome to the club, kid,* he thought.

Fraser jerked his head at the line of soldiers manning the barricade. "Round up your platoon, Sub," he ordered. "There are hannies around the armory and the motor pool! Get over there and shred 'em. Got it?"

"Yes, sir." Bartlow bit his lip uncertainly.

Fraser ignored the man's hesitation. "And get your weapons lances armed, for God's sake. We need something better than popguns if we're going to take on tanks!''

The subaltern nodded.

"Move it!'' Fraser snapped. The subaltern flinched and backed away, shouting for his platoon sergeant. Fraser turned back to contemplate the breach in the north wall. The self-propelled gun had turned and was moving toward the northwest tower. Trent and his recon troops had stirred up trouble there, relieving the pressure on the main perimeter and knocking out the snipers in the tower. They couldn't hold out long, though; sixteen legionnaires wouldn't stand off a tank and the rocket-armed hannie troops who were pouring into the compound behind the vehicle.

Without heavy weapons on the firing line all they could do was pick off the hannies who were too stupid to take cover. The legionnaires from the company's six weapons lances were supposed to be drawing their gear from the armory. Until they came, Bravo Company's chances looked grim . . .

Gunnery Sergeant Trent grunted and slid deeper into the ditch as his second clip ran dry. *What does it take to discourage these bloody monkeys?* he wondered as he slapped his last 100-round clip into place in the receiver of the FEK. The hannie regulars were taking heavy casualties, but it didn't seem to be hurting their morale. They just kept on coming, pouring through the hole in the wall. With rubble and the tank for cover, they were getting enough troops into the compound to pose a serious threat to the legionnaires defending the perimeter.

A rocket like the one that had killed Cole streaked over the trench, then another. The self-propelled gun spoke again. Trent crouched low in the ditch, playing a waiting game.

Trent's lances didn't stand a chance on their own. At this point there was only one way to turn the tide . . .

A hannie soldier jumped and landed barely two meters away, holding one of the short, stocky, native autorifles with a determined grip. Trent triggered a short FEK burst that sent the soldier spinning sideways to collapse in the trickle of water at the bottom of the ditch. Two more hannies appeared at the top, firing wildly. A round *pinged* off the plasteel legpiece just below his left kneecap. His finger tightened on the trigger three times as he pumped needles into the natives.

More hannies were reaching the ditch now. Many were oblivious to the legionnaire, their rifles chattering and barking as the soldiers plunged straight ahead. Trent killed two more natives before they could take a more deadly interest in him. Then he saw the target he'd been waiting for.

Popping to his feet, the sergeant sprayed FEK fire on full-auto into a clump of locals. Ignoring their ululating screams, Trent sprang forward before any others could react. He kicked a dead hannie aside and scooped up the blood-soaked blunderbuss that had been pinned underneath the body.

As he raised the tube awkwardly to one shoulder, Trent struggled to recall the adchip briefings on native weaponry. *That* switch was the safety . . . and *that* one controlled the primitive electronic sight. Ignoring the sighting system, Trent lined up on the slow-moving vehicle and yanked back on the trigger. The rocket ignited and *whooshed* away, trailing flame.

Without waiting to watch the shot, Trent ducked and rolled for the cover of the ditch. As he landed at the bottom, the roar of the explosion drowned out the jabbering cries of the natives. His light intensifiers blanked out for an instant, then adjusted.

Raising himself cautiously to the lip of the ditch, Trent peered over the top. A smile tugged at the corners of his mouth as he surveyed his handiwork. Smoke trailed upward from the hole near the bottom of the vehicle's forward chassis, just over the left-hand tread. The tank was turning again, trying to line up on the company perimeter, but the left tread was flopping loose. The vehicle was still dangerous, but it wasn't going anywhere. The hannies were wavering now as they realized their most potent weapon was damaged.

"Come on, Sarge!" someone yelled behind him. Two FEKs on full-auto hosed across the hannies. From above, on the tower platform, more Legion rifles joined in. A hatch on the tank opened, and a squat local started to climb out, only to be knocked down by a shot from the legionnaires on the tower.

Trent realized his own FEK was gone, lost in the scramble for the alien rocket launcher. Drawing his 10mm PLF rocket pistol, he ran toward Pascali and Legionnaire Reinhardt.

*We shook 'em,* he told himself as he dived behind the corner of the tower next to Corporal Pascali. *We shook 'em . . . but they haven't broke yet.*

Legionnaire Spiro Karatsolis crouched low, sheltering behind the corner of the fort's tiny chapel, and peered cautiously around the neoplast wall toward the much larger structure that housed the Fort Monkey motor pool.

The dead body of Legionnaire Vance sprawled between the two buildings was a grim reminder of the effectiveness of the unseen native snipers who had the unit pinned. Half the man's head was gone, thanks to a high-caliber hannie bullet.

Karatsolis hefted the FEK in his hands. Compared to the turret-mounted plasma cannon of his beloved Sabertooth fire-support vehicle, the infantry weapon was a popgun. But it would have to do.

"Last chance to back out, man," Corporal Selim Bashar said behind him.

"Yeah, sure." Karatsolis took another look at Vance. "Let's do it."

They had worked their way this far forward of the rest of the legionnaires of the transport platoon without drawing fire. If they could just make it the rest of the way . . .

Even one FSV would make the difference, both here and up on the north end of the fort. He'd heard Sergeant Persson calling for assistance from the lieutenant, but even if help was on the way those hannie snipers were too well hidden for infantry to root out quickly. But a Sabertooth wasn't vulnerable to sniper fire.

Bashar slapped him on the back. "Ready," he said tersely. The swarthy Sabertooth driver wasn't armed, but he carried a satchel of tools slung over one shoulder. If Karatsolis could cover him long enough for the Turk to reach the motor pool, Bashar would deal with the booby traps they'd discovered before. Or at least that was the plan.

Karatsolis rolled out from behind the corner, his finger

tightening on the trigger of the FEK. The weapon whined, spraying needles at the south wall. He paused a moment, and a native rifle raised a gout of dust at his feet. Throwing himself sideways, he fired at what he estimated was the source of the shot. He shouted as he fired. "Move! Move, Basher!"

The Turk bounded across the compound at a dead run, zigzagging to avoid the sniper bullets. He dove, rolled, and came up next to the motor pool door, flashing Karatsolis a quick thumbs up. Another bullet missed his head by inches. The Greek gunner swung his FEK and squeezed off another long burst, and was rewarded by a scream. A hannie body tumbled from behind the cover of a ventilator housing on top of the armory across the road from the motor pool, landing heavily on the ground below.

Now that he had one of their hiding places spotted, Karatsolis switched from needle rounds to 1cm grenades and fired a quick three-round burst at the housing. *That should discourage anyone who's still up there,* he thought as the explosions lit up the compound with a brief false dawn.

He took advantage of the distraction to run, firing randomly again as he crossed to Bashar's side. The Turk was hunkered down beside the door studying a tripwire that ran almost unseen in the dirt.

"Not bad shooting for a goatherd," the corporal commented coolly as he located the mine the tripwire ran to and disarmed it by jamming a screwdriver into the firing mechanism.

"You do all right yourself, Basher . . . for a rug merchant." They both came from New Cyprus and kept up a long-standing feud over the merit of Karatsolis's farmboy origins versus the city background Bashar had grown up with.

Bashar grinned and gestured at the door. Karatsolis kicked it in, FEK at the ready, half-expecting an explosion or a fusillade of shots to meet him.

The lights came up automatically as the sensors detected the two legionnaires. Inside, the ranked Legion vehicles awaited, neatly parked in their workbays, ready for action. His heart leapt at the sight of the old, battle-scarred Sabertooth in Bay Five. Though in theory, maggers—transport platoon crews—were interchangeable among vehicles, there was still a tendency for specific crewmen to become attached to individual vehicles. Bashar and Karatsolis regarded that FSV as their own. They'd christened it *Angel of Death* and lavished as much attention on the ancient veteran as some men did on a mistress.

Lying quiescent in the workbay, the Sabertooth didn't look very threatening. The flat manta-ray shape with its sleek bubble turret was half-hidden by a clutter of tools, workbenches, and spare parts. But once it was powered up, with magrep modules for lift and four General Dynamics ground-effect turbofans for thrust, the Sabertooth would become a living thing, as deadly as the carnivore on Medea that had given the vehicle class its name.

Side by side, the two legionnaires ran to the FSV, eager to come to grips with the enemy.

*Zydryie* Wyzyeet steadied kys bolt-action sniper's rifle and scanned the Demon Fort in search of targets. Ky was having trouble getting used to the new nightscope that registered differences in temperature rather than light. It was a new device, issued only to the most elite units of the Dryien army, and this was kys first chance to use it in the field. The fuzzy, greenish images it showed were mostly dead bodies or patches of vegetation; none of the offworld demons were showing themselves now. Since the two humans had reached the big building they used to shelter their vehicles, no others had ventured into the open.

Two humans surely couldn't do much even if they penetrated the booby traps outside the building. Still, Wyzyeet cursed silently. Kys superior wasn't known for tolerance, and kys failure to stop the two demons might result in Wyzyeet's demotion from the ranks of the Soldiers of the Eternal Mists. Only the very best of Dryien's soldiery could aspire to serve in the elite commando unit. Aided by agents among the native servants employed by the demons, the commandos had penetrated the fort in perfect silence, set their traps, and prepared their ambush. Cut off from their armory and their vehicles, the offworlders would be easy prey for the main assault.

Wyzyeet felt uneasy. Those two humans had made it

past the snipers. Their vehicles were certainly power-ful . . .

Raw sound hammered at kys ears, and an explosion of blinding light made Wyzyeet duck down involuntarily. Kys night vision was gone, but when the *zydryie* looked back into the compound ky could see the demon vehicle clearly enough.

It was broad and flat, with a sleek bubble turret that mounted a menacing weapon some said was magical, plus missile launchers mounted on either side of the hull. And it *floated,* as if held up by an unseen force. Huge fans roared under the body of the machine, but Wyzyeet knew of no fan that could hold up so monstrous a weight.

The vehicle floated a few *kwyin* above the ground, scarcely higher than a full-grown *kyen.* It pivoted slowly in place like a beast questing for a scent.

Ky remembered the stories other soldiers told of the demonic devices that could see a kyen in total darkness . . . or through solid walls. Devices that made the night-scope like a child's toy by comparison.

These were the demons who had cast down the Ancient Gods and shattered their great Sky Fortress.

Wyzyeet's hands shook. Ky hesitated, torn between duty and fear.

Then the great cannon on the demon vehicle's turret flared once, a searing pulse of light and heat. Wyzyeet never even felt the ball of superheated plasma that consumed kys body and a three-meter section of the south wall.

# Chapter 4

An officer knows inside a week if he clicks or doesn't click in the Legion.

—Major Fernand Maire
French Foreign Legion, 1918

Kelly Winters cringed at the sound of gunfire from the top of the slope, the crack and chatter of native weapons mingled with the high-pitched whines of old-style FEK gauss rifles. The fighting up there sounded fierce . . . and it sounded like the legionnaires in the garrison were badly outnumbered.

Crouching low behind a clump of twisted, thorny bushes, she lowered the injured native to the ground and checked kys pulse. *You should have known there'd be no safety up in the fort,* she told herself bitterly. *Damned legionnaires.*

Why had the Commonwealth sent legionnaires to garrison the Enclave, anyway? Everybody knew they were nothing but malcontents and troublemakers—everybody who wasn't dazzled by the "romance" of the Foreign Legion, that is. She'd been forced to use them as her primary construction crew in putting together the Enclave, the landing strip, and the fort itself, and the road net that connected the Enclave with the capital and the inland zyglyn plantations. Slovenly, disrespectful, equipped with outdated gear and attitudes to match, the legionnaires weren't much good for peacetime work. From the sound of it they weren't doing much better at fighting, either.

But she didn't have much choice. The locals were in complete control in the rezplex, and she'd seen a patrol heading for the landing field an hour earlier. The legionnaires at the fort were still putting up a struggle, at least.

And both she and the native needed medical attention. Her injured native ally had passed out soon after she'd administered first aid and had been drifting in and out of consciousness ever since. She bit her lip as she examined the blood-soaked bandages on the native's leg. Infections were easy to come by in Hanuman's mid-latitude regions. Without competent medical aid and a dose of regen therapy, the little alien would probably lose the limb. *If either of us live that long,* she thought grimly.

Underneath makeshift bandages, her arm still throbbed where the hannie soldier's neck quills had opened half a dozen deep, painful stab wounds. Now that she was reasonably safe, the adrenaline wasn't pumping any more, and she felt sick and exhausted. She wanted to close her eyes, to sleep.

But she knew that sleep would just bring back the memories. The massacre . . . the hannie soldier dying under the smashing blows of kys own rifle, killed by her own hand. Her own hand . . .

No. She couldn't let herself remember. Not yet.

It took a major effort to focus on her surroundings again. A glow from downslope relieved the darkness . . . Monkeyville was burning. At least it gave her enough light to examine the hillside.

Were the shots above coming closer?

She froze in place as several small, dark shapes scrambled down the hill, heedless of their surroundings. They were hannies, soldiers by the look of them, but only one was armed. As she watched ky threw away the weapon, then suddenly toppled, kys torso erupting in a spray of blood and flesh and metal slivers. The native twitched a few times as ky hit the ground, then lay still.

"Come on, lads!" a human voice cried out in Terranglic. "We've got the little bastards on the run! Let's get 'em!"

A legionnaire ran past her position, still shooting at the fleeing natives. In the glow of the burning rezplex, Kelly could see him clearly. His uniform matched the darkened hillside but seemed to shimmer a little where the firelight hit it. Plasteel body armor covered his arms, legs, and chest over his duraweave coverall, and his bulky helmet was made of the same material. Armor, equipment, even his FEK had the scarred, battered look of gear that had either been badly maintained or seen long, harsh duty.

Another man appeared and fired at the fugitives, apparently oblivious to the fact that they were unarmed now.

"I'm glad to see you can fight *someone*, soldier," she said harshly. "Next time try for some of the dangerous ones. You know, the ones who can shoot back."

The soldiers reacted instantly to the noise, pivoting toward her with weapons held ready. "Hold your fire!" she called. "I'm a Terran . . . a Navy officer."

A corporal appeared out of the shadow, studying her closely. His watchful expression didn't waver. "Lieutenant Winters, isn't it?"

Kelly nodded.

"I'm Corporal LeMay," he said. "How many with you?"

"Just a native," she said, trying to match his brisk, professional manner. "I don't know if anyone else managed to get out . . ."

He cut her off with a curt gesture. "Never mind the details, Lieutenant," he told her crisply. "No telling how much time we have before they re-form."

"What about the hannie, Corp?" one of the legionnaires asked, pointing to her injured ally.

"Leave it. Don't have no orders about lokes."

"Belay that, mister," Kelly snapped. She wasn't going to abandon the native to the mercies of the Dryien army. "Ky helped me escape. Bring ky with us."

The corporal looked stubborn, then shrugged. "If you say so, Lieutenant," he said resignedly. "Kraisri, get the hannie. Ma'am, we'd better get back to the fort."

Kelly took a step, suddenly conscious of the weakness in her knees, of the sweat dripping down her face and neck, of the pounding throb in her wounded arm. Her arm . . . it felt swollen under the bandages.

"LeMay . . . ?" She tried to speak, but her tongue felt swollen. Breathing was difficult, as though unseen hands were closing about her throat. "LeMay . . ."

The ground swept up and collided with her face. From a very great distance, she could hear LeMay calling her name.

Then there was only darkness.

* * *

The noise of the turbofans was music, a triumphant fanfare that put fresh life into the beleaguered legionnaires at the barricade. Colin Fraser found himself grinning from sheer relief as he opened fire once again. The scarred hull of a Sabertooth shot past, the flare of light from its plasma cannon illuminating the name painted on the side of the turret: *Angel of Death*. The FSV was living up to the name as the plasma gun and the hull-mounted CEK chaingun swept the north wall. A second native tank that had squeezed through the hole created by the first took a plasma round square in the front, leaving a wide hole surrounded by half-melted armor right over the driver's compartment.

Nearby, an M-786 Sandray APC grounded with a roar of braking fans, the rear troop ramp dropping as it set down. Grim-looking legionnaires filed out at a trot. First came Corporal Dmowski, carrying a Fafnir rocket launcher, while the next two, armored head to toe in plasteel, cradled onager plasma rifles in their arms. Other soldiers followed. Bartlow's platoon was still on the south side of the compound, mopping up the hannie commandoes, but at last Fraser had the heavy weapons units who could turn the tide. And the vehicles, two Sabertooth FSVs and four Sandrays armed with CEKs.

*Now maybe we can teach those monkeys a lesson about fighting the Legion.* Fraser allowed himself another grim smile. He clicked to his command channel. "First and Second Platoons, attack on my signal!"

"First Platoon confirms," Subaltern Fairfax said over the commlink.

"Second Platoon, acknowledged." That was Subaltern Watanabe, the soft-spoken native of the Japanese colony on Pacifica.

Fraser peered over the top of the barricade one more time, then clicked to another comm channel. "Sergeant Trent! Are you there, Trent?"

"I'm here, L-T," the sergeant's voice responded promptly. Trent sounded out of breath, preoccupied.

"Time to show the lokes some firepower, Gunny. How're your people doing?"

"Three down from First Platoon Recon." There was a pause. "With all due respect, L-T, I wonder if you could stop talking and start shooting? Those little bastards are still trying to get at us.''

Fraser smiled in spite of himself. Would anything shake Trent's unflappable style? ''Acknowledged, Gunny.'' He keyed in the command channel again. ''Now!''

The explosion and the impossibly bright flare of plasma rounds blanked out Fraser's LI display for a second, until his helmet electronics could compensate for the glare. All six of the company's armored onager gunners were sweeping the north side of the compound with their plasma rifles, and the effects were devastating. As Fraser's vision returned, he could see hannie soldiers throwing down their weapons and fleeing for safety. Onager and FEK fire pursued them.

The whine of FEKs mingled with the deeper-throated hum of the MEK lance-support weapons as the rest of the legionnaires surged forward across the barricade, firing as they charged. A few shots rang out in answer but quickly fell silent.

And then, suddenly, it was over. The compound was quiet, the night peaceful again, as if the battle had never been.

Lieutenant Colin Fraser listened to the silence. The attack was over . . . or was it? Something had caused the Dryien army to turn on the Legion. Until that *something* was dealt with, the legionnaires would still be in danger.

The silence seemed somehow more threatening than the fury of the battle.

Slick winced as Dmitri Rostov probed at his shoulder. ''Careful, for God's sake!''

Rostov grinned. ''You deserve it, nube,'' he said. He came from the Russian-settled frontier world of Novy Krimski, but he spoke flawless Terranglic. ''That was a damn fool stunt you pulled, trying to take those ales with a knife.''

He didn't answer. He was tired, his arm hurt, and the last thing he needed was another lecture on teamwork.

When the judge had passed sentence on him for trying to break into the freighter and stow away on the London/ Orbit shuttle, Slick had been almost relieved. The Fifth Foreign Legion—what youngster didn't spin romantic dreams of serving in the company of those tough outcasts in their distant off-planet outposts? He'd talked Billy into the caper to get away from Terra's swarming beehive cities, out into the Colonies where life was exciting. The Legion shouldn't have been punishment at all! The idea of serving with the misfits, the adventurers . . . The chance to be *part* of something, and not always on the outside . . . it should have been a dream come true.

But he was quick to discover the bitter truth behind the romance.

From the moment he'd arrived for training at the main Legion depot on Devereaux, Slick had been miserable. The NCOs were either sadists or martinets, while most of the other legionnaires were concerned with proving how tough they were. Dreams of camaraderie were quickly overshadowed by the realities of being an easy target, a nube, someone to cuff or humiliate or ignore. But they still expected him to be part of the team.

*I'll show them I don't need their team,* Slick thought. A planet like Hanuman didn't offer the disgruntled legionnaire any place to try desertion. His only alternative was to win some respect, to show that he could make it on his own.

"All right," Rostov went on after a long silence. "Far as I can tell it's a clean wound, and nothing's broken. Strauss'll probably hurt you worse next time he decides you need an obedience lesson."

Slick nodded curtly. "Thanks, Rostov," he said.

"Just doing my job, nube," the other legionnaire replied cheerfully. He lowered his voice again. "And listen, kid . . . what you did was stupid, but it took guts. You're all right . . . in a kind of a dim, thick-skulled sort of way. Know what I mean?"

Rostov packed up the first aid kit, whistling happily. Pulling on his fatigue jacket carefully, he looked over the tower parapet. The hannies were gone, now, scattered by the furious Legion counterattack.

*I'm still alive.* The realization was only starting to sink in. *I'm alive . . .*

And Rostov seemed more friendly, more willing to accept him. Maybe he really could fit in.

Maybe.


"So I guess we have our orders." Lieutenant Colin Fraser leaned forward over the desk. It felt wrong to be sitting in Captain LaSalle's chair, presiding over the company staff meeting. But the word from the capital was positive: LaSalle was dead. Right or wrong, Fraser was in command now.

It wasn't fair. He'd been attached to the Legion less than two months, on Hanuman with Bravo Company barely a week. He still didn't understand these outcasts, these misfits who seemed determined to close ranks and go their own way and tell the whole universe to be damned. They were strangers to him, more alien than the hannies. How was he supposed to make combat decisions that risked the lives of these men?

He glanced around the office. Gunnery Sergeant Trent and all three platoon leaders were present. So were the company's four warrant officers, the specialists whose authority lay outside the regular chain of command. This one room held the entire surviving command staff of Demi-Battalion Alice, the Legion's garrison in Dryien-jaiyeel—for the next few hours, at least.

"Commandant Isayev has confirmed the evac order," Fraser went on. "The transport lighter *Ganymede* will be here by dawn. Come noon, we'll be back in Fwynzei, safe and sound. We have to be ready to pull out by then. Doctor Ramirez, what's the medical situation?"

WO/4 Eduardo Ramirez raised his head tiredly. The doctor was best known in camp for his capacity for alcohol consumption, but he had been hard at work since the beginning of the Dryien attack three hours before and hadn't taken a drink in the entire time. He looked, Fraser thought, more like one of the patients than the unit's medical specialist. "Battle injuries all treated, sir," he mumbled almost inaudibly. "Nothing very severe. Almost anything that got through armor killed the target."

"God rest their souls," WO/4 Fitzpatrick added softly. Father Michael Fitzpatrick—he was known to one and all within Bravo Company as "the Padre"—was the unit's chaplain. He was a Catholic from Freehold, one of the colonies that had been cut off from contact with Terra during the Shadow Centuries. Although his brand of Catholicism didn't recognize the primacy of Rome, it was a popular religion in the Colonies. At least half of Bravo Company was made up of Catholics of one kind or another, and the Padre served their spiritual needs as well as any conventional Vatican-backed priest.

"Good." Fraser looked over at the platoon leaders. "Tighten perimeter security for the rest of the night, gentlemen. No repeats of tonight's little performance. I want this evac to go smoothly."

"We'll do our best, sir," Fairfax said. Bartlow nodded agreement.

"Are we giving up on the people in town, and on Charlie Company, sir?" Watanabe asked.

"There's nobody left in the capital to give up on." Donald Hamilton, the WO/4 responsible for native affairs and intelligence, tapped the arm of his chair nervously. "*Ganymede* rescued a couple of eyewitnesses to the massacre in the Fortress of Heaven. Everybody else is dead. Including Captain LaSalle. I gather *Ganymede's* going to make a couple more search sweeps overnight, but it doesn't look good."

Fraser nodded slowly. "We have to mag out, Subaltern. There's been no word from Charlie Company, and with more hannies moving in around the base of the plateau it won't be easy to send anyone out."

"The lieutenant's right," Trent said bluntly. "Hell, how long could a platoon-sized outpost last if they got hit the way we did?"

"We could probably run a search from the lighter," WO/4 Hendrik Vandergraff, the unit's science and technology analyst, suggested. "They can't do much to us once we're aboard, and we could scout around for radio sources."

"Maybe," Trent said. "Don't think I'd like to tangle with the whole Dryien air force, though. Those cargomods they drive might not be much, but they could damage a transport. Now if we had an assault boat—"

"We don't," Fraser said. "If there's a chance to locate other survivors, we will, but the commandant wants us to pull out of here and back to Fwynzei intact. We don't risk Bravo Company on the off-chance there's a couple of other Terrans still blundering around out in the jungle. Got it?"

"Yes, sir," Vandergraff said. Fraser thought he heard Trent say something like "The Legion takes care of its own" under his breath, but he ignored the sergeant.

"Last thing," Fraser went on. "Hamilton, you're supposed to be an expert on our hannie friends. Any special recommendations?"

"Don't underestimate them," he said curtly. After a moment, he added, "Sir. They're a potent threat even if they don't have our weapons and armor." He paused again. "Specific things to consider . . . hmmm. First, maintain a tight watch tonight, and have the off-duty platoons sleep with weapons ready so we don't get caught with the heavy stuff in the armory again. Keep all the armed vehicles deployed around the compound. And for God's sake make sure there aren't any locals inside the fort!"

Fraser nodded thoughtfully. "All right, let's get things rolling. One platoon on watch, the others packing up or getting some rest. See Gunny for a schedule. I want to be ready for the lighter when it gets here."

"And ready for the hannies, too. I bet we'll see them first." Trent added, rising. He made it sound like a casual social call, not another bloody assault.

"That's a bet I won't touch, Gunny," Fraser said quietly. He looked away. *I don't understand these people. I don't belong with the Legion. Not as Exec . . . certainly not in command.*

He thought of Trent, so self-assured, so dedicated to his soldier's life. A warrior born and bred. A legionnaire.

*I just don't belong.*

"Idiots! Fools!" Zyzyiig slammed a fist down on the table. "How could two regiments be driven back by a handful?"

Shavvataaars, the Semti Chief Advisor to the Throne of the Eternal Mists, spoke with a whispering, sibilant hiss, pausing frequently as he struggled with kyendyp vowel-sounds. "That journey is done now; it cannot be retraced. The demons are trapped in their jungle lair, where your troops may still destroy them all. But you cannot afford delay, my dear *Asjyai*. Their transport ship may fly them all to safety, and you cannot afford to allow the Terrans to regroup and mount a counterthrust against you here. They must learn that Dryienjaiyeel is not safe for their kind.''

It was galling to have success so near, yet still hanging undecided, a ripe jungle fruit just out of reach on a high tree limb. The youthful usurper, Jiraiy, was dead, and with the child the offworlder demons who had led ky from the ways of the Ancients. The army was in total control here in the Fortress of Heaven, and the process of rooting out the false *yzyeel's* supporters in the capital was going smoothly. By morning, the new *yzyeel*, Zyzyiig's chosen candidate, would be secure on the Throne of the Eternal Mists.

But the offworlder skyship floating in the harbor remained intact, until artillery or armor could be summoned to the capital from the outlying provinces. And the demon soldiers, the offworlder *Foreign Legion*, were still holding out. But two full regiments were already in place below the offworlder fortress, and two more crack armored units were on the way. The three smaller camps where the interlopers had settled in the deep jungle were gone now, two of them overrun, the third evacuated. That would free up another regiment, but it surely would not be needed.

''You are sure the demons will withdraw?'' Zyzyiig asked. ''Might they send help to their garrison instead?''

''They cannot,'' Shavvataaars replied. ''Their strength is not that great, and their attention will soon be elsewhere. Nothing shall stand in the path of the Great Journey. But the Time of Cleansing cannot begin until the demons have been cast out.''

Dryienjaiyeel would be free of the offworlders, of the northern merchants, of everyone who exploited the zyglyn trade and interfered with the savages of the deep jungles. And the People of the Mists could return to their own ways again under the protection of the Ancients, Shavvataaars and his sibs.

*Yes . . . yes, the Cleansing will soon be complete.*

''Best if I go to command the assault in person,'' Zyzyiig said. ''Then there will be no mistakes.''

The Semti's rasping voice sounded worried now. ''That is not wise, my Companion of the Journey. Such will only delay the moment of decision, perhaps aiding the demons to evade their fate.''

Zyzyiig crossed arms firmly. "My decision is made, Honored One. I will lead the troops into battle and see these *legionnaires* crushed as the mists melt away in the morning sun."

# Chapter 5

Most legionnaires have nothing to lose and life it-
self is not held very dear.
—Legionnaire Adolphe Cooper
French Foreign Legion, 1933

Gunnery Sergeant Trent peered cautiously over the embankment of the slit trench. "What've you got, Pascali?"

"Heat sources there," Corporal Pascali replied, pointing. "And there . . . there . . . down there. Goddamned big ones, Sarge."

Trent switched to his IR helmet display. In the eerie
green light of the infrared screen, the bright plumes of
heat stood out like brilliant stars on a dark night.
"Hmmm . . . power plants. Vehicle engines. Looks like
our monkey friends aren't settling for half-measures this
time."

Sunrise was still almost an hour away, but a pre-dawn
glow was already suffusing the eastern sky. Hanuman's
rotation period was close to thirty-four standard hours
long, and everything—day, night, twilight—seemed to
stretch out endlessly.

The trouble was, the hot, moist climate made heavy
morning mists inevitable. A thick fog clung to the lower
slopes of the Monkeyville plateau, masking the jungle
. . . and the native troops assembled there. Visibility was
better around the Enclave itself, but not by much. Even
infrared was obscured to some extent.

*Perfect conditions for an attack,* Trent thought. He
keyed in his radio to the command frequency. "Alice
One, this is Guardian."

"On line, Guardian," Legionnaire Garcia replied
promptly. "Go ahead."

"I've got four confirmed heat sources on the north

road. Probably vehicles. Better tell L-T the monkeys are on the warpath again.''

'' 'Firm. Wait one.'' Static crackled as long seconds passed. Then Garcia's voice came back on the channel. ''Acknowledged, Guardian. Lieutenant says to come back inside and take charge of the main perimeter. Strauss and Braxton will reinforce the trenches.''

''On my way.'' As Trent cut the channel, an alarm siren wailed behind him, inside Fort Monkey.

Those vehicles were climbing the main road from the northwestern valley. No doubt there were more behind them, and enemy troops filtering through the jungle and up the slopes to support the armor. It looked like the long-expected hannie attack was finally grinding forward.

''They want me inside,'' he said crisply. ''Pascali, take charge out here. L-T's sending the other two recon lances, and I'll get you a couple of heavy weapons for support. Don't fire until they're right on top of you. We want to sucker as many of the little bastards as we can.''

Pascali nodded. ''We'll nail 'em, Sarge,'' she said confidently. She and Reinhardt were the only survivors from her recon lance, but two legionnaires from one of the First Platoon's rifle lances had been drafted to join them on guard. They looked ready to wipe out the hannie army without any help at all from the rest of the company.

He slapped the top of her helmet and scrambled out of the trench.

The trenches had been Subaltern Watanabe's idea. With most of the native troops gathered on the northwest side of the plateau, and the only decent road running straight up into Fort Monkey from the north, it seemed likely that the main threat would be to that side—the same area they'd attacked the previous night. Two slit trenches on either side of the road and thirty meters from the north gate would be a nasty surprise to hannies who thought they knew the terrain. Trent smiled. Watanabe was shaping up into a real legionnaire—tough and cunning.

Of course, there was always the chance the hannies would try to bypass the main route. They had troops on all sides of the fort, but getting tracked vehicles across the rugged ground surrounding the plateau would be quite a challenge. It looked like they were going to take the easy route, and they'd pay for that.

He crossed the road and headed for the hole the hannies had blasted in the north wall on their first attack. Bravo Company's second FSV was grounded in the opening. Despite the alarm siren, Legionnaire Ignaczak was still lounging in the open turret hatch, eating from a ra-pack while he studied a pornographic magazine.

"Button up, Zak," Trent called. "We've got company coming, so put that shit away and get ready."

"We'll kick ass, Sarge," the gunner replied. He stuffed the magazine into his fatigue jacket and sealed it up. Taking a last mouthful from the ra-pack, Ignaczak crumpled the package and tossed it carelessly into the compound behind the Sabertooth.

"Better go after it, Zak!" another legionnaire called from the parapet above. "That's a week in cells for littering!"

"Yeah?" Ignaczak shouted back. "Then what do those monkeys get for knockin' down the wall last night?"

"Well, shitfire, Zak," the other man answered, patting his FE-MEK barrel and grinning. "They're not in the Legion. I guess we'll either send 'em home without their dinners or shoot 'em. How 'bout it, Sarge?"

"New directive from the Colonial Office, Gates," Trent responded. "We're supposed to make them go to camp sanitation lectures."

"That's cruel, Sarge," Gates said, shaking his head and laughing. "Real cruel. We'd better just put 'em out of their misery."

Trent laughed and broke into a trot across the parade ground. The banter was a good sign; the legionnaires were ready for a fight.

And a fight, Trent reflected as he watched Bravo Company boiling out of the fort's barracks buildings, was exactly what they were likely to get.

"Go! Go! Go!" The corporal's voice was hoarse with excitement.

Slick jumped into the trench, wincing as the motion jarred his bruised ribs. DuPont climbed in after him, taking care not to bump his laser rifle. Though the Whitney-Sykes HPLR-55 was rugged enough to be the standard infantry weapon of most Terran Army light infantry units, the Legion snipers who used the laser rifle were inclined to handle them with exaggerated caution. The least little flaw in the alignment of the crystals could spoil the Legion's reputation for fielding the best snipers in the Commonwealth Defense Forces.

Rostov and Vrurrth were last, and paused to pull the chameleon tarp into place. Except for narrow gaps along the front of the trench, the tarp completely covered the legionnaires' position. The microcircuitry worked into the weave of the cloth would analyze the reflective qualities of nearby terrain and adjust the tarp's colors accordingly. The same principle was used in duraweave battledress coveralls and made the cloth—and anything it covered—a nearly perfect match for most backgrounds.

Across the road Braxton's lance was already in place beside Pascali's improvised unit. Thirteen legionnaires awaited the hannie army, joking, swearing, laughing . . . Thirteen legionnaires, and Slick.

As he chambered a round in his FEK and poised the rifle on the rim of the trench, Slick found himself recoiling from the others. Overnight he'd had his baptism of fire, his first exposure to the realities of battle. But he still felt totally out of place here. Rostov had started to make him feel welcome, but these legionnaires were still almost as alien as the monkeys creeping through the mist.

Fear gnawed at his stomach. The trench was constricting, like a box . . . or a coffin. *No room for stealth this time*, he thought. *What the hell am I doing here?*

"*Ganymede, Ganymede*, this is Alice One," Fraser said into the handset of his C³ unit. He was hunched over the computer map table in the front compartment of an M-786C, the command variant of the Legion's ubiquitous Sandray APC. "Say again your ETA, *Ganymede.*"

"Alice One, *Ganymede.*" Captain Garrett sounded tired, irritated. "ETA is thirteen, I say again, one-three, mikes. What's your situation, Alice One, over?"

"*Ganymede*, I have hostiles advancing on the north wall," Fraser responded. "I can't cover the fort and the landing field, too."

The captain's voice took on an even sharper edge.

"Well, you're the one who knows the score. How do you want to play it, Alice One?"

Fraser released the transmit key and looked down at the computer-generated map of the compound. Bravo Company was already mustered on the perimeter, ready to meet the hannie attack. The command APC was near the center of the compound, together with a handful of other Sandrays, ready to deploy as needed. He glanced at Legionnaire Garcia, who sat at one of the other C³ terminals monitoring reports from the rest of the unit.

They could wave off the transport until the natives were driven off, but Fraser didn't like the idea of more delays. It had taken all night to get the ship to Monkeyville, and that had given the hannie army time to muster for a big push. What if the hannies just kept throwing troops at the legionnaires all day? If numbers finally overpowered Bravo Company, they'd want *Ganymede* down and waiting to dust them off in a hurry.

But if she set down at the Enclave's landing field south of the fort, *Ganymede* would be exposed, vulnerable to any attack mounted from the southeast through the deserted civilian facilities of the Enclave. A pair of Sandray APCs were sufficient to keep an eye out for patrols working along that side of the plateau, but they couldn't cover the landing field. And Bravo Company just didn't have the men to spare to cover the landing field in the middle of an enemy attack.

There was one other solution . . .

"*Ganymede*, Alice One," he said at last, keying in the handset again. "Can you put down in the open space on the east side of the fort? Over."

"Wait one," the captain answered crisply. Fraser could visualize him calling up the computer files on Monkeyville to cross-check sizes and distances. "Alice One, that's affirmative."

"Then that's the drill, Captain. That'll keep you under my guns."

"And away from the natives, I hope," he said. "This bucket wasn't designed to play around in a hot L-Z, Lieutenant. We're not armed, and even that primmie stuff the monkeys have is enough to put a hole in the old girl."

"I hear you, Captain," Fraser said. "We'll do our best for you. Alice One, out."

He replaced the handset. Fraser examined the map again. *Did I make the right decision?* he wondered. *Damn it! I wish LaSalle was here.*

But LaSalle was dead, and if his men didn't hold the hannies on the perimeter there would be a lot of legionnaires joining the captain before dawn came.

And whatever happened, it would be Colin Fraser's responsibility.

"Assault column in position, *Asjyai,*" the radio operator said.

The army command post was a ramshackle hut in a small jungle clearing near the base of the Demon Plateau. It was crowded with radio equipment and the big table where topographic maps of the area were spread out to accommodate tactical planning. There wasn't much room left over for personnel, so most of Zyzyiig's staff waited outside for orders. The arrangement had advantages; ky could think and plan better with fewer underlings clamoring for their leader's attention.

Zyzyiig stroked kys muzzle slowly. "What about the turning column?"

"*Jyiedry* Ghyzyeen reports it will be ready to attack in another five *dwyk, Asjyai,*" ky replied. "The terrain to the east is very difficult for the armored vehicles."

"Tell Ghyzyeen I want action, not excuses," Zyzyiig growled. "They must be ready to strike just as soon as the enemy is fully engaged."

"Yes, Honored."

Behind them, Shavvataaars stirred. "You would do well not to underestimate the offworld demons," he whispered. "They will detect your maneuver."

"I handle this *my* way!" Zyzyiig snapped. Ky glanced back at the Semti, suddenly aware of who and what ky was speaking to. Zyzyiig was a civilized kyen, far too sophisticated to believe that the Semti were really the Ancient Gods of Dryien myth. But they were an old and powerful race, long-lived, wise . . . and vital allies. "Honored One," ky continued, "I have planned this carefully. Two attacks on the ground will keep the demons off-balance. Armored vehicles can kill them. So can rockets, and we have issued launchers to soldiers in both columns."

"Many of your soldiers will complete their journeys," Shavvataaars said. "The demons will not be caught by surprise this time."

"I know, Honored One. But if we can keep the enemy occupied on the ground, our last surprise will have a chance of getting through." Zyzyiig smiled grimly. Ky turned again to face the radio operator. "Order the assault column to attack!"

"Here they come! Get ready!"

Slick tightened his grip on the FEK and fought the temptation to fire. Green shapes glowed against a darker green backdrop on his IR display: heat sources, the larger, brighter ones hannie vehicles, the smaller but more numerous ones individual native soldiers creeping forward to the attack. It was quiet, except for the distant clank of vehicle treads. The enemy movement was slow and cautious. Were they expecting the legionnaires to spring a trap, or was the fog hampering their advance? Probably the latter, since hannie IR gear was still scarce in Dryienjaiyeel's army . . .

"Wait for the onagers to fire, *mes amis.*" Platoon Sergeant Henri Fontaine was in command in the trenches now. Second Platoon's senior NCO had joined the three recon lances with two heavy weapons units, bringing the total strength of the advanced force to twenty-four men—nearly a quarter of Bravo Company's strength. There was a lot of firepower here . . . but would it be enough against the weight of the hannie attack? "Steady . . . pick your targets . . ."

A burst of native machine-gun fire erupted from the left, loud in the pre-dawn stillness. More hannies joined in the firing, accompanied by a chorus of shouts. Slick couldn't make out what they were yelling, but from the way the gunfire fell silent he guessed the monkey officers or non-coms were trying to get control over nervous troops.

It helped to think of the enemy soldiers as being just as nervous as he was. Slick shifted his FEK, lining up on the closest heat source. The closest troops were no more than twenty meters from the concealed trenches now. The vehicles were still lagging behind the infantry, hindered as much by the rugged terrain as by the visibility. When would Fontaine give the order to fire? Couldn't he see how *close* the monkeys were?

The onager gunner next to Slick chambered a round with an audible *cha*-CHUNK. Clad from head to toe in plasteel armor, with a modified helmet that covered his entire face and contained sophisticated sighting gear that slaved the aim of his plasma gun to the movement of his eyes, Legionnaire Childers was the very image of the ultimate high-tech soldier. The man's weapon shifted minutely in its ConRig harness as Childers lined up on his target, one of the vehicles lumbering up the main road.

"Onagers . . ." The tension was plain in Fontaine's voice. "Ready . . . fire!"

Childers squeezed the trigger. Slick blinked back tears as a blinding flash of raw light and heat surged from the barrel of the onager and hurtled toward its target trailing a visible streak like some impossibly straight bolt of lightning. The French who had first developed the plasma weapon had called it the *fusil d'onage,* or "storm rifle." Seeing it in action, Slick didn't think the label was strong enough.

All around him, the rest of the defenders were shooting now as legionnaires threw back the tarps to improve their fields of fire. Corporal Dmowski had the other onager in action over in Pascali's trench, and the two plasma rifles kept up a measured, accurate fire. Kinetic energy rifles whined, while the deep-throated hum of a pair of heavier MEKs droned a deadly harmony. The hannie line faltered under the weight of a barrage equal to what a regiment of their own troops might have poured out.

Slick fired, then ducked down involuntarily as a native anti-tank rocket leapt from a blunderbuss launcher toward him. The rocket passed over the trench, exploding harmlessly near the base of the fort's north wall. When he peered over the rim of the trench again, Slick saw that one of the vehicle heat sources was now much brighter. Raked by multiple onager hits, a hannie tank was on fire.

The scene reminded him of the carnage inside the fort after the first assault . . . had it only been a few hours ago? There were dead hannies everywhere, but more were advancing to take their places. He fired at them mechanically, hardly caring if he scored a hit or not. The deadly hail of Legion firepower would mow them all down long before they could be a threat.

Another rocket skimmed above the trench, much lower than the first. Again Slick couldn't help ducking, though he knew the thing was only really a threat if it scored a direct hit. Even without plasteel, his uniform would keep out most shrapnel and ordinary bullets, and this morning Slick had added plasteel plates over his chest and back. In this kind of fight, armor counted more than freedom of movement.

"Come on, nube!" DuPont grabbed his uniform collar and hauled Slick to his feet. "Get with it!"

"Incoming! Incoming!" Rostov yelled. Something screamed overhead and exploded behind them, showering the trench in dirt.

"What the hell?" DuPont shouted. "I didn't see any of the tanks firing!"

"That wasn't a tank," Childers said, firing his onager again. "Too big. Must've been one of their big howitzers, down in the jungle somewhere."

"Who's sighting for it?" DuPont asked wildly. All his bravado had fled. "Where are the bastards calling in the fire, dammit?"

"Steady, *mon brave,*" Fontaine's voice cut in smoothly on the radio circuit. "Keep the line clear. I'll see what the lieutenant wants us to do."

Slick fired a spread of grenades, more by reflex than design. He felt trapped in the narrow confines of the trench, trapped and helpless under the fall of those shells. Not even full plasteel body armor would save the defenders once the enemy artillery found the range . . .

"Lieutenant! Sergeant Fontaine reports the natives are calling in arty."

"Damn!" Fraser turned in his seat to face Legionnaire Garcia. He had hoped that the poor jungle roads would make it impossible for the hannies to bring up heavy guns. The natives didn't have much in their arsenal capable of breaking the Legion defenses, but artillery was definitely a threat. "What size guns?"

Garcia shook her head. "He's not sure, Lieutenant. One-oh-eights . . . maybe one-twenty-ones."

Fraser looked down at the map table. "All right. Order Fontaine to pull back . . . heavy weapons first. That'll buy us some time."

"Yes, sir." She turned back to the radio.

Fraser swiveled his seat to face a control console. The command version of the Sandray lacked the weaponry of the ordinary APC model, substituting a satellite dish for the usual turret arrangement. It did, however, mount something the other M-786s lacked: a launch rack for surveillance drones. His fingers danced over the controls, programming one to search out the enemy artillery.

First they had to know what they were dealing with. Then the legionnaires would take steps to counter the threat.

Another shell arced toward the defenders. It fell short this time, the explosion ripping through a clump of hannies in an improvised foxhole thirty meters from Slick.

"Goddamn it!" DuPont shouted, "They're bracketing us!"

"Once they get the range . . ." Rostov said. His voice was cold and flat.

"All right! Listen up!" Fontaine broke through the clatter. "The lieutenant knows what's going on. Weapons lances, fall back to the main gate. Recon lances, cover them. On my mark . . . move!"

Rostov was helping Childers scramble out of the trench, while farther down the line Childers's lancemate, Legionnaire Hsu, was already running for the fort wall, the elongated tube of a Fafnir missile launcher slung over one shoulder. There was a renewed volley of FEK fire from the trenches as the recon lances laid down covering fire. Slick opened up at a hannie soldier fifty meters away, saw the tiny native spin backward and fall . . .

"Incoming!" The call came again, this time from Strauss. There was another screech as a howitzer shell

rose from the jungle fog, streaking heavenward, then arcing over and down, plummeting straight toward the
trench. Slick stared up at it in horror, unable to react at
all, unable to move, to think, even to scream . . .

# Chapter 6

The goal of a Legionnaire is the supreme adventure of combat at the end of which is either victory or death.

—Colonel Pierre Jeanpierre
French Foreign Legion, 1958

"Grid coordinates five-seven by one-zero-nine," Fraser said, reading the display underneath the video monitor that was relaying the view from the surveillance drone. "Six targets. Computer IDs them as one-twenty-one mike-mike field guns. Recognition named Hellhound."

"Five-seven by one-zero-niner," Trent's voice answered over the comm channel. "Six targets, ID Hellhound. Copy."

"Confirmed," Fraser said. "Pound 'em flat, Gunny."

"Count on it, L-T," the sergeant responded. "Count on it."

"All right, Zak," Trent shouted. "Let 'em have it!"

Trent thought he could hear the distant *crump* of the hannie guns loosing a full barrage now that they had their target bracketed. He was crouched beside the Sabertooth parked in the gap in the north wall. The sounds of fire from the trenches were slacking as the defenders pulled back. If those guns weren't silenced fast . . .

Beside him the Sabertooth seemed to vibrate as one of the two Grendel missiles left its launch rack with an ear-splitting roar. The second Grendel followed moments later, riding a column of smoke and fire.

Trent hit his comm switch. "Fafnirs . . . lock target profiles and fire!" Corporal Toshiro Ikeda nodded and aimed his Fafnir rocket launcher skyward. "You heard the man," he said. His fingers danced over the tiny keyboard that controlled the rig, programming in silhouette and IR signature data. "Ready . . ."

The corporal stabbed the launch button savagely, and the missile leapt from the tube with a roar like a wounded beast. Moments later, three more missiles followed. The man-portable Fafnir rocket launchers used programmable guidance computers to recognize preselected targets. They were ideal for tracking down unseen enemies, though their warheads were smaller than the vehicle-mounted Grendels.

"Missiles running . . . running . . ." Legionnaire Ignaczak's voice droned in Trent's earphones. His two Grendels, unlike the Fafnirs, were set for controlled teleguided flight; after the Fafnirs found their targets, the Grendels could smash whatever was left of the hannie battery. "I've got one . . . two hits. Three. Three down, Sarge! Sending in the big boys now!"

"Fafnirs!" Trent called. "Fire another spread . . . just to make sure."

As the missiles leapt into the air Trent allowed himself a smile. The hannies wouldn't be trying *that* little trick again!

The explosion erupted less than ten meters away. Slick staggered under the force of the shock wave, dropping his FEK in the mud at the bottom of the trench. His helmet protected his ears from the force of the blast, but he could feel blood trickling from his nose. Sluggishly, he pulled himself up, surprised to find that he was still in one piece.

"Childers is down!" Rostov yelled.

"Help him, nube," Strauss ordered harshly. "The rest of you keep firing!"

Shaking his head to clear the ringing in his ears, Slick started to clamber out of the trench. The ground seemed to be swaying under his feet. Then he saw Childers.

The armored legionnaire was sprawled on the ground a few meters away, close to the shell crater. The man's left leg was twisted around at an impossible angle, broken.

Blood spurted from the stump of his right leg. The

legionnaire's foot, still sheathed in plasteel, lay nearby. Slick stared at the sight, unable to move, unable even to look away. Nausea twisted inside him.

"Help him, kid!" Rostov's voice sounded far away.

Slick sank to his knees, clawing at his helmet, and pulled it free barely in time. Vomit clogged his nose and throat.

"Goddamned nube!" he heard Strauss curse. "Vrurrth, help Childers. Rostov, get the nube out of here!"

Gasping for air, Slick saw the big Gwyrran crouch next to the fallen onager gunner. Vrurrth's massive fingers were surprisingly deft as he stripped away plasteel leg armor and tied off a tourniquet above the man's wound. Gently, he lifted Childers, armor, weapon, and all, hoisting the fallen legionnaire over one huge shoulder and sprinting for the cover of the fort.

"Come on, kid, move it!" Rostov said, pulling Slick to his feet and shoving him in the same direction. There was a far-off scream of more incoming shells as the rest of the legionnaires retreated, firing back to discourage the hannies from pursuing too close. Rostov caught Slick as he tripped and staggered, urging him on again. Nearby, another legionnaire fell, his back ripped open by a hannie rocket.

Slick closed his eyes, trying to block out the scene, but the horror wouldn't go away.

The warning light on the computer-generated battle map strobed urgently. Fraser stared down at it in sinking despair. *Not now, damn it!* he thought. Panic threatened to overwhelm him. *Not* there!

He fought for control. The light indicated that something had set off the fort's remote sensors on the east side of the compound. As he watched, the computer identified the intruders and displayed symbols on the map . . . native infantry and armor pushing over the rough terrain toward the east wall.

And the lighter was only minutes away from landing on that side of the fort . . . the place *he'd* pronounced safe. *Damn those hannie bastards!*

"Garcia!" he snapped. "Get *Ganymede* on the line. Instruct her not to land until she gets confirmation."

Without waiting for her acknowledgement Fraser keyed in his private line to Trent. "Gunny, there's trouble on the east side of the fort. Computer says we've got at least a company of monkey infantry with eight tanks coming up. Get some men over there and turn those bastards back. We've got to secure the area for the transport to land."

Trent's reply was calm and measured. "I'll take care of it, L-T." Was there a rebuke in his voice? "Permission to use Bashar's Sabertooth?"

"Anything you need, Gunny," Fraser told him, trying to suppress his uncertainty. "Just clear that area!"

"Lieutenant!"

"What is it, Garcia?" He tried to sound calm, in control.

"*Ganymede* reports a flight of primmie aircraft. Bearing three-four-seven. Heavy stuff . . . bombers, maybe."

*As if we didn't have enough trouble!* Fraser nodded wearily. "Acknowledge."

Artillery, flanking columns, bombers . . . what next? And when would Bravo Company finally run out of resources to deal with whatever the hannies were going to come up with?

Fraser stared down at the map. It looked like the legionnaires were running out of time . . . and luck.


"It's huge, *Asjyai!* Huge!"

Zyzyiig's neck ruff stirred in anger. *The offworlders and their demon technology!* First they had crippled the artillery battery the troops had hauled so laboriously over mud-choked roads to support their attack. Now, it seemed, one of their huge air vessels was in the sky over their fort. If this craft mounted weapons like the ones their soldiers used . . .

"Be not so ready to give in to defeat, *Asjyai,*" Shavvataaars whispered behind him. It was as if the Semti was reading his mind. The thought sent a chill up Zyzyiig's spine. Perhaps the legends were true . . .

"The vessel your soldiers describe is of the type the demons refer to as Camerone-class," the Semti continued. "It is a transport, unarmed, ill-armored. They never intended such craft for operations in a combat area.''

"Then . . .'' Hope was rekindling in kys heart.

"The vessel is no threat to your soldiers,'' Shavva-taaars confirmed the unspoken statement. "They need not fear. The Cleansing may continue unhindered.''

Zyzyiig smiled, reaching for kys radio. Perhaps there was time after all.

The wall burst inward in a roiling cloud of smoke and splintered masonry. Sergeant Trent fired a spray of grenades into the opening before the dust could settle. "Pour it on, boys! Let 'em know you're here!''

Beside him, Legionnaire Fiorello squeezed off a plasma bolt from his onager. The flare as it found a target backlit the smoke, giving the scene an eerie, hellish quality. Other legionnaires of Third Platoon added in their firepower, and hannie screams testified to their accuracy.

A tank gun barked, sending a shell whistling through the opening. It struck the back of a supply hut thirty meters behind Trent. Machine guns hammered.

The first hannie tank rumbled through the new gap in the east wall, firing again as it came. This time, the shell found its mark, an MEK gunner crouched behind an improvised barricade of upturned cargomods. Fiorello's onager flashed again, tearing a hole in the tank's front chassis armor. The vehicle ground forward, followed by another. Hannie troops charged out of the smoke firing rockets and screaming defiance.

With a whine of strained turbofans a Legion Sandray shot past, slewing sideways in front of Trent's position. The APC's gun chattered, spraying death. Natives scrambled for cover or fell, torn by dozens of needle shards. The lead tank fired again, but the Sandray's composite-laminate armor absorbed the impact easily. A second Sandray appeared from the left of Trent's defensive line, pumping high-volume autofire into the hannies. The gap in the east wall was a seething cauldron no infantry soldier could survive.

Farther down the line, a second explosion opened a new hole. As another hannie tank crashed through the debris, Corporal Bashar's Sabertooth opened fire. The turret-mounted plasma cannon illuminated the battle-field like a brief, false dawn. Superheated metal smashed into the hannie tank, vaporizing the vehicle's gun mount and leaving the chassis a twisted, smoking hulk.

"Score one for the cavalry!" someone shouted.

Fiorello's third shot exploded right over the lead tank's engine compartment, tearing a hole through armor plating and complex machinery. The vehicle rolled to a stop as smoke poured from the gash, a thick, oil-blackened cloud. The second tank smashed into it, pushing the cripple aside.

Bashar's Sabertooth pivoted on its fans, ready to make the kill . . .

"Sabertooth One, this is Alice One. Break off and await new orders!" Garcia's voice sounded urgent over Trent's headphones.

"Confirmed," Bashar replied blandly. The FSV continued its turn without firing.

"Goddamn it!" Trent roared. "What the hell do you think you're doing, Garcia?"

"Lieutenant's orders," Garcia replied. "He wants the Sabertooth redeployed."

Trent thought about overriding the order. With the FSV on the east wall, there was no way the enemy would manage a breakthrough. Without it . . . well, the onagers would still keep their tanks at bay. But Fraser had promised him the Sabertooth for support . . .

"We've got enemy aircraft inbound, Sarge," Garcia said quietly. She seemed to be reading his mind. "And Sabertooth Two's got troubles on the north wall. We need Bashar for anti-air."

"Right," Trent said at last. "We'll make do here."

He raised his FEK to fire another burst of grenades.

*We'll make do . . . unless they've got more surprises for us . . .*

"Six bogies, bearing now three-three-niner, speed five hundred, altitude five-five-zero, range nine hundred, closing." The lieutenant's voice sounded tinnily in Legionnaire Spiro Karatsolis's ear. "Tentative ID is native propellor-driven bombers, recognition code Boomerang. Repeat this is a tentative ID only."

"Roger, Alice One," Karatsolis replied. He ran his fingers over his tracking board, slaving his computer to the feed from the command van. Data readouts flashed confirmation of Fraser's verbal information. "Receiving your input. Ready to fire."

"Just be goddamned careful of the transport!" Fraser snapped.

Corporal Bashar glanced up and back from the Sabertooth's controls. "Sounds like the lieutenant's getting jumpy, huh?"

"That's what they pay him for, Basher," the gunner responded with a grin. "Officers worry . . . we just pull the trigger and collect the bounty."

As Bashar guided the FSV past the barracks, Karatsolis programmed the two Grendels. "Fire on the rail!" he warned, hitting the launch buttons in quick succession. Bashar compensated for the recoil so smoothly that the Sabertooth barely rocked.

Monitors flashed on above the Grendel control console, giving Karatsolis a warhead's-eye view of the missiles' flight paths. The *Ganymede* filled the two screens as it circled to the northwest of the fort. Karatsolis smiled and gripped a joystick. Those hannie bombers would get the surprise of a lifetime, and thanks to the transport they'd barely have time to see it coming.

The view on the screens lurched and plunged as the two missiles dived together, dropping under the lighter, then up . . . up . . . Karatsolis disengaged the teleguidance and switched to heat-seeking mode, making sure the transport's IFF code was registering. The lead Grendel locked on an enemy bomber. The second started to follow, but the legionnaire overrode and the missile selected the second highest signature to home in on. An instant later, the two screens flared and went blank almost as one. Two of the six targets went dead on the Sabertooth's fire-control board

"Two down!" he yelled.

"Two for the goatherd," Bashar agreed. "Kind of reminds me of that time on Ossian. Remember?"

Karatsolis swung his chair to operate the turret controls. "Tracking!" he shouted, ignoring Bashar's comment. The turret rotated smoothly. In front of him, another monitor lit up to display sighting data for the

Sabertooth's powerful onager cannon. The legionnaire raised the plasma gun skyward, probing for targets. His left hand called up the feed from Fraser's computers and superimposed the information on the aiming display.

The bombers had split up. One pair was dropping low, while the others climbed, angling behind and over *Ganymede*. The transport lighter screened the second pair . . .

He dropped the barrel so that one of the low-flying bombers was centered in the video monitor. A few quick keystrokes locked the target image into the computer and slaved the turret to the aircraft's motion. "Clear!" he called, and Bashar fired up the turbofans again. The turret swung under computer control as the Sabertooth moved, keeping the image of the aircraft locked on the screen. Seconds later, crosshairs lit up over the target in red, and Karatsolis squeezed the trigger that fired the onager cannon.

The noise was deafening, the heat almost unbearable as the cannon fired, flinging a packet of raw plasma at the target. The superheated metal lanced toward the airplane like summer lightning, and in an instant the target was gone, vaporized.

"Tracking!" he repeated, and even before Bashar had halted the vehicle he was already starting to line up for the second shot. This bomber had no more chance than the other. The plasma bolt found its mark and destroyed the aircraft before the crew knew what had hit them.

But where were the other two. . . ?

"Basher! Move around . . . give me a better angle!" The last two aircraft were still masked by the lighter. They'd be close enough to drop their loads soon . . .

*Damn!* Ganymede *was still in the way. Damn! Damn!*

*Wyzzeer* Gyeddiig pulled back on the yoke and pushed all four throttles forward, feeling the *Fwyryeel* bomber shudder as its nose came up and the four props revved to three-quarters power. So far the demons below hadn't fired on kys plane, but it was only a matter of time. If their lightning weapons didn't find a mark, their tame servant-rockets would. Ky had watched four of the six aircraft in Flight Predator knocked out of the sky by the devil-weapons. So far only luck had protected the two survivors . . . luck, and the screening bulk of the demon skycraft lumbering in a slow circle above the Demon Plateau.

*Zeeraij* Dreeyg, kys copilot, pointed downward. The ground battle was still raging around the demon fort. Flight Predator was supposed to deliver the knockout blow that would break the offworlders, but with two aircraft left and certain destruction awaiting them if they ventured too close, how could they hope to carry out the mission? Without a powerful strike, and soon, the ground attack was sure to fail. Those demon weapons were as deadly on the ground as they were to aircraft . . .

Lightning leapt from ground to sky, engulfing the other bomber in fire. Gyeddiig fought the controls to keep the aircraft stable as the shock wave buffeted them. They were alone now.

"We're not going to make it," Dreeyg said softly. "Even if we turn back and get clear, the *Asjyai* will have our ruffs."

"Not that there's much hope of getting clear," Gyeddiig commented. Ky banked the aircraft. The huge bulk of the alien air ship loomed ahead.

The *Asjyai* had told them these demon craft were powerless, unarmed, and so far this one certainly hadn't fired. It was moving slowly, like a dirigible but without visible propellors. Would it be as vulnerable as a dirigible?

If they couldn't strike a blow against the demons on the ground, couldn't they at least damage the sky vessel? Its fall might discourage the demons, disrupt their defense of the fort below . . .

Grimly, Gyeddiig adjusted the bomber's course and switched on the intercom. "Bombardier . . . arm all weapons."

Dreeyg was looking at the pilot with wide, horrified eyes. "You're not—?"

"Bombs armed, *Wyzzeer*," the bombardier reported.

Gyeddiig pushed the throttles to full. "Ancients and Eternal Mists!" ky shouted.

The bomber plunged toward its helpless target.

# Chapter 7

People grow old quickly here. Yesterday, they
were baptizing us—today they're giving us the last
rites.

—Legionnaire Forster's dying words
French Foreign Legion, April 1908

"My God, Fraser, we've been hit!"

The words brought Fraser out of his seat. *"Ganymede!*
What's your condition?"

Over the open comm channel he could hear Captain
Garret shouting orders while other voices babbled in the
background. He caught the phrase "drives failing . . .
crash . . ." but little else. Fraser rushed to the rear of
the APC, calling for the driver to drop the ramp.

Outside, he gaped at the scene. *Ganymede* hung suspended over the east side of the camp, less than a hundred meters off the ground. Smoke and flame billowed
from her stern section, where the hull was twisted and
crumpled around a wide gash. As Fraser watched, the
stern sank visibly. The ship stirred, lifting slightly, turning; for a long moment, it looked as if the crew was
regaining control over the damaged giant.

Then she faltered again as the main repulsion fields
failed. The ship dropped.

The ground shook at the impact, and a sound like a
hundred thunderclaps washed over the fort. Dust and
smoke obscured the scene, but as it thinned Fraser could
see the transport's broken hull lying astride the remains
of the east wall. Flames were rising from the wreck.
Something exploded, sending a fireball mushrooming
back into the sky. Mingled with the roar of flames, the
screams of the wounded—human and native alike—were
a nightmare sound.

Fraser realized that he wasn't alone. A cluster of on-lookers had gathered nearby, at the door to the medical hut. Like him, they all seemed stunned by the crash, shocked into immobility.

He forced himself to tear his mind away from the horror. "Don't just gawk!" he yelled. "Get over there. *Help* those poor bastards! Come on, Doc! Move!"

Ramirez snapped out of his paralysis and pushed the others to work—the Padre to round up medical supplies, the other two warrant officers to round up vehicles. A bulky Sandray rigged for engineering work stirred from the ground, its bulldozer blade dropping down into the ready position in front of the driver's cab.

Fraser turned, glancing into the command van's darkened interior. "Garcia! I'll be at the crash site!"

The C$^3$ tech shook her head. "You can't, Lieutenant!"

"Damn it, don't argue with me!" He stopped himself. Garcia was right. Whatever he wanted, he still had an obligation to the unit. Reluctantly, he turned his back on the chaos outside. "All right. Tell Ramirez . . . tell him to save as many as he can . . ."

He sank into his seat, drained. The transport crew . . . Third Platoon . . . Sergeant Trent . . . He shuddered, picturing the butcher's bill.

And the battle wasn't over.


"Sarge! Come on, Sarge, wake up!"

Gunnery Sergeant Trent groaned and opened his eyes. He was lying in the dirt behind a tumble of cargomods, half buried by dirt and debris. Somewhere near by, close enough for him to feel the heat and hear the crackle, a fire was burning. His leg hurt, the same leg he'd twisted before. Blood trickled down his forehead and dripped in the dirt.

Legionnaire Krueger was kneeling beside him, his face grimy but determined. "Come on, Sarge!"

"Enough, Krueger," Trent growled. He raised himself to his hands and knees and looked around. "What the bloody hell happened?"

"The transport, Sarge. It crashed." Krueger looked away. "It just crashed . . ."

The lighter lay like a broken toy across the ruined east wall. The ship's tail rested on a flattened, twisted pile of

wreckage that had been one of the hannie tanks. Hull
plates had fallen away over much of the length of the
vessel, exposing the ship's interior in a dozen or more
places. Smoke boiled suddenly out of one of the holes as
explosions rippled inside the wreck.

Trent started to rise. Something in front of him caught
his attention . . . Legionnaire Fiorello, his body cut
nearly in two by a jagged piece of hull plating. It had
sliced clean through the soldier's plasteel bodysuit.

Two meters to the left and it would have caught Trent
instead.

"What are our casualties, Krueger?" he asked, shaking his head to clear it.

Krueger shrugged. "Sergeant Qazi and Mr. Bartlow
are okay, Sarge. And I saw a couple of the other guys
moving around a minute ago. The two seven-eighty-sixes
were right under that thing when it hit . . ."

The medical APC was racing towards them, followed
by a gaggle of other vehicles. Trent picked up his FEK
and started to meet them, favoring his sore leg.

Someone was moaning softly, the sound almost drowned
out by the roar of the fires. Another one alive . . .

How many had survived? How many? The question
was a searing pain deep within him, a knife in his gut.

Every legionnaire's death would twist that knife deeper.


"Retreating! What do you mean, retreating?" Zyzyit-
ig smashed a tight-clenched fist against the table. "They
will continue the attack, by the Ancients!"

*"Asjyai,* Regiment Godshammer has lost all but two
tanks," the radio operator protested. "The demon sky
vessel crushed them when it fell. More than a hundred
soldiers were lost . . . and that does not include the ones
killed in the fighting!"

Zyzyiig whirled, neck ruff puffed out full. "Say the
wrong word and you will be the next casualty, *Zydryie!"*

The radio operator crossed arms. "I . . . I am sorry,
Honored," ky said, subdued. "But . . . the flank column
is already in full retreat. How can we rally them now?"

"Call for my car," Zyzyiig ordered. "I will go there
and *personally* see to them."

"Y-yes, Honored One." The *Zydryie* turned back to
kys radio gear.

"Do not allow your anger to deflect you from the path of success, my Companion," Shavvataaars said softly, intercepting the *Asjyai*.

"Demons take you!" Zyzyiig spat. "Get out of my way!"

"The moment is not ripe to complete this journey," the Semti insisted. "You cannot force your soldiers to act against their natures, and for the instant their nature demands retreat. Recovery."

"You said yourself that we must not waste time in overrunning these demons," Zyzyiig said. "Now you say we should wait?"

"The moment has changed. An attack in the night might have broken them. Before the fall of their vessel, they might still have been overcome. Now, though, your troops lack the will for victory."

"What of the demons? Their skycraft crashed! They must be demoralized . . ."

The Semti spread his thin, long-fingered hands. "Indeed they will be, my Companion. The difference is that time will help your soldiers to recover their courage. According to my sources, that transport was the only one the Terrans had available to remove these legionnaires. They are trapped here. And time will only serve to sap their strength, as their knowledge of these facts ripens."

Zyzyiig stepped back. "You are sure of this?"

"Very sure, my Companion of the Journey. As always, time withers all opposition. Now they are trapped. Your army can destroy the demons at leisure . . ."

Zyzyiig paused, pondering the alien's words. "Cancel the order for my car," ky said at last. "Pass the word to disengage. We will let the demons live . . . for now."

The command APC grounded with a shudder as the magnetic fields collapsed, its rear ramp already opening. Fraser climbed out slowly, afraid of what he might find.

Most of the fires around the crashed transport had gone out, extinguished by fire-fighting foam or smothered under dirt piled high by the bulldozer blades of the Legion construction vehicles. One of those was still at work near the stern of the wreck, pushing crumpled hull plating aside so a party of legionnaires could reach wounded crewmen trapped inside.

Close by the command van, the medical APC was parked in the center of a circle of wounded men. There was no sign of Doctor Ramirez; presumably he was in the tiny field surgery inside the vehicle. Legion medics moved among the wounded, performing triage. Other soldiers carried stretchers to waiting APCs to take wounded men back to the fort's medical hut.

Not far away, Father Fitzpatrick knelt beside one casualty, his hands sketching the cross in the air as his lips moved in prayer. Last rites . . . how many times had the Padre administered them today?

At least the hannies had pulled back long enough to give the legionnaires time to look after the wounded . . . and the dead.

Sergeant Trent was crouched over a piece of wreckage a few meters beyond. As Fraser came up beside him, Trent looked up.

Fraser cleared his throat. "What's the situation, Gunny?"

Trent answered. "It isn't good, L-T," he said softly. "Best count so far is twenty dead out of Third Platoon . . . most of them in the crash. Six more seriously wounded."

"God!" Fraser looked away. "Two thirds of the platoon . . ."

"Yeah." A shadow seemed to cross Trent's face. "Six dead from First and Second Platoons in the fighting on the north perimeter. We lost two onagers and a Fafnir launcher . . . two Sandrays and their drivers, too."

"What about *Ganymede?*"

"We've pulled fifteen wounded off," the sergeant replied. "Most of them pretty bad. When she hit, she set off ammo and fossil fuel aboard the vehicles under her . . . and she was carrying ammo in her hold, too." He shook his head. "I'm surprised anyone lived through it."

"God . . . and all those refugees aboard . . ." Fraser remembered Captain Garrett saying there were two hundred Commonwealth citizens in the capital for *Ganymede* to pull out. Two hundred civilians crammed into the vessel's troop bays . . . "Did any of the bridge crew make it?"

Trent shook his head. "No. No ship's officers at all. A couple of corpsmen, the rest ordinary shiphands."

"Well . . ." Fraser wasn't sure what to say next. "Well, keep at it as long as you think it's practical, Gunny. We . . . can't afford to keep too many men tied up for too long, though. The hannies could still try again."

"Yes, sir." Trent paused. "What's the word from Battalion, L-T?"

"Out of touch," Fraser replied. "Next sat pass is seventy minutes."

The sergeant frowned. "Let's hope they move faster getting us out this time. All we'd need is for the monkeys to come up with another surprise or two."

"I hear you, Gunny." He hesitated, looking at him. Trent had been a tower of strength since the first hannie attack. Even though exhaustion was plainly written in every line of his face, the man was still going on. "Look, Gunny . . . thanks. Thanks for everything you've done today. We wouldn't have made it . . . *I* wouldn't have made it without your help."

Trent shrugged. "It's what we're trained for, L-T," he said simply.

"Yeah." Fraser looked back at the smouldering wreckage again, feeling inadequate. Trent's unflappable calm was something he'd never understand, much less live up to. *How can I lead these people when I don't even know what makes them tick?* "Carry on, Gunny. I'll be in HQ if you need me."

Trent saluted stiffly and limped away.

Walking back toward the command van, Fraser tried to shut out the sights and sounds around him. So many people killed . . .

*It's what we're trained for.* The words haunted him. *I wasn't trained for this! I shouldn't have tried to bring the ship into the fort. They're dead . . . and I killed them. I wasn't trained for this!*

Slick leaned on his shovel and mopped sweat from his forehead. Although his fatigues were climate-conditioned, the heat and humidity were enough to keep his bare head damp even when he wasn't working. Shoveling dirt into sandbags to fill in the gaps remaining in the east wall after the engineering vans had finished clearing the debris was hard, sweaty work.

Less than an hour had passed since the end of the battle, but it was still vivid in his mind. In a way, the heavy labor was welcome; it kept him from thinking too much about the fighting. He knew the image of Childers, one leg gone below the knee, bleeding to death before his eyes, would haunt him for the rest of his life. Childers was dead despite Vrurrth's first aid. *Maybe if I hadn't frozen . . .*

"Back to vork, nube!" Strauss shouted. Slick grunted and dug the shovel into the dirt again. It was almost good to have the corporal shouting at him. At least that was better than being ignored.

For a while, after last night, Slick had thought he was gaining a measure of acceptance. Now the rest of the lance, even Rostov, seemed barely willing to acknowledge that he existed.

*They think I'm a coward,* Slick thought bitterly. *Maybe they're right . . .*

That was something he didn't like to admit to himself.

Growing up on the streets in Old London . . . there hadn't been much room for cowards there. Slick and Billy had lived by their wits from the day their parents had died in that rezplex fire. Twelve years old, with a younger brother to look after, living on whatever they could beg or steal . . . Slick had always seen himself as a survivor, not a coward. He'd been scared a time or two, but he'd always kept on going.

Except the night Billy died, of course . . .

If he had reacted faster, perhaps he could have kept Billy from falling. Or, today, he might have saved Childers. *Maybe I am a coward.*

A coward would never win acceptance among the legionnaires. Someone like DuPont could get scared under an artillery barrage and still fight. But being too paralyzed by fear to keep a man from dying . . . that was unforgivable.

Slick dropped the shovel and dragged the full sandbag into place, conscious of the way Rostov and DuPont turned away as he came close. All his life he'd been looking for some place where he could be a part of something larger, like the Red Brethren, or the Legion. Or a family. The Brethren had turned him out because he hadn't been willing to kill a man.

Now the Legion was closing ranks against him because he hadn't saved one.

At least the first time Billy had been there. This time there was no one to turn to.

He had never felt so totally alone.


"Lancelot, this is Alice One," Fraser said. "Lancelot, do you copy, over?"

Fraser was alone in the communications shack. He had ordered Garcia to grab a few minutes of sack time, and Trent and the subalterns were still out supervising the repairs to the perimeter. With the orbital communication satellite overhead, he had transmitted a full report to Battalion HQ. Now all he needed was some kind of response, some word of what would come next.

"Alice One, Lancelot." The voice was crusty with more than just static. Commandant Viktor Sergeivich Isayev, senior officer of Third Battalion, First Light Infantry Regiment of the Fifth Foreign Legion, sounded stiff and formal. "Copy your last transmission."

Fraser waited expectantly, hoping Isayev would continue. But the comm channel gave him nothing but static. "Lancelot, request further instructions," he said at last. "When can we expect another evac mission, over?"

There was another long pause before the commandant replied. "Alice One, there will be no evac. Repeat, no evac." Isayev's voice softened. "Lieutenant Fraser, *Ganymede* was the only ship we had available for you. *Magenta*'s in for repairs, and *Ankh'Qwar* left two days ago for the systerm to rendezvous with the carriership *Seneca*. I couldn't get you a ship in less than a week, Fraser . . . even if the resident-general would allow it."

"Sir?"

"The resident-general is concerned that the situation in Dryienjaiyeel might spread. He's issued orders restricting Commonwealth forces to Fwynzei until further notice." The commandant paused. "There's no way he'll risk more men, Fraser. I'm sorry."

"Then what are our orders, Commandant?" Fraser fought to keep his tone level.

"It's your discretion, Fraser," Isayev replied. "If you think you can hold out until we can get you relief, do so . . . but I can't tell you how long that will be. Otherwise . . . you know the score better than I do, son."

"Yes, sir." Fraser swallowed. "I understand."

"Just remember that you're in the Legion now, Fraser. Remember Camerone. And Devereaux."

"Are you telling me to hold on here to the last man, Commandant?"

Isayev coughed. "What you do with those men is your decision, Fraser. Just make sure whatever they do brings credit to the Legion. If you stand, then stand with courage. If you die, do it with honor."

"We'll do our best, Commandant," Fraser said slowly.

"I know you will, Fraser. Lancelot out."

Fraser's hand was shaking as he replaced the handset. Bravo Company had been abandoned.

# Chapter 8

*I could not expose them, as an officer of the
Legion, to such a dishonorable solution.*
                    —General Pierre Koenig
                    French Foreign Legion, 1942

"So there's the situation," Fraser finished grimly.
"We're on our own."

The headquarters building was full for this meeting.
Fraser sat behind LaSalle's desk, with Garcia nearby to
operate the computer in case they needed reference material or other data. All three of Bravo Company's subalterns were there, together with their platoon sergeants.
Watanabe had one arm in a sling, while Platoon Sergeant
Fontaine wore a bandage on his head that gave him a
piratical air. A fourth platoon sergeant, Persson, represented the transport platoon; his unit's officer, Subaltern
Lawton, had been at one of the Charlie Company outposts when the crisis began.

The unit's four warrant officers were clustered together
in one corner. Ramirez looked exhausted. The Padre
seemed more discouraged than tired, with a look of despair Fraser thought he could understand easily enough.
Fitzpatrick had watched too many men die today.

Gunnery Sergeant Trent rounded out the gathering.

"Well, the damage to the east wall can't be repaired
in less than two days," Trent said. "But we've plowed
up dirt to block the worst gaps, with some sandbags
thrown in where we could. It's not what I'd call defensible, but at least the monkeys won't get in too easily."

"I'm more concerned about the remote sensors,"
WO/4 Vandergraff put in. "The crash knocked out a
good chunk of the east-side perimeter, and I don't have
enough in stores to replace them all. That's going to be

a weak spot until we can cannibalize enough spares out of other electronics.''

"Sensors aren't all we're short on," Trent added. "We've got a good mix of supplies, but a few more battles like what we did this morning'll eat up our ammo faster'n anything. If the hannies keep launching attacks on us—''

"They will," WO/4 Hamilton, the native affairs specialist, said. "Depend on it, they will. We're becoming a symbol to them. If they're trying to oust the Commonwealth, our presence here will goad them into more attacks.''

"If so," Trent continued, shooting an irritated look at Hamilton, "I think we could run into some pretty serious supply problems. We can handle two or three more pitched fights . . . but as long as they can keep coming, time's on their side.''

"Shouldn't we try to get Battalion to change their minds?" Ramirez spread his hands. "I mean, they can't be *serious* about leaving us on our own, can they?''

Sergeant Fontaine snorted derisively. "Another civilian heard from!" he muttered. The words were loud enough, though, for everyone to hear.

"What was that, Sergeant?" Fraser asked softly.

Fontaine met his look with an icy stare. "Any legionnaire knows the only thing we can count on is getting screwed by the damned civs!" Qazi, Third Platoon's senior NCO, nodded agreement.

"That's enough, Sergeant," Fraser said dangerously.

"If it was up to Commandant Isayev, there wouldn't be a problem," Trent put in. "The Legion takes care of its own. It's when the politicians get involved that we get the short end of the stick . . .''

"What about negotiating with the locals?" Vandergraff suggested. "Surely we could strike some kind of deal. Even if we had to surrender, it would be better than sitting here waiting to be slaughtered.''

"Surrender, hell!" Sergeant Fontaine said.

"Legionnaires don't surrender," Karl Persson added.

Fraser opened his mouth to speak, but Hamilton beat him to it. "It just won't work," he said quietly. "You all heard what happened in the capital last night. We can't negotiate with them.''

"But if we open a dialogue . . ."

"If the hannies wanted to talk surrender with us, don't you think they would have given us the option before now?" He shook his head. "Haven't you heard the way they refer to us among themselves? We're demons . . . and this thing is turning into some kind of Holy War to get rid of us. They don't want us as prisoners. They want us dead."

"There can't be any question of surrender," Fraser agreed, nodding. "As for making a deal . . . they're the ones that started this. With all due respect, Padre, turning the other cheek isn't going to get us very far. If they want to offer some kind of solution . . . we'll see. But I think Mr. Hamilton is right. The only kind of settlement the monkeys are looking for is one we aren't going to like at all."

"Then what's left, Lieutenant?" Subaltern Bartlow asked.

It was Trent who answered. "We can't stay here and we can't give up," he said. "Looks to me like our best bet is to try to pull out."

"You're the one who said we can't get an evac," Fairfax said.

"So we do it ourselves," Trent answered. "Overland."

There was an explosion of comment from around the room. "Overland?" Fairfax began. "How—"

"We're surrounded up here," Bartlow was saying. "We're trapped—"

"Do you have any idea. . . ?" Vandergraff said.

Fraser held up his hand. "One at a time!"

"You're talking about a march of nearly fifteen hundred kilometers to reach Fwynzei," Vandergraff persisted after the others had fallen silent. "Through Hanuman jungles and across the Raizhee Mountains . . . some of the worst terrain on the planet. That'll take a hell of a lot longer than waiting here for another transport."

"*And* we'd be crossing hostile territory," Fairfax added. "Their army isn't going to sit still and let us go marching out, you know."

"Once we break contact, we'll be home free," Trent insisted. "Even if we have to fight once or twice, our

ammo stocks'll be good for it. That's better than what
we'll have if we try to fight it out here.''

''It's still a hell of a long way,'' Persson pointed out.
''Hauling the wounded, I don't know if we'll have enough
vehicles to mount everybody. There won't be any room
for error, at least. It'll slow us down if we have to move
at a marching pace.''

''We'll still move faster than the lokes, though,'' Qazi
said. ''We can let the men rest aboard the APCs while
the column keeps moving.''

Hamilton nodded. ''The Dryiens aren't fully mechanized, anyway. That tracked junk they use isn't cut out
for long-distance jungle movement, while our MSVs can
handle damn near anything we're likely to pass through.
Hannies on foot'll fall behind pretty quick, so all we'll
really have to worry about are the garrison troops between here and the border. The worst problem is Zhairhee, right below the pass to Fwynzei. There've been
reports of a troop buildup there. 'Maneuvers,' the monkey staff calls it.''

''What about supplies?'' Fairfax asked. ''Can we even
make it that far?''

''That's your department, Ham,'' Trent prompted.
Sergeant Qazi doubled up his duties as a platoon sergeant
with the responsibility for Bravo Company's logistics.

Qazi stroked his pencil moustache thoughtfully.
''We've got more stuff here than we can carry in the two
supply vans,'' he said. ''If we cut down our troop capacity some more, we can stock up pretty good. Say a
month's worth . . . six weeks with rationing.''

''That's cutting it tight,'' Fontaine said. ''Fifteen hundred kilometers of rugged ground in six weeks . . .''

''We can supplement our food from local sources,''
Vandergraff admitted grudgingly. ''Biochemistry's com-
patible . . . there'd be some vitamin deficiencies, but
those won't start hurting anybody in six weeks.''

Fraser had deliberately kept quiet while the discussion
unfolded, taking in everything. It sounded like Sergeant
Trent's idea would work . . . but the task was daunting
at best. ''I guess we don't have a lot of options,'' he said
at last. ''Gunny, looks like your scheme's the only one
we've got.''

Trent shrugged. ''It's the only one that has a chance

of getting anybody out alive, L-T,'' he said. ''Like they say, 'March or Die.' Don't get me wrong. This ain't gonna be a picnic. We'll lose a lot of men . . . and there's no guarantee we'll make it at all.''

''It still sounds better than any other options I've heard,'' Fraser replied. ''All right . . . I want you people to start sizing up the job. We need to be sure we can handle this once we get going. There won't be time to turn back later.'' He looked around the room, studying them. Not everyone was convinced, but they all looked more hopeful now that they had something to shoot for. ''You each have your own responsibilities. Coordinate through Gunny Trent. I want a report in six hours. Understood?''

''Okay, let's run over what we've got,'' Trent said at last.

He had appropriated the command APC; its computer terminals were tied in to the company HQ network, and it offered him privacy to go over the unit's options. Ramirez, Qazi, Persson, and Legionnaire Garcia were with him.

''The vehicles we have left give us a lift capacity of 194 men,'' Persson said, consulting his wristpiece. ''That's assuming no wounded . . . and no extra space for supplies or equipment.''

''We'll lose some space to litters for the casualties,'' Trent said. ''What do you need, Doc?''

Ramirez consulted his wristpiece computer. ''We have twenty-seven wounded. If we stack the litters, I can make do with . . . hmmm. Looks like I'll need the medical van, an APC, and something else . . . say one of the engineering rigs. We'll need to mount extra fittings to hold stretchers, but that shouldn't be too hard.''

''Good.'' Trent looked at Qazi. ''What about the supplies, Mohammed?''

''If we strip the place, and I think we'd better, I'll need a hell of a lot of space to carry it all,'' the Arab sergeant replied. ''For starters, let's talk about throwing everybody but the crews out of both supply vans, both fabrication vans, and one of the APCs. That *might* do the job . . . but I'd be happier with a couple of the engineering vans carrying supplies instead of troops, too.''

"There's a problem," Persson put in. "Three of the engineering rigs are in pretty bad shape. They were pulled for maintenance last week, but Battalion never sent the parts to repair them. They'll break down inside of a couple of days."

"So if we take two for supplies and one for the Doc . . ." Trent trailed off.

"We can mount everyone in the company," Persson finished. "But just barely. We'll have ten guys clinging to the outside of APCs or crammed in where there ain't room. First time we have a breakdown, we're slowed to marching pace."

"That's better than I thought it would be," Qazi said. "Hell, we'll all ride out!"

"There's gonna be breakdowns, Ham," Persson said. "We're talking about loading up a lot of high-tech MSVs and pushing them to the limit with nothing but field maintenance. We'll be lucky if half those puppies make it to the border."

"It's still worth trying," Trent said. "With everybody mounted, we'll be able to break contact with our buddies down there in the jungle and put some distance between us and the Dryien army."

"Yeah," Persson said. "Maybe . . ."

"What's the matter, Swede?" Qazi asked. "It checks out, doesn't it?"

Persson grunted. "Sure. But everything's riding on the Exec. He ain't a Legion man, know what I mean? Too much of the old officer-and-gentleman about him . . . not much in the guts department."

"Knock it off, Swede," Trent growled. "I don't want to hear that kind of talk!"

"Ah, hell, Johnnie, you know I'm just tellin' it like it is! The way I heard it, he screwed up on his last assignment and got transferred to the Legion 'cause he had friends in high places to keep him from being court martialed!"

"And *I* heard he got reassigned because of some political mess," Qazi added. "If he's screwed up in that kind of peacetime shit . . ."

"I said *knock it off!*" Trent repeated harshly. "L-T can hack it, as long as you screw-ups do your jobs!"

"But, Johnnie . . ."

"I mean it, Swede! Things are gonna be tough enough without you trying to second-guess the L-T, so just lay off! He's doin' all right . . . and he'll get us out."

Qazi and Persson nodded reluctantly. "If you say so, Sarge," the Arab said.

"I do. Now let's finish up." Trent turned away, making a pretence of studying his 'piece. The two sergeants didn't have the whole story on Fraser's transfer to the Legion, but they had parts of it right. The lieutenant's previous CO was the man blamed for sending the faulty intelligence reports that had led to the loss of two battalions of Commonwealth Regulars on Fenris. From what Trent had heard, it was Fraser's testimony that had damned the man at his court martial . . . but he had some influential friends. Not powerful enough to save the officer, but with sufficient pull to ruin Fraser's career. The lieutenant was given the "opportunity" of serving in the Colonial Army . . . and like so many officers under a cloud had wound up in the Legion.

Fraser wasn't trained as a combat officer, and he was out of his element here. Trent was sure of it. But the sergeant wouldn't allow that kind of talk to spread, for fear of what it might do to the unit's morale. He'd make sure the lieutenant didn't screw up.

Or he'd die trying.

"Lieutenant Winters? I hope I'm not disturbing you." Kelly Winters looked up from the laptop terminal across her knees. "What is it?"

The young officer in the Legion lieutenant's uniform looked tired and worried. "I'm Fraser. Acting CO of this post. Doctor Ramirez said you'd asked to see me."

They'd brought her unconscious to the fort's tiny hospital, where the unit's doctor had treated her for anaphylactic shock. Apparently she'd had a strong reaction to the alien proteins of the hannie soldier's quills. She'd spent some time in a regen chamber, dead to the world, but after the *Ganymede* crash they'd pulled her out to make room for some casualties who needed far more treatment. For the most part, Ramirez and his assistants had ignored her since, except as strictly necessary.

She was going stir-crazy from lack of news. Just what

was happening outside the cramped confines of the small storeroom they'd converted into a private room for her?

"You're in charge? I thought Captain LaSalle was—"

"Captain LaSalle was in the capital when the hannies turned nasty. He's officially listed as missing, but . . ." Fraser spread his hands. "I'm afraid you're stuck with me."

She studied him. He wasn't anything like the unit's old Exec, a worn-out lieutenant whose only real love was the bottle. Fraser looked like a competent, ambitious young officer on his way up in his profession. What was he doing with the Legion?

"I wanted to find out about evac plans, Lieutenant," she said at length. "After what happened with *Ganymede* . . ."

He shook his head. "There won't be another ship, Lieutenant. HQ won't authorize it. We're preparing for an overland withdrawal now."

"Overland! We're a thousand kilometers from friendly territory!"

"Fifteen hundred," he corrected dryly. "But we can't stay here. The Dryiens will get us sooner or later unless we break contact."

Kelly didn't answer. The prospect of crossing an entire continent . . . Could legionnaires do it? Or would they fall apart as soon as the going got tough?

"Doctor Ramirez assures me you'll be able to travel," he said after a long pause. "We'll make you as comfortable as possible, but I can't guarantee the accommodations will be very pleasant."

"Don't worry about me, Lieutenant," she said sharply. "I can take care of myself all right."

"That I don't doubt," Fraser answered. "You were the only one to get out of Monkeyville alive. That took some doing."

"What about the native? I thought ky—"

"Oh, right. Myaighee, I think the doctor said kys name was." Fraser smiled reassuringly. "Your loke friend's well enough, under the circumstances. Still in regen, I guess."

She sank back on the bed, relieved. Fraser wasn't so different from the other legionnaires after all. Not even enough compassion to think about a native who'd risked so much to help the Terrans. "Just make sure ky is treated well, Lieutenant. My loke friend is a damned sight more a hero than any of your so-called soldiers."

Fraser raised an eyebrow, then nodded. "I see. I'll be sure the doctor does everything possible. Good day, Lieutenant Winters." He spun on his heel and left the room.

"Sounds good," Fraser said, nodding approval. "With everyone mounted, we'll make good time."

The entire staff was assembled again to go over the final details of Sergeant Trent's proposed overland withdrawal. Fraser had tried to keep his face unreadable as he listened to the sergeant's report. His doubts about his own abilities were only reinforced by the slim resources at their command.

Right now Bravo Company had only 106 officers and men available, plus Kelly Winters. There were twenty-seven wounded to be cared for. And while Trent's report was encouraging in suggesting they could leave the fort mounted, their assortment of available vehicles was none too reassuring. There were only two Sabertooth FSVs at Monkeyville, plus a total of nineteen Sandray APCs of various types. The four standard carriers designed to hold two full lances each were the only ones mounting kinetic energy cannons, and two of them were going to be carrying supplies or casualties instead of troops. Each of the other vans was designed to carry only one lance plus specialized equipment: computer and comm gear for the command model, mobile workshops and parts stores for the two fabrication vans, and so on. Only the nine engineering vans—three of them apparently broken down beyond repair—mounted weaponry, and that only low-powered lasers designed for felling trees or fusing tunnel walls, not combat armaments.

All in all, it would be a delicate balance, and Fraser wasn't happy at relying on such slim resources to make the long journey north. Not that they had any choice.

"All right, get the men ready to move out," he said. "We'll break out of here tomorrow morning."

"Just how the hell *are* we getting out, Lieutenant?" Subaltern Bartlow asked hesitantly. "I mean, the lokes really have us in a bag up here. How do we break out?"

"We blast a hole and go through," Fairfax said. "Simple enough."

"We'll take casualties, though," Watanabe said thoughtfully. "This time *they'll* have the defensive positions . . . and we can't afford to waste our ammo on one battle."

"Yeah," Fraser agreed. He looked down at his desk. Tactics weren't his specialty, but some kind of tactical trick would help them. "We need surprise . . . a diversion . . ."

Trent looked thoughtful. "If you'll let me have Garcia and Tran for a few hours, L-T, I think I might have just the trick you're looking for . . ."

# Chapter 9

*Bah! No bunch of [deleted] savages can stand against the Legion!*
—Colonel Wilhelm Lichtenauer
following the Battle of Concorde Station
Second Foreign Legion, 2191

Angela Garcia wiped sweat from her forehead and silently cursed the fault in the climate-control circuits of her uniform. Less than an hour after dawn the temperature was already close to 30°C and climbing steadily. The humidity-laden mist seemed to wrap tight around her.

She was hunched over Bravo Company's portable C³ unit in an improvised foxhole at the edge of the *Ganymede* crash site overlooking the eastern edge of the Monkeyville plateau. Legionnaire Tran and Gunnery Sergeant Trent crouched on either side of her, the sergeant scanning the fog-shrouded landscape with his IR scope while Tran helped Garcia set up the terminal for the task ahead.

"Anything, Sergeant?" she asked softly.

"Not yet, Garcia," he replied. "Second and Third recon lances are in position . . . but there's no sign of the bad guys yet."

"Damn." Garcia bit her lip and squinted up through the mist. The fierce heat of Morrison's Star would soon burn away the morning fog, and once that happened the chance for surprise would be gone. "Maybe wc should we call it off, Sarge."

Trent spat expressively. "Give it a few more minutes, Garcia," he said. "We'll find a few witnesses soon."

"All right, Sergeant. You're the boss."

Garcia looked back down at the computer terminal and checked the settings again, more for something to do than because there was any need for another run-through.

She wondered how Fraser was managing without either of his C[3] technicians to help coordinate the main body's escape.

He had wanted to take charge of the diversion personally, but Trent's arguments against it were too strong. The company needed him on the spot if and when the enemy took the bait and gave him his opening to lead the main body out of the fort. So Fraser was stuck in his command van, waiting for the signal to move out, while Trent supervised the operation that was supposed to give him the chance he needed.

Tran cocked his head sideways and said something too softly for Garcia to hear, speaking into his throat mike. The junior C[3] tech flipped a control on the terminal pack and looked up at Sergeant Trent. "Second recon lance has something, Sarge," he said. His finger moved over the computer-generated map display. "Hannie patrol . . . *here,* moving south. Just outside the sensor line, and acting like they know it's there."

Trent pulled his chin thoughtfully. "Didn't think the little bastards knew about 'em," he said. "Well, let's give them a show, Garcia!"

Her fingers danced over the terminal controls.

*Zydryie* Kiijyeed held up a hand to stop the column and cocked kys head, listening to the morning mists.

The sounds coming from the heights above were demon-spawned, not a part of the natural voice of the mists at all. Ky had heard that sound before. It was the noise made by the demon float-tanks when they moved. Ky had been a common soldier on city security duty when a parade of their float-tanks passed through the capital streets back when the demon army first arrived in Dryienjaiyeel.

Here, surrounded by jungle and mist, the sound took on new terror for Kiijyeed. Everyone in kys unit was talking about the terrible vengeance wrought by the guns the demon vehicles mounted. The casualties taken by Regiment Godshammer even before the skyship had fallen . . . Immortal Ancients! How could ordinary mortals fight such demon weapons?

The help the Ancient was giving the army seemed paltry by comparison with the power of that weaponry. It was good to be able to locate the devices that helped the demons track the Dryien troops around the perimeter of their fortress, but what did that really do to protect them from danger?

Especially now. It sounded as if the demons were sending their vehicles *this* way, toward kys patrol. The *Asjyai* had warned that the demons might attempt to break out from their plateau to wreak vengeance on the countryside. Could they be seeking out the trail Regiment Godshammer had used to bring up the tanks used in yesterday's attack? This side of the perimeter was weakly held at best.

Kiijyeed signalled to kys radii operator. Headquarters had to be informed . . .

The noise grew suddenly louder as a huge, flat-bodied shape burst out of the mists only a few *kwyin* away. Kiijyeed recoiled instinctively, dropping the radio handset and snatching at kys submachine gun. The alien APC roared past as if the driver hadn't seen the patrol. Behind it, a second shape thundered through the fog.

Throwing kyself to the ground, Kiijyeed scrabbled for the radio handset again. This was surely the breakout attempt the *Asjyai* was waiting for. Troops had to be shifted to block the demons before they broke through the lines and spread over the countryside, harrying, destroying . . .

As ky gripped the handset the radio operator flopped sideways in the dirt, half of kys face burnt away silently, invisibly, by some unseen demon weapon. Kiijyeed fought down terror as ky opened the radio channel.

"This is patrol three! Patrol three! The demons are attacking! Sector four . . . demon attack!"

The sinister whine of demon *effeekaa* rifles seemed to come from everywhere. Two more of kys soldiers died almost instantly, while a third was screaming horribly and clutching at the stump of kys arm, cut off at the wrist by the hail of demon bullets.

"Patrol three under attack by demons! They are breaking out. . . !"

Kiijyeed hardly even felt the needles that pierced kys body in a dozen places. The handset dropped from nerveless fingers as ky died, still gasping out kys last warning . . .

* * *

"Cease fire! Cease fire!"

Corporal Strauss's words grated harshly in Slick's earphones. He dropped behind a fallen tree, FEK at the ready, and scanned his surroundings on IR. None of the hannie soldiers was moving any more. It had been a perfect ambush, short and sharp. Dark shapes rose out of the mist around the killing field.

"Report!" That was Sergeant Trent, speaking on the general comm channel.

"Red Lance," Strauss replied. "All clear here. Patrol eliminated. No casualties."

"Same for Blue Lance," Corporal Braxton added. The two full-strength recon lances had been responsible for the ambush, while Pascali's understrength unit remained in reserve. Trent had directed the legionnaires into position hard on the heels of the decoy vehicles. The timing had been perfect—after the hannie patrol had sighted the three engineering vans, they'd been given just enough time to report the movement to their HQ before being silenced. If all went according to plan, the natives would shift forces to investigate. And the more they shifted, the easier the *real* breakout would be.

"Very good," Trent said. "All right, Red and Blue . . . get moving. Position number two. Spread out and start planting your Galahads. Rostov, Cunningham, start unloading your gear and setting the charges. Get moving, people!"

"You vill help Rostov, nube," Strauss ordered curtly.

Slick followed the two demolitions experts as they headed for the nearest of the three engineering vehicles, now grounded a few meters beyond the ambush site.

The vehicle certainly looked convincing, Slick thought, as he moved up alongside it. With the engineering fittings stripped away and the laser turret disguised by a little sheet metal and some ingenious camouflage paint, the engineering van looked a lot like an ordinary Sandray troop carrier. With luck, it would convince frightened hannies that the main weight of the Terran breakout was coming through the east perimeter.

In fact the three vehicles were being remotely controlled by Legionnaire Garcia. As a computer and electronics expert, Garcia knew enough about programming to preset simple autopiloting instructions in the onboard computers and then use a $C^3$ terminal to transmit updated orders as needed. With the recon lances deployed to spot the enemy and provide a little on-site firepower, the legionnaires could manage a convincing simulation of a breakout attempt—convincing enough, everyone hoped, to fool the natives, at least.

Rostov opened the rear door, revealing a stack of cargomods inside. Bravo Company had been well-provided with PX-90 explosives and detpack programmable detonators for use in their engineering work. Now the demolitions gear would serve a more lethal purpose, supplementing the unit's assortment of M46 Galahad antipersonnel mines in a defensive perimeter that should help protect Trent's diversionary force when the hannies arrived in force.

With a scowl, Rostov tossed the first case of explosives to Slick. Although he knew the explosives were completely safe unless equipped with suitably programmed detonators, he still flinched involuntarily as he caught it. Rostov's eyes were full of contempt as he turned away to pick up another cargomod.

*They all think I'm a coward.* The words had become a litany echoing through his mind. Slick tried to push the thought away, deny it, reject it . . . but it kept coming back.

If the diversion worked the way it was supposed to, the full weight of the hannie army would be pushing this way soon. Part of him shrank from the thought of another fight. Another part, though, welcomed the prospect.

He wasn't going to run from combat this time. When the battle began, Slick would be in the thick of it.

They wouldn't call him a coward then.


"Good . . . good . . . come a little left now." Colin Fraser studied the video image carefully, noting the movement of vehicles and men. "Steady on that view."

"Got it, Lieutenant," WO/4 Vandergraff acknowledged.

"What do you make of it, Mr. Hamilton?" Fraser asked the other warrant officer.

Hamilton leaned forward to look over his shoulder at

the view relayed from the drone hovering low over the main hannie camp. "They're moving, all right. Looks like our monkey buddies are falling for it."

Fraser stood up, ducking to avoid the low roof of the command van. "Take over here, Mr. Hamilton," he said. "Let me know when they're committed."

"Yes, sir." Hamilton slid into the chair beside Vandergraff.

Moving forward, Fraser stuck his head into the driver's cab. Platoon Sergeant Persson looked up from the control board.

"Everything ready?" Fraser asked.

"Looks like it, sir," Persson replied. "All the 'rays are loaded up. Bashar and Mason have the FSVs in position."

"Good. We'll mag out as soon as the monkeys are busy with Gunny Trent's little show."

Fraser could hardly control the excitement rising inside him. Now there was finally a chance to *act*, instead of just sitting and waiting. Sergeant Trent's arguments had been convincing . . . but he still wished he had insisted on taking charge of the diversion. It was frustrating to sit back in the safety of the fort, waiting and worrying while others risked everything. Getting them out after the rest of the company was clear of the fort was going to be dicey.

But Trent was right. His responsibility was to the whole unit . . .

In the back of the command van, Legionnaire Hengist and the Padre were waiting in silence. Fraser caught the Padre's eye from the compartment door.

"Know any blessings for a mag-out, Padre?" he asked, keeping his tone light.

Fitzpatrick raised his hand in benediction. "May the Good Lord bless and keep this mag-out . . ." he intoned solemnly, ". . . moving just as fast as possible."

Hengist laughed. "Think He's looking out for us, Padre?"

"Of course, my son," the priest responded "God watches and cherishes the very worst sinners. I can't think of anyone He loves more than the Legion."

Fraser turned away, smiling again. He hoped God *was*

watching over them. In the next few hours they'd need all the help they could get.

Slick tamped wet dirt down around the cylindrical base of his last Galahad mine, then flipped open the plasteel lid covering the arming controls and touched the pressure pad labelled "TEST." A green light glowed briefly as the mine's sensor array went through a brief diagnostic check. At the same moment Slick heard the tone in his earpiece that indicated his helmet's IFF system was operating. Any legionnaire with a working transponder could walk through the minefield without fear . . . but once the Galahad was armed, any other living thing that passed within ten meters of the deadly little cylinder would trigger it. The open-topped tube contained ten separate egg-shaped bomblets. Each time the mine's computer brain registered a valid target and no nearby friendly forces, one of those bombs would be hurled into the air where it would explode, showering the area with a hail of lethal shrapnel.

Satisfied, Slick armed the mine. Between Rostov's explosive charges and the pattern of Galahads, the hundred-meter stretch in front of the position Trent had designated as the main line of defense was now a death zone. The hannies would have to take this route—it was the only one suitable for their vehicles on the whole east side of Monkeyville. Anyway, in a few more minutes the engineering vans would be back in action, drawing the enemy's attention again.

He stood up and picked his way up a steep slope toward the location Strauss had chosen for him. The corporal had assigned Slick a spot on the end of the Red Lance line, probably to keep him on the periphery of the action in case he froze up again. But Slick wasn't planning to be left out. He'd show Strauss . . . he'd show them all.

As he settled behind one of the stunted, twisted trees typical of Hanuman's jungle growth, Slick felt rather than heard a distant vibration. He'd finished his work just in time. Hannie vehicles were coming.

Slick checked his FEK's battery charge and ammo counter, then flipped down his helmet display screen and called up the map Garcia was transmitting over the $C^3$

net from Trent's observation post. Pascali's lance was out ahead of the main line, scouting out the enemy as they headed for the diversionary force. Red symbols crawled across the screen, creeping slowly toward the thin blue line that represented Bravo Company's forlorn hope.

"Yeah, L-T, six to eight tanks, maybe a hundred infantry. They'll be on top of our mines in about ten minutes." Trent smiled wolfishly. "Looks like they got our invitation!"

"Just about what we were looking for, Gunny." Static crackled around Fraser's reply. "The drones are showing a lot of activity on this end. They've started shifting most of their boys your way. If we hit 'em hard, we'll break through without much trouble."

"Roger that," Trent said. He glanced over at the C³ display. Garcia was peering at a video image relayed from the lead decoy vehicle while she entered new commands to the autopilot through the keyboard. "We'll let 'em know we're here, L-T. Don't make a move until we've got the buggers' attention."

Fraser's reply sounded stiff. "We'll keep to the plan, Gunny. You just make sure you get disengaged in time."

"Don't worry about that!" Trent said. "We're not sticking around here any longer than we have to!"

"Roger. Alice One, clear."

"Guardian clear." Trent turned his attention to the battle map on his helmet display. The hannies were moving up steadily . . .

"All right, Garcia," he said softly. "Time to bait the trap."

The morning mists were all but gone now, broken up by the heat as Morrison's Star rose higher above the horizon. *That's one advantage gone,* Slick thought. *Let's hope our other surprises make up for it.*

His display map showed the hannie forces closing in, less than half a kilometer away now. The jungle hid the enemy, but Pascali's lance was still tracking their advance . . . and the three decoy vehicles remained in front of them, continuing to stimulate the movement of a larger Terran force trying to get past the native lines. Periodically Slick heard cannonfire as native tanks challenged

the empty APCs. The last few shots had been close . . .
*really* close . . .

With a roar of turbofans, one of the engineering vehicles burst from the treeline in full retreat, crossing the
minefield at top speed. The Galahads ignored the friendly
target, and the charges Rostov and Cunningham had
placed were rigged for radio-controlled detonation. Any
observer would have assumed that field was safe to cross.

The APC moved straight across the open ground and
up the gentlest part of the slope. The sound of the fans
died and the vehicle stopped moving, resting on its magnetic suspension near the crest of the hill. Then, slowly,
the fields collapsed and the Sandray settled to the ground,
hull-down behind the shelter of the rising ground. The
turret, though, remained visible. Slick could see Corporal Pascali climbing down off the back of the vehicle.
Trent had ordered the scouts to hitch rides aboard the
computer-controlled vehicles so they could join the
defenders along the perimeter.

Then the second and third APCs appeared almost together, farther down the line of trees, weaving past ob-
stacles before they revved up to make the final run across
the open ground. Somewhere back in the jungle another
tank gun coughed. An explosion raised a gout of thick
black mud from a pool of stagnant water a few meters
ahead of one of the Sandrays. Legionnaire Reinhardt,
lying on top of the flat manta-ray shape and facing the
jungle, squeezed off an FEK burst.

Slick braced his weapon on the improvised barricade
in front of him and tried to keep his breathing regular.
*This is it!*

A squat, massive metallic shape crashed through the
trees below him, clanking into the clearing with the im-
placable momentum of a juggernaut. Around the tank,
hannie foot soldiers were fanning out into a loose skirmish line. An officer with a gaudily-painted muzzle
jabbered orders, gesticulating wildly as ky urged the
troops forward.

Movement to his right made Slick shift his head. Another party of native infantry was emerging from the
treeline. Most were armed with blunderbuss rocket
launchers or bulky heavy machine guns, but they were

moving fast considering their loads. Slick drew in a quick, sharp breath.

These natives were ignoring the easy route up the slope. They were moving straight up the most difficult part of the hill, well clear of the minefield and the defending legionnaires.

Despite the difficult terrain and the burdens they were carrying, those hannie soldiers would be behind the Legion line in another few minutes, and those weapons they were carrying were a lot more dangerous to the Terran troops than the standard enemy longarms.

The trappers were about to be trapped . . .

# Chapter 10

What matters is the action, the combat which places you on a different plane from the rest of the herd.

—Colonel Pierre Jeanpierre
French Foreign Legion, 1958

A green light on the C³ terminal lit up, and Garcia smiled in satisfaction. The final program was in place; the three diversionary vehicles were committed.

"It's set," she told Trent.

Trent nodded acknowledgement. The engineering vans had stopped maneuvering. Now they were deployed in a loose defensive line, and their drilling lasers were programmed to fire on command. That, in combination with the explosives Rostov and Cunningham had planted, would keep the hannies busy for a while.

She frowned at the terminal video display, watching the images relayed from the middle vehicle. This remote-controlled battle was like a distant, unreal game, a dreamchipper's fantasy. No, not even that . . . a dreamer's visions *seemed* real enough while he was under.

Garcia wondered how the soldiers down on the perimeter were feeling. This would be all too real for them.

Her screen showed a native tank advancing slowly into the minefield with hannie soldiers fanned out around it. She tracked the hannie vehicle, calling up a set of crosshairs and centering them over the target. Something moved to one side of the scene, a small, oblong something that rose a meter off the ground and exploded in a glittering shower of metal fragments. A pair of hannies went down with blood welling from wounds in their chests and arms.

"Now!" she called. Her finger stabbed the remote firing control, and red light bathed the front of the tank.

The last battle of Monkeyville had begun.

The bursting Galahad down in the minefield made Slick duck and turn. The flanking party had driven all thought of the main body out of his mind.

Down below, hannies were gibbering and running. The nearest tank glowed red under the intense light of the laser focused on it from one of the engineering vans. Although their lasers were not intended as combat weapons, they had the power to fell trees and fuse tunnel walls . . . and a few seconds was enough to superheat the target's armor. The front chassis just above the main gun dripped and melted. An instant later something inside exploded, raining debris over the panicked native soldiers. Farther down the line, one of Rostov's PX-90 charges went off directly under a lighter tank, ripping open the bottom of the AFV.

Slick jerked his attention back to the flanking party. They had heard the explosions too, but a spur of the hill blocked their line of sight. An officer or NCO was urging them on, pointing wildly at the top of the slope and screeching rapid-fire orders—or maybe invective—and physically pushing one laden soldier from behind. It looked so much like something Corporal Strauss might have done that Slick smiled.

But what to do about them? Slick considered calling for help, then rejected the thought. *They think I'm a coward already* . . .

If he needed help handling a few lokes, they'd be sure of his cowardice. He had to act by himself. That was the only way to win back their respect.

As he rose from his hiding place and sprinted a zigzag course for the top of the hill, Slick was surprised at just how important winning their respect had become.

The command van lurched once as Legionnaire Hengist swerved to avoid an obstacle. Colin Fraser braced himself against the door frame and peered over the driver's shoulder at the monitor showing the vehicle's path ahead. "Rev her up, Hengist," he ordered. "Persson, pass the word. Show a few revs."

The van shuddered once as the fans whined louder. Suspended on magnetic fields and driven by two powerful turbofans, the vehicle began to glide forward, gathering speed. Fraser braced himself against the motion and looked over the driver's shoulder at the video display from the vehicle's forward cameras. Ahead of them, Corporal Weston's supply van was surging forward.

Fraser raised his voice over the noise of the fans. "The path forks off about a half a klick ahead, sergeant. Tell your drivers to be ready to turn."

"Yes, sir."

Hengist swerved again, this time to avoid the smoking remains of a hannie self-propelled gun on the right side of the road. Bashar's Sabertooth had literally opened the trail for the rest, cutting through the unprepared hannie outposts before they realized the legionnaires were even coming. With most of the enemy's strength and attention focused on the diversionary force, Bravo Company's breakout was running smoothly.

But they couldn't stay on the main northwest road for very long. The jungle was too thick down in the lowlands to allow the Legion vehicles any freedom of movement, and the drones had shown another large hannie mechanized column farther down the road pressing hard to join the siege of Monkeyville. Bravo Company couldn't afford to let itself be trapped between the reinforcements and the bulk of the native army, which wouldn't stay distracted too much longer . . .

One trail did break off from the main road, winding north into deeper jungle. They had to secure that fork in the road and hold it until Trent's rearguard could be extracted. That would be the most dangerous part of the entire plan.

Persson pointed to the flashing map display between the driver and passenger seats in the cab. "Bashar's up to the fork, Lieutenant!" he shouted. "He reports all clear."

"Right," Fraser replied. "Pass the word. Get the APCs off the road!"

Without waiting for a reply he turned back into the command center, staggering as the van sideslipped, then sinking gratefully into a chair next to Vandergraff. He took control of one of the drones and steered it north-

west. Time to find out how long they'd have to get Trent
out . . .

Slick dropped to his belly and lay still, hardly breathing. The chameleon coating on his fatigues and armor
faded from the grey-brown of the rocky slope to a mottled yellow-green as sensors embedded in the uniform
read his surroundings and the suit's miniature computer
transmitted the appropriate electrical impulses through
the climate-control mesh that triggered the color change.
In the tall grass at the top of the hill, Slick would be
nearly invisible.

Below him the ten hannie troopers were still climbing,
but more slowly now. The exertion was probably starting
to get to them, Slick thought. Hanuman's natives were
strong for their small size and tough, capable of surprising feats of endurance, but yomping that heavy gear up
the steep hillside must surely have taken a toll by now.

The first local appeared less than five meters away. Ky
was carrying a blunderbuss rocket launcher and several
reloads. The weapon seemed impossibly large for the
native, but after a few seconds' rest the soldier was moving again, crossing the flat hilltop and scanning the battlefield below with a clumsy-looking optical imager.
More troops followed . . . three more blunderbusses, a
pair of HMGs, then two soldiers with ordinary native-
issue rifles, belts of ammo draped over their shoulders
and chests, and folded tripods slung across their backs.
They joined the HMG gunners and started setting up the
weapons in commanding positions overlooking the valley.

The officer and another soldier were last up. A shout
from the first trooper made the leader hasten to kys side,
where the two hannies jabbered together with frequent
gesticulations. Slick thought he heard the native word
that meant "devil." He remained motionless, his mind
racing. The natives were too spread out. So far they
hadn't offered a target he could take out all at once. There
wasn't much time . . .

The first native was raising the blunderbuss and training it on the ridgeline below. Slick tensed, hesitated. Ky
was aiming about where DuPont had been posted with
his sniping laser. He had to act, despite the danger.

He rolled into a crouch and brought the FEK up, spraying caseless kinetic energy rounds into the soldier with the blunderbuss, and the officer. The trooper's fingers tightened convulsively on the weapon's trigger as ky fell, and a rocket roared from the tube. Officer and soldier collapsed in a bloody pile, and Slick swiveled his rifle toward the nearest of the machine-gun teams.

Needles slashed into the natives at 10,000 mps, flinging them backward as they tried to wrestle their weapon into line. The gunner sprawled against a rock in an untidy heap; kys loader balanced for a moment on the crest of the slope before tumbling out of sight. A blunderbuss roared and Slick felt the heat as the rocket passed inches from his head. He kept on firing, and three more hannies went down.

The FEK clicked and whirred, the hundred-round magazine empty. Rising to his feet, Slick cursed and shifted to his grenade launcher, firing a stream of 1cm projectiles into the second hannie machine-gun position. The gunner's scream was cut short as one of the warheads struck soft flesh and exploded, tearing the soldier in half. Slick didn't have time to react to the sight.

Something smashed across his back. The fatigues absorbed some of the blow, but it still knocked Slick to his knees, and the FEK spun out of his hands into the tall grass. The native swung kys rifle butt again, but Slick rolled with the blow and caught the weapon in both hands, pulling hard. The native, already off-balance, staggered and let go. An instant later ky was on him, long fingers extended to grope for Slick's neck.

An explosion a few meters away showered them with dirt, and the native's attention wavered. Slick drove his fist into the hannie's stomach and the soldier rolled off him, hitting the ground hard. In a flash, his other hand closed around the knife in his boot-top. A quick upward stroke finished the hannie before ky could recover.

A second explosion made Slick stagger as he rose. He shook his head to clear it, realizing dimly that the blasts were from Legion rifle grenades, not hannie weapons. The hannies were all down, dead or dying.

"Cease firing! Cease firing!" he screamed into his radio. He flipped down his helmet display to try to get a fix on whoever was firing. "Rostov, this is Grant! I'm on the hill you're firing at! Cease fire!"

The last explosion raised a shower of rock splinters from a nearby boulder. Slick's map display went dark as a rock the size of his fist slammed into his helmet.

Then a different kind of darkness engulfed him.

"Damn!" Angela Garcia swore softly as the video image on her screen blacked out. "That's two down."

She shifted the pickup to receive from the number three van. The hannies had backed off from the minefield, but their tanks were concentrating heavy fire on the Legion APCs from the edge of the jungle. The Sandrays were well-armored by native standards, but they couldn't stand up to the punishment of a head-to-head slugging match with main battle tanks. She fired the APC laser at the closest target, but the driver quickly dropped the tank into reverse and backed into the trees before the beam could do more than scorch the chassis armor. The hannies might be primitive, but they weren't stupid. They'd learned how to deal with APCs.

And their troops were getting wary of the minefield now. The locals might not have the technology to produce mines with multiple warheads, but they'd grasped the concept quickly enough. There were reports of flanking parties trying to turn either flank of the defensive line. As they found the direct route blocked, they'd be pushing more troops to the sides.

"Corporal Pascali reports three casualties," Tran was telling Trent. "One dead in her lance . . . another in Braxton's. And one of Strauss's men is wounded. Damn fool went off on his own without telling anyone and took friendly fire out on the flank. Rostov and Vrurrth are marking the pickup now."

"All right. Pull back by teams to the next position." Trent frowned. "Damn! I was hoping we'd hold 'em longer there." He paused, then shook his head. "The hell with it. All right, get 'em moving!"

Garcia turned back to the terminal and started programming the retreat orders into the vehicle's autopilot.

*"Asjyai! Asjyai!* The demons have broken out of the fort on the northwest side!"

"What?" *Asjyai* Zyzyiig whirled to face the panting messenger by the tent flap. "What are you talking about?"

"It's true, Honored! Many of their floating demon-cars, and heretic soldiers with them!" The messenger flinched under Zyzyiig's stare. "They destroyed our tanks and scattered the troops along the road! The demons are between us and the Regiment Fearmongers!"

Beside Zyzyiig, the Semti stirred. "I told you not to send so many to respond to that first report," Shavva-taaars said. "These legionnaires are more resourceful than you believed . . . or more ruthless. Expending part of their force in a false breakout called for considerable courage. The Terran demons rarely show such under-standing of the needs of war. Their commander is one I would wish to Journey with . . ."

"He won't live long enough for your Journeys!" Zyzyiig snapped. The demons were getting away! He turned to the radio operator. "Order Fearmongers and our reserves to converge on them!"

"Honored . . . it will take an hour to launch the at-tack!" the messenger protested. "And the demons con-trol another way out!"

"You will not catch them, *Asjyai*," Shavvataaars said calmly. "Their vehicles are too fast for you."

Furious, Zyzyiig rounded on the Semti. "This is *your* fault! You said we had them where we wanted them, that they could not escape!"

"I also said that patience was the greatest of all wis-dom," the Semti replied coldly. "Had you been less ea-ger, you might have had sufficient forces assembled to meet this attack."

Zyzyiig felt kys neck ruff rippling. Taking a deep breath, ky forced the anger back. "If we cannot stop the main force, we can at least crush this diversion. Order the Regiment Deathshead to press the attack!"

"Vengeance will gain you nothing," Shavvataaars said. "You would do better to regroup in case these le-gionnaires do not remain in flight. They could still cause much damage, left unwatched."

"You want me to call off this attack, too? I won't do it." Zyzyiig spat. "Ancient or not, you have interfered with my command once too often. You have your prep-

arations to make to the north, Shavvataaars. I suggest
you get to them, and leave the demons here to me!''

"Keep your head down, Garcia!'' Sergeant Trent fired
an FEK burst and glanced at the C³ technician. She was
crouched behind a rock, her FEK held ready.

The last engineering van had fallen prey to hannie tank
guns almost half an hour back, and the legionnaires were
on their own now. The three recon lances, less four dead
and two wounded, were holding a narrow perimeter
around Trent's original observation post. The natives
were pressing their attack more fiercely than ever, flinging in troops and vehicles with careless disregard for casualties. Apparently they didn't realize, or perhaps didn't
care, that this wasn't the real breakout force. The monkeys seemed determined to destroy Trent's force no matter what.

That was bad . . . very bad. The plan had counted on
hannie pressure letting up as soon as they realized that
Bravo Company was trying to escape. Maybe the diversion had worked *too* well.

"Tran! Give me the command channel!''

He nodded acknowledgement and passed him the
handset. Now that it wasn't being used as a remote control for vehicles, the portable C³ terminal was on his back
again. Garcia lifted her FEK and fired as Trent started
broadcasting.

"Alice One, Alice One, this is Guardian. Abort rescue! Repeat, abort rescue!'' Trent swallowed once, fighting off despair. The rearguard had counted on him . . .

"Guardian, Alice One,'' Fraser's static-crusted voice
came back. "Negative! Rescue unit on the way. Hold out
. . . three more minutes.''

"Damn it, L-T, they'll be charging into the middle of
half the Dryien army! The monkeys know how to knock
out our APCs! Abort the op, for God's sake!''

Corporal Bashar's voice came on the line. "Not a
chance, Sarge! Ain't no primmie bastard can hit *my* baby.
Anyway, you still owe me twenty sols from that poker
game last week!''

Trent swore. "You can't collect if you're dead, Basher!
Call it off!''

"Shut up and let me rescue you, Sarge!" The line went dead.

Trent replaced the handset and peered cautiously around the rock. Thirty meters away a hannie tank was lumbering slowly forward across bare, rocky ground. Suddenly a grey-brown figure lunged out of the cover of a rockslide and leapt on top of the vehicle, poking his FEK into the open hatch. Corporal Strauss's finger tightened on the grenade launcher trigger, sending a stream of small but powerful rifle grenades into the low-slung vehicle. Smoke and flame gouted from the hatch and the driver's slit as Strauss jumped clear, hosing a squad of hannie infantry with autofire as he ran for cover.

Farther away another hannie tank fired once. Then the sleek shape of a Grendel missile skimmed over the ridge beyond the vehicle. It seemed to pause for an instant like a hound casting for a scent, then plunged downward into the tank.

The explosion hadn't subsided when the Sabertooth topped the rise, fans revving at full speed. Legionnaire Karatsolis guided the plasma gun to bear on another target and fired. The Sabertooth pivoted on its fans, maintaining a steady barrage. Behind it, a Sandray appeared, its CEK chattering as it passed through a cluster of hannie troops.

"Recon lances! Let's savkey! Go! Go! Go!" Trent realized he was shouting into the radio. So much for his image of unflappable calm.

The legionnaires were scrambling from their defensive positions, laying down their own covering fire to augment the heavier guns on the two vehicles. Trent watched as Legionnaire Rostov helped Grant, who had recovered enough to walk, into the back of the Sandray. The rest of the recon troopers quickly climbed aboard and the APC skittered sideways to make room for the Sabertooth. As it touched down, Trent was already urging Tran into motion. He sprinted across the open ground and reached the rear door while the ramp was still dropping.

Garcia was next. A hannie machine gun opened up, and slugs slammed into the legionnaire's legs. She stumbled and fell.

Trent fired a three-round grenade burst at the machine-gun nest and leapt from cover. He barely paused to help

Garcia up, half-carrying her. It looked like her uniform had stopped the bullets, but he knew the kinetic energy of those hits would still have been enough to hurt, maybe even cause a fracture. She gritted her teeth. ''Thanks, Sarge,'' she gasped as he pushed her into the back of the Sabertooth. Tran helped her up and stretched her out on one of the troop benches, rolling up the trouser leg to examine the injury. Trent slapped the ramp button and sank onto the other bench, exhausted.

With a roar, the Sabertooth lurched forward, the plasma gun still firing wildly.

Trent could hardly believe they'd managed to escape.

# Chapter 11

The Legion takes care of its own.
                    —traditional slogan
              Fourth Foreign Legion, c. 2650

"It's no good, lieutenant. It'd take a week in a repbay and a list of spare parts as long as a Toeljuk's tentacles to get this baby running again."

Colin Fraser frowned. "You said these carriers were working, Sergeant."

"They were, Lieutenant," Persson replied patiently. "As of the last check-up . . . and before you tried to take them through the jungle."

Bravo Company's vehicles were clustered in a large clearing surrounded by jungle. Monkeyville was nearly two hundred kilometers behind them now, and there had been little sign of pursuit. Legionnaire Ignaczak had shot down a hannie fighter plane pacing the column in the first hour of the retreat, but beyond that it looked as if they'd broken contact cleanly.

The trail they'd followed north away from the main road had been a good escape route, but an hour after leaving the main road Fraser ordered the column to turn east into the jungle. At that time the decision had seemed valid enough. The trail emerged from the rain forest and rejoined the main road net halfway between the capital, Jyeezjai, and Dryien's second largest city, and Fraser wasn't about to lead Bravo Company into that kind of danger again so soon. And the possibility of more aerial harassment while they remained on the open trail was something he had to consider as well. The two Sabertooth FSVs could knock down aircraft easily enough, but a really large-scale attack might be more than they could handle, especially given the restricted fields of fire on the jungle road.

Now, though, it seemed that his decision had been wrong.

"These Sandrays ain't built to go bouncin' off trees," Persson continued as if to emphasize Fraser's gloomy thoughts. "You can't use them as battering rams without expecting to take some damage."

"All right, Sergeant, you've made your point. How long will it take to transfer the supplies to another APC?"

"Maybe an hour, Lieutenant." Persson paused. "A couple of hours if we do things right and strip the beast."

"Strip it?"

"Yeah . . . pull out the electronics and the magrep modules, break down the fans for spare parts, that sort of thing."

Fraser studied the damaged vehicle. It was one of the two cargo vans, stocked with food, ammo, and other gear. One of its fans had been knocked out, another damaged, and it was sagging on one side from a magrep module failure. He felt his fists tighten at his sides. A breakdown this early in the long journey was a bad sign. This would be enough to force some of the legionnaires to ride on the outside of other vehicles or travel on foot . . . and that would slow the column down.

Forcing himself to relax, he nodded. "All right. Do it the right way, Sergeant. But I'm holding you to that two hours. Don't do anything that'll end up taking longer."

"Yes, sir." Persson turned away, shouting for Corporal Weston.

Specialists in the transport platoon were cross-trained in mechanical maintenance and repair; Persson's men would be able to handle the salvage work on their own. But transferring supplies from the supply vehicle into another Sandray would go faster with some extra help. Fraser sought out Sergeant Qazi and told him to round up a work detail, then headed back to the command van. Trent met him by the ramp.

"L-T, Garcia's got something on the radio," the sergeant said.

Legionnaire Garcia had suffered a sprained ankle and some bad bruising on her legs, but she was back on duty at the van's $C^3$ console. Trent seemed little the worse for wear, but Fraser thought the man looked exhausted. After the fighting outside Monkeyville, that wasn't surprising.

"What is it, Gunny?"

Trent shook his head. "Can't be sure, L-T. There's a lot of static, and the signal's pretty weak to begin with. But it's on the platoon net assigned to Charlie Company, and a couple of clear spots sounded like human voices."

Fraser locked eyes with Trent, startled. If some of Charlie Company had escaped after all. . . ! "Did you try to raise them?"

"Garcia gave it a go, L-T, but there wasn't an answer. She says they're probably using helmet sets, and the range is just too long. All we're getting is stray stuff, nothing coherent."

"Yeah . . . or our hannie friends are using recordings." Fraser looked away.

"Shit, L-T, you're not going to ignore them, are you?" Trent looked angry. "We can't just leave them!"

"God, Gunny . . . I don't know!" Fraser suddenly felt dizzy, weak. One crisis after another, decision after decision . . . and a wrong choice at any turn could kill them all. "I just don't know!"

"I could take out another patrol . . ." Trent was swaying with fatigue as he spoke.

"Forget it, Gunny," Fraser told him. "You've done enough for one day." He paused, wrestling with his doubts. "All right. Pass the word to Watanabe to get his platoon ready to move out—but leave the recon lance out of it. Mount them on one of the APCs, a Sabertooth, and one of the engineering vans. Uh . . . better have a couple of the other vehicles ready in case we do find survivors."

"You're putting Watanabe in charge, then? Good choice . . ."

"I'll take command myself, Gunny. If this is a trap, I'm not sending in any of those kids while I sit on my butt back here. Tell Fairfax he's in charge if I don't come back. And get the column moving again in two hours whether or not we've reported in. We'll catch up."

"L-T, I don't think—"

"That's an order, Gunny!" Fraser interrupted with more force than he'd intended. Now that he'd made the decision, he was impatient to go through with it.

Trent drew himself to attention and saluted. "Yes, sir."

Fraser watched the sergeant as he left in search of Sub-altern Watanabe. So many wrong decisions already . . . would this one go wrong, too?

He didn't want to think of what would happen to Bravo Company if it did.

"How'd we get stuck with this detail, anyhow? Didn't we do enough already?"

Slick grunted, ignoring Legionnaire Rostov's complaining as he manhandled another box of supplies down the damaged cargo van's ramp. The effort made his head throb, but he was glad to be working. Sitting in an APC while it lurched and swerved through the jungle had made his head hurt just as much, and there hadn't been any way to take his mind off it.

Vrurrth picked up Slick's box at the bottom of the ramp as if it was packed with feathers. "The fight, the work," the alien rumbled, looking at Rostov. "The duties make us Legion."

"Easy for you to say, big guy," Rostov told him. "You'd think a fifty-klick hike was a nice way to rest. *I'm* tired."

"Could be worse," Slick ventured. "We might have had to go with the rest of the platoon on that run the lieutenant ordered."

Rostov grinned. "Hell, at least I could get some sleep sitting on my ass in an APC!" He wrestled another box out of the stack and across the floor of the van. Slick took over at the top of the ramp. "It's a good thing we're not going, all the same. Corp'd probably tie you up and leave you in the back of the 'ray if we went out on another op."

Slick felt himself flushing. Since waking up after the fight on the hilltop, he had been starting to feel accepted again. No one was likely to doubt his courage now, not after he'd taken on ten hannies alone! But underneath Rostov's bantering tone he thought he detected a hint of genuine warning.

"What're you talking about? Don't tell me he's still after me for that shit in the trench!"

"I'm talking about this morning, kid. That stunt you

pulled was enough to get you a couple of weeks in cells. If—"

"Stunt? I saved the lance! Maybe the whole god-damned battle, for Chrissake!"

Rostov straightened up from the box in front of him. "You really don't get it, do you, kid?"

"Get what? Why—"

"Look, you may have saved some lives this morning . . ."

"*May* have! There was a blunderbuss aimed right at DuPont—"

"Shut up, kid! I'm trying to help you." Rostov pulled out a slender Medean cigarette and lit it. "Like I was saying, you might have saved some lives out there. But the *way* you did it was stupid . . . criminal, even. Did it ever occur to you to warn somebody about the monkeys?"

"Yeah, right," Slick responded sourly. "With everybody already saying I'm a coward, I'm gonna call for help. No thanks, man."

"Call for *help!* How about you call to report and *ask* for some orders? Hell, what are they teaching you nubes these days, anyway?"

"I used initiative," Slick said firmly. Inside, though, Rostov's words hit home.

"You wouldn't know initiative if it sat up and bit you on the nose, nube. You were thinking with your pride, not your brains. For God's sake, kid, I damn near snuffed you today 'cause I didn't know you were up there. And where the hell would we have been if they'd killed you, huh? You *report* what you see and you *follow orders.*" Rostov spread his hands. "Get with the program, Grant. In the Legion we look after our own. That means we think about our buddies before we think about ourselves . . . and we don't go hogging the glory and risking everything the way you did!"

"That's real great advice, Rostov," Slick said, angry. "Real great. Maybe if I thought I *had* some 'buddies' around here I'd buy all this teamwork crap I keep hearing. Every move I make gets me nothing but grief. If it isn't from Strauss or from one of you guys, it's from one of the sergeants—or from Gunny Trent. I'm not a part of your team, and I don't think I ever will be!"

"Not with that attitude you won't, kid," Rostov said bluntly. "You'll be accepted by the Legion just as soon as you show you're really a legionnaire, not before. As long as you keep playing games, though, don't expect anybody to think you're anything but a dumb nube."

"Enough talk!" Corporal Strauss shouted from outside. "Get back to vork!"

Slick turned back to the nearest box and started shoving it down the ramp, attacking it with some of the fury seething inside of him. Rostov was right about the mistakes he'd made in the fight with the hannies, but the rest . . . ! The harder he tried to understand the Legion, the worse things got. It wasn't like he had volunteered; the court had forced him to join. And it seemed as if there was no way he'd ever fit in on *their* terms.

All he could do, he decided, was survive.

"Can't you push this thing any faster, Mason?" Fraser asked irritably as the Sabertooth slowed down to swing wide around another tight-packed clump of trees.

Sergeant Paul Mason didn't even raise his head from the monitor screen in front of him. "Not unless you want to tear the guts out of her, Lieutenant," he said gruffly. He had the sound of a man protecting a child.

"Survey map says it thins out in another few klicks, sir," Legionnaire Tran said from behind Fraser. He was filling in for Garcia, since she was still recovering from her injury, and what he lacked in technical expertise he made up for in enthusiasm. "We can make better time there."

Mason grunted. "Yeah. Maybe."

It had been a frustrating two-hour trek. Following the line of the radio signal Garcia had picked up, the three Legion vehicles had travelled deep into the jungle. Fraser had been tempted to turn back when it became clear that they weren't heading for any of the three Charlie Company outposts, but his conscience wouldn't allow him to act until he was sure. They'd been delayed repeatedly by the dense jungle growth. In places the short, twisted trees were so tightly intertwined that they seemed like a single organism. Patches like that were impenetrable to men and machines alike, and the only option was to change course and seek an easier way around the obstacle. With Mason worried that the Sabertooth and the two APCs might suffer the same kind of damage as the crippled supply van, they were forced to proceed at a painfully slow pace.

Fraser had been thinking of the detachment as a "flying column." The phrase rang in his mind like a feeble joke now.

By now the main body would be moving again, and each passing hour would widen the gap between them. It would cost more precious time if they had to stop so Fraser's party could catch up . . . but the alternative, keeping the tiny Legion force divided in the heart of a hostile country, was unthinkable.

Another choice gone wrong . . .

"I'm getting something, Lieutenant," Tran said suddenly. He was holding a headphone to one ear. "Sounds like . . . yeah, that's Russo. Charlie Company's command $C^3$ tech. I think they're under attack!"

Fraser took the headphones and slipped them over his ears. Static made the signal ragged.

". . . get the damned Fafnirs over on the left . . . too late!"

"That's firm . . . bastards moving up the road . . ."

"Sub's been hit! Tell Baker to get a medic down here . . . ! Where's the Sarge? He's in charge now!"

Handing the phones back to Tran, Fraser looked down at the $C^3$ terminal balanced on the legionnaire's knees. "Do you have a line on them?"

"Yes, sir. And Garcia's feeding us a second line from the command van. Looks like they're right about . . . here." The terminal's map display showed two lines intersecting at a point about twenty kilometers away. Tran touched a stud and a detail map replaced the first. Fraser bent forward to examine it.

The lines touched at an open area labelled "Shelton's Head." It was at least 110 kilometers from any of the three outposts where Charlie Company's platoons had been stationed . . . more like 200 klicks from the site of the company HQ, where Russo would have been stationed.

"What have you got on this place, Tran?" he asked,

pointing to the name.

Tran called to the data from the computer. "It's a zyg-lyn plantation, Lieutenant," the Viet legionnaire said. "Head of the trail. Surveyed by a free-lancer working for StelPhar by the name of Shelton . . . ten years back. Seems Shelton and his wife struck a private deal with some of the local growers and settled there after he retired. It was Shelton who convinced StelPhar to open the trail from Monkeyville up to his place."

Fraser nodded slowly. "So . . . if they got cut off from Monkeyville, some of the people from Charlie Company might have holed up with this Shelton."

"Looks that way, sir," Tran agreed.

Fraser studied the map again. "On the other hand, it still could be a trap. We don't have any proof that those signals are coming in live. They might have been recorded."

"Maybe so, sir," the legionnaire said. "But if they pulled back here, it would explain why the Sarge couldn't raise them when he did his recon the other night."

"Maybe so." Fraser frowned. "Damn! I wish we had the command van so we weren't going in blind. Drones'd be real handy right about now."

"Won't take long to call for one, Lieutenant," Tran told him. "Let me get Garcia for you."

He hadn't been thinking in terms of help from the main body . . . hadn't been thinking at all, in fact. Of course Garcia could send drones in to scout out the area; flying high over the jungle they'd be over Shelton's Head by the time his slow-moving vehicles made it overland.

Fraser clenched his fists. He couldn't afford to lose track of his assets like that. Not if he wanted to keep his men alive.

"All right, Tran. Get on it." He turned back toward the driver's cab. "You have the coords, Mason? Then rev it as much as you can. If those signals are the real thing, we've got men in trouble out there."

It felt good to have a clear course of action for a change. Fraser almost smiled as he strapped himself back into a seat and braced himself against the motion as the Sabertooth increased speed.

But the smile didn't quite come. He was all too aware of how little he really knew about commanding men in battle. And this time he didn't have Sergeant Trent to help him if he got in trouble.

This time, Fraser was on his own.

# Chapter 12

The Third Company of the First Battalion is dead,
but it did enough that in speaking of it one could
say "It had nothing but good soldiers."
          —Sergeant Evariste Berg
          in his report on Camerone
          French Foreign Legion, 1863

"They're alive! Look, Lieutenant, those're humans down there!"

Fraser leaned closer to peer at Tran's video display. The shapes caught in the drone's cameras were unmistakable. He watched an armored soldier carrying an onager run across the open ground from the plantation building toward an odd-looking blockhouse. No . . . not a blockhouse, the turret of a Sabertooth FSV. Someone had heaped dirt over the front and sides of the hull, leaving the turret with its lethal-looking plasma cannon free. The onager gunner stopped and fired, then ducked into the vehicle's rear hatch.

There were survivors from Charlie Company after all.

"Tell Garcia to circle wider. Let's get an idea of what they're up against."

"Yes, sir." Tran glanced at him. "Uh . . . do you want me to raise Charlie Company, too?"

Fraser hesitated before replying. "No. We don't want to risk tipping off the bad guys that we're this close. If we can hit them by surprise, we might have better luck nailing the bastards."

Tran nodded and put through the call to Garcia.

The view on the monitor widened and blurred as the drone gathered speed, rising. Within moments it stabilized again, and Fraser could study a wider view of the battlefield.

It looked like Charlie Company had given a good account of itself in the fighting so far. Their hannie opponents were mostly infantry, with a small number of light tanks in support. From what Fraser could gather from the drone's camera views and computer interpretation of the images from the command van, the natives were not as well equipped as the ones who had attacked Fort Monkey. Charlie Company had taken casualties, and plenty of them—the best estimate from the computers put the Legion losses at roughly fifty percent—but most of those had probably been due to surprise and early weight of numbers rather than superior firepower. The Commonwealth defenders seemed to be holding their own now against a native force that had lost a lot of soldiers . . . and a lot of cohesion as well.

One good blow could crack the enemy wide open . . .

"Right," Fraser said at last. The three vehicles were grounded less than two kilometers from the plantation by the time he'd put together a battle plan that looked like it would work. Watanabe and Platoon Sergeant Fontaine had joined him in the Sabertooth after deploying their platoon to watch the perimeter around the temporary camp. "Let's get moving before any stray monkeys find out we're in the neighborhood."

As he outlined his plan to the others, Fraser suppressed his own worries. The situation was straightforward enough, and the Legion held all the cards in this hand.

But, deep down, doubt gnawed at his self-confidence, and Colin Fraser couldn't shake the fear that he might be leading these men to their deaths.

Platoon Sergeant Ghirghik flicked his tail back and forth irritably. "How bad is it?"

Terranglic wasn't as well suited to conveying the full range of his anger as his native Khajrenf, but the three humans in the plantation office took a step back as he spoke. Of course, humans were often nervous around members of the Iridescent Race, even an outcaste like Ghirghik. He often wondered how they would react if confronted by one of the true

Ubrenfars, a high-caste Drakhmirg or a Zhanghi warrior.

Had his father not dishonored the Line with cowardice at the battle of Jirghan, he would have been a Zhanghi himself. Instead he had fled his own kind, ending up among the humans. Once he would have called them "weakling humans" as any Zhanghi might have done, but twenty cycles serving in their Foreign Legion had taught Ghirghik that not all humans were weak. Some might almost have been Warriors themselves.

Now they would face their end like true Warriors, here on the planet they called Hanuman.

"We're down to less than two magazines per man, Sarge," Corporal Johnson said. "There's only one Grendel left, and maybe ten Fafnirs. If they all work."

Ghirghik touched his forehead, then gave the human equivalent of the gesture and nodded his head. Among his own kind, the gesture would have been degrading, but humans seemed unable or unwilling to learn any body language but their own. "Go on."

"Connie's starting to run low on juice, and I don't think we can get the powerplant going again," Johnson continued. Connie was Charlie Company's nickname for the Sabertooth FSV they'd managed to salvage from the chaos of the first hannie surprise attack. One of their tanks had put a round through her engine, and despite the best efforts of their lone mechanic, Legionnaire Brecht, their makeshift repairs kept giving way. The vehicle was now a pillbox on the southern perimeter around Shelton's Head, but on battery power it wouldn't be useful for long. "We've only got enough for five or six more shots, at best."

"Not good," Ghirghik said. "What about the men?"

"There's fifty-three guys still on their feet, Sarge," Legionnaire Delandry replied. She was one of the last two medics left with the unit. Although Ghirghik normally had nothing but contempt for the whole idea of medics, he respected the human woman's courage. He had watched her drag an injured comrade out of a trench and across fifty meters of open ground under heavy fire.

It still struck him as foolish to rescue casualties—a Zhanghi warrior would have fought until he died, regardless of wounds—but that didn't detract from Delandry's personal bravery. "That's including walking wounded. We've got five more who're in pretty bad shape, including Subaltern Lawton."

That human had been another surprise. Ghirghik had naturally assumed that the commander of the transport platoon would be like most of his caste—a mechanic and a teamster, not a Warrior. But after the native surprise attacks took out the officers of each separate platoon, it was Lawton who had pulled them together and led them out. Ghirghik hoped the man would recover enough to face his death as a Warrior should, with a weapon in his hands and an enemy in his sights.

Sergeant Baker, the third human, cleared his throat. "What are we going to try, Sarge?" he asked. "If we keep sitting here, they'll take us sooner or later. Once the ammo runs out . . ." He trailed off.

"Are you suggesting we surrender?" Ghirghik showed his teeth in disapproval. Very few humans were likely to misinterpret *that* gesture as one of their "smiles."

"N-no, Sarge," Baker said. "But . . . well, what the hell do we do?"

"We fight. If we have to, we die." Ghirghik flicked his tail again. "At least we will die as Warriors!"

The door to the office burst open. Legionnaire Russo, the $C^3$ operator, stood framed in the door, his face a grim mask. "We got troubles, Sarge. Hassan's spotted movement down the main road. Tanks and infantry."

Ghirghik nodded. "Time to fight," he said. "Get the men ready. Johnson, put a lance out in the jungle on either side of the compound in case they try another flank attack like last night."

"Okay, Sarge." Johnson and Delandry hurried out of the room.

Ghirghik intercepted Baker before he could leave, closing one massive hand over the human's collar. "There will be no surrenders, Baker," he told the man in a low, even voice. "Do not dishonor this unit."

He released the sergeant and followed him out of the

room. Outside, gunfire and explosions heralded the native attack.

Now Legion and Zhanghi alike would see that Ghirghik could face battle as well as any true Warrior.

Fraser drew his FE-PLF rocket pistol and chambered a round. "Almost time, Sergeant," he said.

Platoon Sergeant Fontaine nodded and made a hand signal: *Prepare to attack.* The legionnaires of Corporal Radescu's lance stirred in the undergrowth, checking weapons one last time, shifting to better vantage points, selecting targets.

Next to Fraser, Legionnaire Tran bent over his $C^3$ terminal, watching the twin displays that showed the drone's-eye view of the battlefield and the computer-generated map depicting terrain and positions. Watanabe's understrength platoon was deployed in a scattered skirmish line along the west side of the main road into the beleaguered plantation. Farther down the trail, near Shelton's Head, gunfire interspersed with larger explosions echoed as the native attack got under way. Timing was crucial. He had to wait until the hannies were fully committed without giving them a chance to overrun Charlie Company.

Tension knotted his stomach, and even with his uniform's climate controls Fraser was sweating. This time, he would be leading his men in person instead of watching and directing from safety. Every man would be needed for this fight. He reminded himself that he'd been in the same position during that first hannie attack on Fort Monkey. It wasn't like this was his first time in battle.

But that time he hadn't been given time to think. He'd reacted to the enemy, moving to counter threats as they occurred. This battle, though, would be different. If he failed to anticipate something, the whole attack could go wrong. Men could die . . . *he* could die . . . all because of what he decided.

"Goddamn!" Tran said beside him. "Lieutenant, Charlie Company Sabertooth's stopped firing."

"Hit?"

"I don't think so . . . my guess is they're low on power."

"Without that plasma cannon, those guys are sharv meat," Fontaine said. "They can hold the hannies for a while with onagers and Fafnirs, but not long . . ."

"They've fired a Grendel!" Tran said. "Looks like . . . yeah, the racks are empty. They're leaving the Sabertooth now. Falling back toward the plantation buildings."

"Lieutenant . . ." Fontaine's voice was low but urgent.

Fraser clicked on the radio command channel. "Go! Go!"

He was up and running with the words. Fontaine rushed past him, firing his FEK at the nearest knot of hannie soldiers as he ran. Radescu's legionnaires was in motion as well.

The hannies barely had time to react. Needles tore through the native soldiers before they even realized they were under attack. A few tried to run, but none lasted more than a few meters. Then the firing stopped. There were no more targets here.

Fraser hadn't fired a single shot.

"Right!" Fraser said over the comm circuit. "Mason, start your run. Dmowski! Get your lance into position! Everybody else form on Watanabe. Move!"

The plan was proceeding smoothly so far. Over a stretch of nearly 500 meters the platoon had knocked out the native troops moving up in support of the attack on Shelton's Head. Now Dmowski's heavy weapons lance would block one end of the trail, delaying monkey reinforcements while the rest of the platoon swung around to take the attackers in the rear. Mason's three vehicles, meanwhile, would support the infantry attack and then break into the plantation compound to pull out the besieged legionnaires from Charlie Company.

"Sergeant Fontaine, take Radescu's lance and support Dmowski," Fraser ordered. "I'll join the subaltern for the main attack."

The Frenchman saluted crisply. Fraser turned east and moved out at a trot, with Tran close behind.

Maybe everything would work after all . . .

* * *

Ghirghik knelt over the body of Legionnaire O'Neil and pried the Fafnir missile launcher from the human's dead fingers. Neither the soldier's headless body nor the machine-gun fire slamming into his own torso armor distracted the Ubrenfar NCO as he double-checked the weapon calmly, trained it on the nearest native tank, and ran through the targeting sequence. The missile leapt from the launch tube as if eager to do battle.

As the rocket exploded just over the driver's slit, Ghirghik bared his teeth in defiance. *I am Zhanghi! I am Warrior!*

"Come on, Sarge! We'll cover you!" Corporal Johnson was shouting from the door of the nearest of the plantation buildings. He had an MEK cradled in his arms. Its harsh, grating hum sounded in counterpoint to the whine of nearby FEKs when Johnson fired.

Ghirghik checked O'Neil's pack hastily, but there were no Fafnir warheads left. He threw the useless launch tube in the direction of the enemy and unslung his own kinetic energy rifle. Firing a ragged burst, he sprinted for the door, ignoring enemy bullets.

"Report!" he snapped as Johnson closed the door behind him.

Russo looked up from his C³ terminal. "Two more dead . . . I guess it's three with O'Neil. Delandry says the monkeys are getting close to the med hut. She doesn't know how much longer her gang'll hold out."

"Baker's down to less than half a clip per man," Johnson added. "Hell, I'm about ready to start throwing rocks myself."

"I'm on my last Fafnir round," somebody else said.

"Hey, Sarge," Russo broke in. "I'm gettin' some funny signals on the terminal. Like input from a relay . . ."

"Never mind that," Ghirghik ordered sharply. "Get your weapon."

"What're we doing, Sarge?" Johnson asked.

"We will attack," Ghirghik told him. "Break out into the jungle. Pass the word: take any native weapons or ammo you find on the way out."

"That's suicide!" Legionnaire Griesch said loudly.

"A few of us will make it out," Ghirghik said. "The rest . . . better to die like Warriors than skulk here."

Johnson showed his teeth. It took a moment for Ghirghik to realize the human was grinning in agreement, not arguing with his orders. "I'm with you, Sarge," he said. "Come on, you apes! Let's give 'em hell for the Legion!"

"Legionnaires!"

Fraser took up the battle cry along with the others as they burst out of the jungle in the rear of the hannie attackers. A detached part of him wondered at the transformation in Subaltern Watanabe, normally so diffident and quiet, but now shouting and waving his FEK with an enthusiasm to match any common soldier's.

Not far away, Legionnaire Hsu dropped to one knee and fired a Fafnir missile at a hannie light tank. The warhead struck the vehicle at the juncture between hull and turret, sent a gout of flame and smoke spiralling skyward. An FEK whined somewhere, and a knot of native soldiers toppled in an untidy clump.

This end of the wide plantation clearing was thick with hannies mustering for the assault against Charlie Company. The buildings where the legionnaires had taken refuge were not visible, nor could the sounds of that more distant struggle be heard over the din of the firefight here, but that fighting was playing a key role in Fraser's battle plan. Caught by the Legion attack from an unexpected direction, the natives were completely unprepared. Despite their superior numbers, Watanabe's understrength platoon was handling them easily.

He wondered how Charlie Company was managing in the meantime. Fraser had kept firmly to his decision not to contact the survivors or use any frequencies they might monitor to preserve surprise right up to the moment of the attack. Since the locals had demonstrated their ability to locate Legion remote sensors he had developed a hearty respect for their capabilities. And Kelly Winters had mentioned seeing a Semti working with the hannie general who seemed to have launched the coup. If so, the natives had access to information and equipment outside their own technological capacity . . . It had seemed best to let Charlie Company act and react without the knowledge of the relief force, just to minimize the chance of giving something away too early.

Apparently the gamble had paid off. If the enemy was monitoring Legion communications, they weren't listening to any of the channels Bravo Company was using, and they hadn't been ready for the attack. In a few more minutes, it would be time to let Charlie Company know the cavalry had arrived.

Hsu fired another Fafnir as a hannie tank pivoted. This shot wasn't quite as good. It tore a gouge in the hull armor along the left side but didn't keep the tank from finishing the turn. The vehicle lurched forward on clattering treads while a hull-mounted machine gun hammered at the legionnaires. Hsu fell under the deadly hail, blood seeping from a half a dozen wounds in his arms and stomach where the high-caliber bullets had pierced the duraweave uniform.

Legionnaire Tran snatched up the Fafnir launcher and moved closer. For a horrified instant Fraser stood frozen, watching the turret track toward the legionnaire. With a roar the tank gun fired, hosing Tran with a stream of flame. The legionnaire screamed, dropping the Fafnir, as the fire engulfed him.

The flamethrower tank shifted aim and fired again, narrowly missing Watanabe and another soldier a few meters to the right of Fraser's position.

Fans raced as the Sabertooth appeared in the clearing. The Legion vehicle swerved easily into the path of the flames, its armor proof against the fire. Ignaczak's plasma gun locked on and fired, and an instant later the tank exploded with a curiously flat, dull thud. The blast knocked Fraser flat. He had a brief impression of a pillar of smoke and flame spouting high in the air, raining burning debris across the clearing. A chunk of armor drifted lazily above it all, spinning end for end, hanging for a long moment before falling back to the ground. A hannie trapped under another piece of the vehicle was screaming.

Fraser rose unsteadily, afraid of what the explosion might have done to his men. But the legionnaires were on their feet already, pushing forward across the smouldering field as the remaining hannies wavered. Here and there natives threw away their weapons and fled for the safety of the jungle. Others died where they stood.

Then the firefight—perhaps the entire battle—was over.

# Chapter 13

What are you complaining about? I'm creating glory for you.

—Colonel Pierre Jeanpierre
French Foreign Legion, March 1958

"A glorious tactic, Lieutenant Fraser! Glorious!"

Fraser tried to conceal his unease as he regarded the Ubrenfar sergeant. The saurian's scaled, heavily-muscled body was marked by dozens of gashes, cuts and patches of missing scales but Ghirghik had spurned any offer of first aid. When Fraser's men had finally cut their way through to the survivors from Charlie Company, the big alien had been standing in the center of a ring of hannie dead, FEK dry of grenades and needle rounds alike, wielding a blade like an oversized kukri and singing a discordant Ubrenfar battle song.

Ghirghik had seemed disappointed that he hadn't died gloriously at the height of the battle, but his praise for Fraser's attack on the hannie rear had been unstinting.

Not that everyone agreed with the sergeant. Not even Fraser.

The hannies were gone, dispersed by the sudden onslaught of the legionnaires. But the butcher's bill at Shelton's Head made the triumph seem hollow. Seventy legionnaires had withdrawn to the plantation after the initial hannie attacks. Of the forty-six still alive when Fraser's men reached Ghirghik, over half were wounded—ten of them seriously. Subalterns Jacquinot and Lawton had died, and the two vehicles the legionnaires had brought out were both useless hulks now. Fraser's force had lost five dead and three wounded as well.

It didn't sound that bad . . . except that every casualty

suffered in these remote jungles was irreplaceable. And when primitive hannie soldiers could kill so many high-tech Commonwealth troops, even at the cost of hundreds of their own kind, the Terran victory was a Pyrrhic one at best.

"Goddamn it, Lieutenant, why didn't you let us *know?*" That was Sergeant Baker. He'd lost his helmet, and a hannie rifle butt had cut a deep gash across his forehead in hand-to-hand fighting around the plantation buildings. The heavy bandage over it gave the man a distinctly piratical appearance. "We could have held out long enough if we'd known you were coming! Instead of charging the monkeys . . ."

The Ubrenfar snorted derisively. "It was brilliant," he said. The afternoon sun lancing through the windows glinted off his scales as his tail twitched. "Using us to focus their attention, then hitting them from behind before they could react . . . !"

Fraser looked away. He *had* used Charlie Company, used them as a diversion for his attack. At the time it had seemed clever.

Now, though, he was ashamed. The Ubrenfar's praise was salt in the wound. Everyone knew their callous disregard for life, their ruthlessness in battle.

*So much for clever tactics,* he told himself bitterly. *More lives wasted. Another mistake . . .*

Watanabe cleared his throat. "Lieutenant, last report from Garcia says we've got bad guys gathering down the road. Shouldn't I be getting the men ready to saddle up?"

Fraser nodded slowly. "Do it, Sub. Wounded get first call on the APCs."

The subaltern saluted. "Yes, sir. I'll have Legionnaire Russo take over Tran's C³ duties, if that's all right with you."

"Yeah. Fine." Tran's death was still fresh in his mind. Russo had been Captain Rayburn's C³ specialist in Charlie Company and had come through the fighting unscathed. He'd make a good replacement for Tran.

Watanabe hurried out of the plantation office, shouting for Sergeant Fontaine. Fraser stared after him, ignoring the others in the room. The subaltern was right. They had to get moving, before the hannie army could reform and launch a fresh attack.

Right now, all he could do here was bury his mistakes, together with the dead, and keep moving. It was the only chance of survival the legionnaires had left.

Shavvataaars, Third Talon of the Everlasting Race, squinted in the harsh light slanting through the window of the Excellent's private audience chamber and drew his hood lower over his eyes. *An eternity's curse on this place,* he thought. Hot, humid, painfully bright under the glare of its F-class star, this world the Terrans called Hanuman wasn't far removed from the ancient Semti religious concept of hell.

Not that any rational being would believe such ideas. The Semti had too long manipulated the religious beliefs of others to set any stock in the mythologies of their own ancestors. But the teachings were a part of the Ancient Lore, treasured, tended, preserved. There were times when Shavvataaars looked around this inhospitable world and recoiled in horror from a scene from Journey's End.

But Hanuman represented a chance to reverse the temporary ascendence of the chaotic Terran barbarians and their Commonwealth. Somehow, unthinkable as it had been, their juvenile vigor had won them a victory over the Conclave. The destruction of Kiassaa, the Conclave's artificial capital, had thrown Semti administration into chaos and opened the way for the barbarian takeover. Yet the moment would pass, and in time the Eternal Race would resume its rightful place as guardian and arbiter of the immature species—the Terrans among them. The proper pressure applied now, here, would create the conditions that would bring the ephemerals tumbling down as quickly as they had first risen.

Assuming, of course, that the other ephemerals, the primitives of these hellish swamps and jungles, could be guided to do their part.

At the moment, that assumption was questionable.

"Another demon trick!" *Asjyai* Zyzyiig smashed kys fist on the table. The native officer was using the ceremonial hall as a personal office, having relegated the new *yzyeel* to virtual captivity in a well-guarded wing of the Fortress of Heaven. "Another slaughter! You told me the

demons would lose heart, would be easy to destroy, and
look where it led! They escaped their fortress, and now
they have rescued the other survivors. And hundreds of
kyendyp killed in each fight!''

Shavvataaars regarded the other patiently. Zyzyiig's
own interference had been responsible for most of the
mishaps so far, but of course it would be impolitic to say
as much. The Great Journey, the plan his superiors had
dubbed ''Twilight Prowler'' required the native's continued cooperation, at least until the embers of anti-Terran
sentiment had been fanned into an all-consuming blaze.
Dryienjaiyeel was a primitive country, barbaric even by
Terran standards, but it had a place in Twilight Prowler
that could not be ignored.

''The demons have indeed proved more resourceful
than we might have hoped for,'' the Semti replied in
even, thoughtful tones. ''But remember, my Companion, that they have already suffered a grave setback at
your hands. Otherwise, they would not be fleeing overland.''

''Fleeing!'' Zyzyiig bared kys teeth. ''They attack as
they please, go where they want to go. Is this flight?''

''Yet they are plainly travelling northward, toward the
border. A long and difficult journey to undertake save in
desperation, when a single transport could carry their
entire band to safety in minutes. Our calculations have
proven correct in that much, at least. These legionnaires
have been abandoned. Time will wear them down, time
and the deep jungles. When next your soldiers encounter
them, you will surely triumph. You must exercise patience in this.''

''I am tired of hearing your speeches on patience!''
Zyzyiig flared. ''Your 'advice' and your 'assistance' have
been nothing but speeches!''

Shavvataaars did not answer. This was always the danger in trying to work too closely with barbarian allies. It
was easy to guide a species on a desired path through
subtle manipulation over a span of centuries, very hard
indeed to apply direct control for some fleeting, short-
term goal. Ephemerals lost patience so easily, and their
haste created situations where a slow and measured response was impossible. But the success of the Cleansing
depended on Zyzyiig and kys followers. Without ephem-

erals as tools, the Eternal Race was no match for the barbarians. Not yet.

"Well?" The *Asjyai* was growing less self-assured as Shavvataars remained silent. Zyzyiig's grandparents had worshipped the Semti as gods. For all kys bluster, the native's superstitions weren't far below the surface. "Don't you have anything to say . . . Honored?"

Shavvataaars studied Zyzyiig from under the recesses of the dark hood. The native was growing harder to control with each defeat inflicted by the Terrans. Perhaps it would be best to let matters in Dryienjaiyeel play themselves out and devote his own attentions to the wider aspects of Twilight Prowler. The events set in motion here could not be turned aside even if the legionnaires continued to elude Zyzyiig . . . but it would be wise to develop other aspects of the plan in case the *Asjyai's* growing unreliability became a threat.

Yes . . . that was the road to follow now.

"It is clear to me, my Companion, that you have no further need of my advice," Shavvataaars told ky smoothly. "My job here is done. You can complete the Cleansing without further guidance."

Zyzyiig looked stricken. "But—"

"I have other tasks I must attend to, *Asjyai*," he continued. "Focus your efforts on blocking the escape of the demon refugees . . . until I send you word. When we are ready to complete this Journey, you and your army will have a vital part to play. Be ready."

The Semti turned away before Zyzyiig could reply. Shavvataaars felt a cold thrill of satisfaction as he left the audience chamber. *Twilight Prowler moves forward. Soon enough I will be able to leave this hellworld . . .*

Colin Fraser climbed the ramp into the command van with a feeling of relief. Two long days of maneuvering, dodging hannie patrols through the dense lowland jungles, was over at last. Demi-Battalion Alice—or at least the hundred and seventy-odd survivors of the two Legion companies—had reunited, ready to make the final push for the frontier.

It sounded simple put this way. But the "final push" still had to cover over a thousand kilometers before the legionnaires could cross the mountains and leave Dryien-jaiyeel . . . and a lot could happen in the meantime.

Legionnaire Garcia looked up as Fraser ducked his head to enter the C³ compartment. "Good to have you back, sir," she said.

He nodded curtly. "Thanks. Didn't think we'd make it for a while there."

It had been a near-run thing. They'd been a little too successful in rescuing the Charlie Company survivors: there just hadn't been enough room on the three Legion vehicles to transport them all. The retreat from Shelton's Head had been limited to a speed not faster than the slowest marching soldier. And with so many walking wounded, that had been a snail's pace indeed.

In fact, the natives would probably have cut them off entirely if Trent hadn't persuaded Subaltern Fairfax to turn the main body around and hold open an escape route for Fraser's men. There hadn't been much real fighting, but the action had cost them four Grendel missiles . . . and precious marching time.

Fraser still wasn't sure if he wanted to thank Gunny Trent for saving them, or chew him out for making Fairfax put the main body at risk. The sergeant's dedication to Legion tradition, to the idea that the Legion always looked out for its own, didn't seem quite so admirable when it put so many lives on the line.

Then again, by that reasoning he should have passed Charlie Company by . . .

That was exactly the kind of decision Fraser didn't want to face again.

He settled into his seat at the computer console. "What's the feed from the drones, Garcia?" he asked.

The map screen lit up. "It looks clear to the northeast, lieutenant," the C³ tech said. "But Sergeant Trent figures there must be hannie units trying to close it off by now, probably moving up outside our scouting range. Do you want me to extend the perimeter any?"

Fraser shook his head. "Not yet. We'll assume Gunny's instincts are right. I don't want to risk the drone. We only have two more left, and they have to last us all the way to the border."

She nodded. "If the lokes are out there . . ."

"We'll find them as soon as they do come in range.

Meantime, all we can do is get our asses in gear and get moving.''

He leaned back in the seat and closed his eyes. With one vehicle out of action and the men from Charlie Company added to the column, it really was going to be a matter of marching. The vehicles could carry supplies and wounded, and they could rotate fit men aboard some of the APCs so the march could continue virtually nonstop, but the pace would still be slow. Too slow, he thought bitterly. Terran troops were used to crossing continents in a matter of hours aboard transport ships. Now the hannies were probably going to be able to move faster than the legionnaires.

''We'll move out in an hour, Garcia,'' he said at last. ''But we'll have to get organized first. I want Trent and the subs in here right away. Sergeant Ghirghik, too.''

Survival would depend more on hard marching than on fighting, but the legionnaires had to be ready for both. That meant integrating Charlie Company into the rest of the unit before they moved out. One more delay to deal with.

He only hoped they could afford it.

> Far from fair Terra, from family and home,
> Far from embraces of those that we love,
> Marches the Legion, the damned, all alone,
> Under a strange sky with strange stars above.

The slow, mournful song was more dirge than marching music, and it seemed to emphasize Slick's mood. His FEK was a heavy weight on his shoulder, and each step seemed harder than the last. There was still another hour before the next scheduled halt, after which the lance was supposed to have a four-hour shift aboard one of the APCs. He hoped he could hold out until then.

Even in training on Devereaux, the Legion hadn't marched this much. For three days now, since the lieutenant's return with the survivors from Charlie Company, their longest halt had been no more than an hour. The legionnaires marched in shifts, ate or slept aboard the carriers, and took turns on point, flank, or rearguard, watching out for hannie attacks. There'd been enough of those, too. Slick could still visualize the enemy ambush two days back, when Corporal LeMay fell into the concealed pit and the rest of the flank party, Slick included, had held off a swarm of screaming hannies who seemed to materialize out of the jungle from every direction at once.

They'd pulled LeMay out of the pit afterwards, but the sharpened stakes had gone right through his duraweave coverall. He was one of four men dead in that clash, left behind in the jungle as the column pressed on.

And still they marched. And sang. The Foreign Legion had a tradition that stretched all the way back to Old Earth of marching to a slow beat of 88 paces per minute. The somber beat was matched by the songs, depressing melodies about loneliness, nostalgia, and the whims of politicians.

Back on Devereaux, Slick had once been punished by an NCO for some minor infraction by being forced to parade all night in full battle kit, singing the entire time at the top of his lungs. He was beginning to recall the incident with fondness. At least then he'd known it would end when morning came.

A hand gave him a savage cuff from behind. "Come on, nube! Sing!" It was Strauss, seemingly unaffected by the hours of marching. "I haf my eye on you. Understand?"

"Yes, Corporal," Slick answered meekly. Any other response was likely to get him another cuff.

Strauss gave him one anyway. "You are lucky ve are too busy for punishment, nube. But I vill remember." The corporal moved down the line to talk with Vrurrth.

"Looks like trouble with the Corp, kid," Rostov whispered. "Maybe you'll get lucky and buy it before he comes up with something nasty, huh?"

"Maybe he'll buy it," Slick muttered.

Rostov laughed. "Fat chance, kid. Ain't no bullet taking out the Corp. They're too scared of him!"

Slick didn't answer. He was sick of Rostov, sick of all his lancemates with their rough and ready humor and their air of superiority over the poor helpless nube.

Sick of Strauss and his punishments . . . sick of the Legion.

He'd heard once that as many as a third of all legionnaires deserted before their term of enlistment was up. If they ever made it back to civilization, Slick was determined to try it as well. He didn't belong in the Legion, and he wasn't going to stay any longer than he had to.

The endless march went on.

# Chapter 14

We fight best by knocking off the kilometers.
—General François de Negrier
French Foreign Legion, 1881

"I'm sorry, Fraser, but there's nothing new to report on this end. The resident-general still won't release any transport."

Fraser nodded wearily. He hadn't really expected any change in policy. He talked to Battalion daily, and the word was always the same. "I understand, Commandant. But I have to tell you that things here aren't going very smoothly."

*That* was understatement. Just over a week had passed since the demi-battalion had reunited after the rescue of the Charlie Company survivors, and in that time they'd reduced the distance to Fwynzei by less than five hundred kilometers. The actual distance the legionnaires had covered was much greater, of course, but the twists and turns forced on them by terrain and enemy pursuit had caused them to make wide, time-consuming detours.

Supplies were becoming a problem, too. The extra mouths they had to feed now, and the unexpectedly slow pace of the march, had thrown off all their careful planning.

"If we keep on going as we've been," Fraser continued aloud, "I'm not sure how well our supplies will hold out. Yesterday we raided a primmie village, but I'm not sure if that's going to be wise in the long run."

"How so?" Commandant Isayev demanded.

"The farther north we get, the fewer villages we'll find, sir," Fraser replied carefully. "Up near the frontier is where the Dryiens have been building all those model settlements, and they'll be a hell of a lot better defended than anything the savages have. Every foraging expedition costs us time and could cost me men as well. If we go up against a strong defense, we could lose everything.''

Fraser looked away from the communications terminal for a moment. There was another reason he didn't like foraging, but it wasn't something he could talk about. The memory of the hannie village in flames, the stench of fire and death, was still fresh. The jungle savages just wanted to be left alone, but now the legionnaires were carrying the fight to them. It was necessary to keep the unit going, but Fraser hated the one-sided killing of primitives who couldn't defend themselves.

''Do what you can, Lieutenant,'' Isayev said gruffly. ''I'll keep trying to get some kind of relief mission organized on this end, but I can't say it looks too likely now. Not the way things have been going.''

''Sir?''

''The carriership *Seneca* is a week overdue at the systerm, Fraser. It's probably nothing—some politician or bureaucrat probably ordered him to wait for a VIP or something—but it's enough to throw a murphy into our works here. The resident-general's hoping to divert some troops slated for the garrison on Enkidu. That's why *Ankh'Qwar* isn't home yet; she's still waiting at the systerm.''

''More troops, sir? To retaliate on the Dryiens?''

''Partly,'' Isayev admitted. ''But in the past few days we've had indications of trouble in Vyujiid, too. There was a riot in the Imperial City yesterday. Our intel people think there could be a rebellion brewing up here. If so, we're going to need every man we can get just to protect Commonwealth interests north of the frontier. Even if we get more men, Fraser, I'm not sure how much help we'll be able to spare. Even the transports are likely to stay busy ferrying garrison troops back and forth to troublespots. The Navy's not going to want to risk a repeat of *Ganymede* when every ship's going to be essential.''

''Yes, sir,'' Fraser said. ''I see their point of view. It's just not a very comfortable one personally.''

''At this point, I'd say you've made the best possible choice. If you can get the demi-battalion out of Dryienjaiyeel on your own, you'll have done everyone a good turn. You were smart to pull out of Fort Monkey when you did.''

"Thank you, sir. But I still wish we didn't have to get past Zhairhee."

Isayev nodded. "I've seen the satellite photos. I don't know if that buildup's there just for your benefit, or to forestall any retaliation from here, but there's a lot of activity between you and the frontier. You'll just have to dodge it as best you can . . . unless I can organize some kind of help in the meantime."

"Yes, sir," he said again.

"Stay in touch, Fraser," Isayev told him. "I know it feels like we've abandoned you . . . hell, the resident-general and his flunkies would like to. But you're part of the Legion, and the Legion takes care of its own. Good luck, Lieutenant. Lancelot clear."

"Alice, ending transmission." Fraser leaned back in his seat and stared at the blank screen for a long time. If the Commandant was right about trouble elsewhere on Hanuman, the chance of assistance was smaller than ever. The Legion really was on its own.

All they could do now was press on, knock off as many kilometers as they could . . . and pray they didn't run into something they couldn't handle.

Kelly Winters lowered herself wearily onto a log and sighed gratefully. After two hours of marching, any chance to sit down, even for just a few minutes, was a welcome relief to aching feet. Everyone in the column took a turn marching, except for the seriously wounded casualties aboard the ambulance vans. She'd spent an entire shift a few days back beside Father Fitzpatrick, and yesterday she'd spotted Lieutenant Fraser and his electronics tech at the head of the column.

Somehow it seemed right. The legionnaires, for all their mismatched backgrounds and ill-mannered behavior, seemed to respond to that sort of sacrifice. Kelly was even beginning to detect some signs of thawing towards her.

Once she would have put that down to being one of a handful of women among a preponderance of men. The Legion ran about ten-to-one in favor of males, and the proportion was about that in the demi-battalion now.

But she doubted sex had much to do with anyone's attitude by this time. Dirty, smelly, her uniform unwashed and caked in jungle mud, her hair cut short after she'd tangled it in a thorny clump of *kiizaij* vines, Kelly had never felt so totally asexual in her life. And she was exhausted, completely exhausted. For all their superior airs, the legionnaires were feeling the fatigue almost as much as she was. Lust wasn't nearly as high on anyone's list as a good night's sleep.

Or a shower. Kelly wanted a shower even more than sleep.

She looked up as roaring turbofans drowned out the sounds of the jungle. An engineering van glided past, raising whitecaps on the sluggish, muddy water of the river that had stalled the column's progress. Without the obstacle they wouldn't have called a halt this early in the day, so in a way it was a welcome sight. But it also represented more lost time, more chances for the pursuit to catch up again.

Myaighee had told her it was the upper reach of the Jyikeezh River, main artery of a drainage basin the computers said was larger than the Amazon on Terra. Even this far from the sea, the Jyikeezh was broad and slow-moving, deep enough to be a serious obstacle to troops on foot. There were supposed to be some easier crossing points a few dozen kilometers upstream, but rumor had it Gunny Trent had persuaded Lieutenant Fraser to cross here to throw the enemy off the scent.

That sounded like Trent. Calculating, competent, but a manipulator. Why Lieutenant Fraser let him dominate the unit was beyond her.

Clever though this maneuver might be, it was still causing trouble. With too many legionnaires for the available vehicles already, and two Sandrays and a Sabertooth detached on a combination scouting run and foraging expedition, getting troops and supplies across was taking time. A long time.

The engineering vehicle grounded thirty meters away and dropped its rear ramp. Some legionnaires nearby started gathering stacks of supplies and manhandling them toward the vehicle. Despite her feelings about the Legion, Kelly had to admit the men seemed ready enough to work. It felt wrong to be sitting back when others were

busy, but Sergeant Trent had already made it clear that
the best thing she could do to help was stay out of the
way.

That went for Myaighee, too. The little alien had finally been released from regen treatment. Like everyone
else, ky alternated between marching and riding. With
no one of kys own race for company, Myaighee spent a
lot of time with Kelly.

It seemed strange, but she frequently felt she had more
in common with the alien than with the legionnaires.

One of the legionnaires staggered and dropped his load
before he could reach the APC. Someone laughed loudly.

Then the man was screaming, writhing on the ground
and clutching at his leg. Kelly was up and running at
once, reacting without conscious thought. She dropped
to one knee beside the man.

His lower leg from boot-top to knee was covered by
some kind of soft, pulsing tissue. ''Medic! Someone get
a medic!'' she yelled, groping for the first aid kit on the
man's web gear. He was still screaming, and his face was
a mask of anguish.

She prodded the creature wrapped around his calf with
a stick. It seemed to tighten its grip, and the soldier
screamed again.

''Don't touch it, ma'am,'' someone said behind her.

Kelly looked up in surprise at the fresh-faced legionnaire. He seemed vaguely familiar . . . Her eyes focused
on the caduceus insignia on his shoulder, and memory
clicked into place. Legionnaire Donovan was a medic in
First Platoon, and had tended her back in Fort Monkey.
He didn't look much like a medic, with his grimy fatigues and the battle rifle slung over his shoulder. Like
all specialists in the Legion, Donovan was a soldier first
and a medic second.

''Spineleech,'' Donovan added grimly. Kelly backed
away and let him take her place.

''Poisonous?'' Kelly asked.

''Might as well be,'' Donovan said as he began fumbling in his pouch. ''Alien proteins. Causes massive an-
aphylaxis. Damn. He's going into shock already . . .''

The soldier was shaking spasmodically as the medic
slipped a plastic airway down his throat. Kelly could see
the swelling in the man's face, the mottled discoloration,

could hear the thick rasp of his breath. Working quickly, Donovan produced a laser cutter and began to work on the pulsing tissue mass enveloping the injured man's leg. There was sizzle of burning flesh, the stink of charred meat. Then the thing relaxed its grip and dropped off in two pieces.

Kelly saw the gripping surface of the creature, a mass of sucker disks and needle-slim quills still dripping blood. The legionnaire was convulsing now, bucking under the grip of two other soldiers who tried to hold him down as the medic pressed a hypospray against his neck. He tried to scream and made a strangled sound against the airway.

"Call Doc," Donovan told one of the legionnaires. "Gates'll need a litter. And someone check around the bank to see if there are any more of those ugly bastards. Look for holes right near the edge of the water. Watch yourselves! They're damned fast!"

"Will he be all right?" Kelly asked.

Donovan turned bleak eyes on her, then shook his head. "He's suffering from a massive allergic reaction. When they get hit this bad, regen just isn't fast enough. Best we can do is keep him under until . . ."

Kelly shuddered and turned away, remembering her own brush with anaphylactic shock. It was horrifying being unable to do anything but watch the boy die. What was his name? Gates.

She walked away in a daze. Just another day in the jungle. Another young kid dead.

It always seemed to be the kids who bought it, the nubes. The old vets seemed indestructible, like they could take any hardship and keep right on going. They were too smart to let their guard down and too cunning to be outmatched by anything . . . or anyone.

She sat down on the same log and stared wearily at the slow-moving water. These legionnaires were something outside her experience, and they were making her take a long, hard look at everything she'd believed in. She still resented many of them—Sergeant Trent, for instance, with his patronizing "leave it to someone who can do the job" attitude. For most of these soldiers, if you weren't a legionnaire you just didn't count, and that was galling.

And yet these same men and women weren't just braggarts. They really were capable of incredible efforts. It was hard to picture a Commonwealth Marine doing any more than these troops, and the Marines were supposed to be the best of the Commonwealth Regulars. On the march, the legionnaires were tough. And in battle . . . in battle, they seemed unstoppable.

Kelly Winters was surprised to realize just how much she admired them.

The *Angel of Death* floated motionless in the center of a hannie village, a high-tech dragon in the midst of primitive mud huts. Flames crackled from the nearest of the ruined structures, testament to the determination of the savage natives who had defended it. A grizzled hannie missing most of the quills of ky's ruff had set fire to the hut while one of the legionnaires had been inside.

Now the hannie was dead, the legionnaire was smeared with burngel, and the pitiful building burned.

Spiro Karatsolis snapped the MEK support weapon into place on a pintel mount next to the turret hatch and scanned the village with a practiced eye. Using the onager cannon against primitives would have been akin to using a SAM against a bothersome fly, but the MEK would serve to cover the troops on the ground in case any of the natives mustered up the courage to attack again.

Around the floating FSV, legionnaires moved quickly, purposefully, rounding up supplies to load on the engineering van hovering near the edge of the river.

Three raids in four days . . . Karatsolis was beginning to hate these foraging runs. These hannie villagers weren't the real enemy, but they were hostile to just about anything that moved through the jungle, so raiding them was the only way to secure supplies short of hunting and gathering on the march.

But it didn't make the job any more palatable.

Karatsolis had seen it all. He was working on his second hitch in the Colonial Army, with a tidy little nest egg in the Battalion Bank and every prospect of making corporal when this tour was up. He'd have made it long since if it hadn't been for that time he'd tried to desert back on Tanais. When he retired, he'd go back to New

Cyprus and buy himself a farm. Or perhaps he'd settle on Thoth. That had been a nice world, not spoiled by developers. Maybe that girl—what was her name? Elena?—was still looking for someone to marry.

Meanwhile, he was a legionnaire, and a good one at that. Shooting savages wasn't his idea of a good fight, but if that was what had to be done, he'd do it.

"Hey, Spear, don't doze off on us, man!" Bashar called. The Turk had his own hatch unbuttoned. "Remember that time you fell asleep and the Gwyrran rebel made a break for it?"

"I got him, didn't I?" Karatsolis responded. "Anyway, I wasn't asleep. I was just checking to see if *you* were on the ball. Which you weren't."

Bashar snorted. "Sure. That's your story, and you stick to it."

"This ain't much like Gwyrr, though," Karatsolis went on. "Too fucking hot."

"Hot, cold, who cares. Just another planet full of ales." Bashar spat over the side of the Sabertooth.

"Better watch it, Basher," Karatsolis warned. He pointed across the village at Sergeant Ghirghik. The big Ubrenfar was in command of the raiding party, which consisted of the Sabertooth, the engineering van, and a standard Sandray troop carrier, with three lances from the unit's newly-formed Fourth Platoon. Ghirghik had been made platoon leader.

That was only right. The new platoon was mostly made up of survivors from Charlie Company and would respond better to Ghirghik than to any leader the lieutenant might have appointed from Bravo Company.

But the Ubrenfar made Karatsolis uneasy. It was hard to think of an Ubrenfar as an ally, even in the Legion where there were very few planets and races that *weren't* represented one way or another.

"Ah, don't sweat it, Spear," Bashar said. "Hell, I heard old Ghirghik swearing about the damned ales himself last night! He's—"

Bashar was cut off by the sudden *whoosh* of a missile swooping just meters away from the Sabertooth, followed by the thunder of an explosion as it hit a nearby hut. Someone screamed; another voice shouted for a medic.

"Goddamn!" Karatsolis swore, dropping into the turret and sealing the hatch behind him. "That wasn't any hannie rocket!"

The whole Sabertooth seemed to quiver and come alive as Bashar powered up the turbofans. "Whatever the hell it was, it's after us!" the Turk replied.

The FSV pivoted smoothly and shot toward the trees to the west. Bashar's hull-mounted CEK sprayed round after round of kinetic energy fire into the jungle while Karatsolis activated his turret controls and chambered a round in the plasma cannon.

Neither man spoke, but Karatsolis knew Bashar was thinking the same thing he was. Another missile could lance out of those trees at any moment. If it did, the *Angel* might not be able to take it.

The FSV crashed between two squat, greyish-orange trees, still firing. A video pickup showed Karatsolis a handful of hannies in Dryien army uniforms running away from the oncoming vehicle. One of them threw away something bulky as ky fled.

He checked his sensor arrays. Nothing on the MAD . . . no sign of vehicles of any kind. He unbuttoned the turret and raised himself through the hatch again, taking a grip on the MEK's trigger and swinging the weapon to track the fugitives. The weapon hummed, and needle slivers sliced through air, vegetation, and hannie flesh.

The whole battle had taken only seconds.

The Ubrenfar sergeant deployed a lance to scout the perimeter for further signs of the enemy, but they turned up no evidence of other troops in the area. Corporal Johnson, however, brought back one trophy from the search.

"What the hell is this thing?" Bashar asked as they examined it together back in the center of the village.

The Ubrenfar turned it over in his hands. It was a bulky tube, too big for most hannies to carry easily, with a simple control box near one end and a fold-out eyepiece for targeting.

"It's about fifty years ahead of anything the monkeys have, that's for sure," Karatsolis said quietly. "The missile that bugger fired was a fire-and-forget job, and the hannies don't have anything like that. We're just lucky the little bastard rushed the shot."

"Looks like Gwyrran manufacture to me," Corporal Johnson added. "I saw a lot of their old military-issue stuff when I was on Gwyrr, and this is a lot like it."

Ghirghik pointed to a line of angular markings below the controls. "I know this writing," he said slowly. "We captured many weapons when we rose against the Semti. This is their language."

"Semti?" Bashar frowned. "What do those ghouls have to do with this?"

"Makes sense," Karatsolis said. "The Gwyrrans were their favorite combat troops before the Conclave fell. And they were worshipped by the hannies. Looks like some of them still have access to an armory somewhere."

"There's no proof the Semti are helping the monkeys . . ." Bashar trailed off.

"Remember the way the hannies got past the remote sensors back at the fort? I think the Dryiens are getting some high-powered help." Karatsolis looked at the Ubrenfar.

Ghirghik nodded slowly. "We must report this to the lieutenant. If it is true . . ."

If it was true, Karatsolis thought, then the Legion might end up facing a hell of a lot more than it could handle.

# Chapter 15

Only soldiers like these could endure, with undi-
minished discipline, the sniping, shelling, and casualties which are their daily lot.
                              —from a press report
                    on the Legion peacekeepers in Beirut
                          French Foreign Legion, 1983

"Lieutenant? Wake up, Lieutenant. They need you in
C-cubed."

Fraser's eyes focused slowly on the Padre's face. Fatigue dragged at every muscle, and his whole body ached.
He remembered an instructor at the Academy telling him
once that a real soldier could grab a few minutes' sleep
anywhere, but a cramped passenger seat in a moving
Sandray didn't make much of a bed.

"What is it, Father?" he asked, stifling a yawn.

"Targets, Lieutenant. Looks like a squadron of aircraft inbound from the direction of the capital.
Mr.Bartlow has been tracking them. Best computer estimate is that they're ground-attack planes carrying some
pretty heavy bomb loads."

He came fully awake with that. The battle at the fort
had proved the legionnaires could deal with native aircraft . . . but images of *Ganymede* lingered, a brutal reminder of what the enemy could do if any of their planes
slipped through the Terran defenses.

They'd left the river behind two days before, continuing the march north. Although they'd avoided further
contact with ground forces, a drone from the command
van had spotted a force of Dryien troops mounted on
tracked personnel carriers trailing the rearguard. The report from Sergeant Ghirghik of possible high-tech weapons in hannie hands had been enough to make Fraser

worry about further contact. Add the almost tangible presence of Zhairhee, the garrison city now no more than three hundred kilometers to the northeast . . .

It hadn't been easy to get to sleep despite his fatigue. These incoming aircraft made the unit's prospects that much more bleak.

Legionnaire Russo and Subaltern Bartlow were huddled close over one of the video displays when Fraser entered the C³ compartment. Warrant Officer Hamilton was at another terminal.

"Confirming now," Hamilton said without looking up. "Tornado tactical support aircraft. Prop-driven. One pilot. External bomb racks and twin HMGs."

"How many have we got on the screen?" Fraser asked.

Bartlow straightened up with a look of relief. "Twelve, sir," he said. "We've got the drone pacing them now."

"Pacing them?" Fraser bit back a curse. "Russo, set the drone on a search sweep. Let's see if they've got anything else out there."

Charlie Company's C³ tech glanced at Bartlow and nodded. "Already programmed, sir." His fingers danced over the keyboard.

"Bartlow, get on the comm panel and alert the unit. Disperse the vehicles and have the men go to ground. And tell the Sabertooth crews to get some Grendels in the air."

"Number One Sabertooth is down to four missiles, Lieutenant," Hamilton reminded him.

"I know, Mr. Hamilton," Fraser snapped. "But we can't just ignore those bastards and hope they'll go away."

"Fafnirs'll take 'em down, sir," Russo said.

Fraser nodded. "Right. Deploy the weapons lances. But get some Grendels flying, too . . . just in case. Mr. Hamilton, try to ID the base those planes came out of and give me an idea of where else the hannies might try an airstrike from."

He took Bartlow's place at the command console as the others responded to the flurry of orders. Unlike his subordinates, he had nothing to do now but watch the screen and the cluster of moving lights that represented the enemy.

And worry.

* * *

Legionnaire Spiro Karatsolis closed his fingers around the joystick that controlled the Grendels in the air. "That's it, baby," he said softly. "Easy . . . easy . . . yeah! There! Eight . . . ten . . . twelve of the bastards."

Bashar's voice was loud in his headphones. "Sabertooth One has targets. Repeat, Sabertooth One has target acquisition."

"Roger that," Russo replied. "Stay with them."

"What's he think I'm going to do? Shell a clump of trees?" Karatsolis adjusted the missiles' course to center the native planes in the video monitor. The four Grendels were loitering over the rear of the Legion column, slaved together so that all of them responded to one joystick, using superheated air sucked through maneuvering thrusters to maintain station.

"Nah," Bashar shot back. "He's just afraid you spot a sheep and lose interest in fighting. Love at first sight, or something." The Turk dropped the bantering tone abruptly. "Fafnirs in the air."

Karatsolis checked his sensor display. "Got 'em," he said. "Tracking . . . targets are breaking formation."

The native aircraft dropped out of their tight welded-wing grouping, scattering. On the sensor display the pattern of moving traces swirled in a confusing dance, targets, rockets, and Grendel missiles dodging and weaving together.

"Damn!" That was Legionnaire Ignaczak in the second Sabertooth. "Looks like they're learning. I read two planes playing decoy for the others. What do you think, Spear?"

"Concur," Karatsolis replied tersely. His fingers were running over the terminal keyboard, programming new instructions. Two hundred meters above the forest floor and two kilometers away, the four Grendel missiles responded to the new commands. Their thrusters revectored to channel the air streams aft, and rocket burners cut in to add more speed. Like the hannie planes, the Grendels dropped out of formation, no longer slaved to a common controller. Each had a separate target now among the native aircraft that had not received attention from any of the Fafnirs. At the same time, Karatsolis knew, Ignaczak would be setting up similar programs for Sabertooth Two's five Grendels.

"Targets locked in," Ignaczak reported. "Missiles running."

"That'll teach the primmie bastards not to mess with the Legion," Bashar said.

"New targets! New targets!" That was Russo, a nervous edge in his voice. "Another flight. Coordinates feeding now!"

"Goddamn!" Ignaczak shouted. "Where'd the buggers come from?"

Karatsolis checked the computer feed with a sinking feeling. "Hedghopped in on us," he said. The coordinates told the story. While the first hannie flight made its approach openly, more aircraft had circled wide, skimming just above treetop level, unobserved by Legion sensors. "Those primmie bastards know what they're doing, Basher."

"Fafnirs, prepare new fire mission," Russo was saying. "Sabertooths, report status."

"Sabertooth One dry," Karatsolis reported.

"Number two, four missiles left," Ignaczak added. "Plotting fire program."

"Wait one."

On his screen, Karatsolis saw the first lights winking out as the Legion missiles found their targets. Usually a successful strike gave him a lift, an almost sexual release. This time it left him cold.

The monkeys had outmaneuvered the Legion. What else were the hannies planning to throw at them?

Fraser stared at the tactical screen, his stomach a hard knot. The second hannie attack wave was bearing down on the Legion column from the east. That second attack group had probably come from Zhairhee, skimming in at treetop level to avoid detection as long as possible. With missile reloads running low, it was going to take every bit of luck the Terrans could muster to meet the new threat.

They were already banking too heavily on luck as it was. The drone's search sweep had brought the enemy formation in view with bare minutes to spare.

*Damn! If Bartlow had set up the search sweep right*

*away . . . !* But Bartlow had made a natural mistake. He was inexperienced.

Anyway, blaming the kid wouldn't change things. Fraser was CO, not Bartlow, and in the end it was Fraser who was really responsible.

"Fafnirs have fired, sir," Russo announced. The traces appeared on the monitor at almost the same moment.

Hamilton leaned over the back of Fraser's chair. "They're breaking formation again," he said, pointing. "Somebody in that bunch of monkeys has been going to school, Lieutenant. That kind of wild weasel maneuver would only be useful against high-tech weapons. The lokes never had to deal with homing missiles before."

Fraser glanced up at him. "Sounds like Ghirghik was right, then. Do you think there might be Semti behind this?"

"Could be. The monkeys are getting tips on how to handle our technology from somewhere. They knew enough to dodge the remote sensors around the Enclave . . . and they didn't seem very frightened of *Ganymede*. Like they knew she was unarmed."

"Yeah." Fraser stared at the screen a moment longer. "Russo, tell Sabertooth Two to launch Grendels."

"It won't be enough," Hamilton said quietly.

"I know. But we have to cut down the odds somehow." He scowled. The trees here were thick enough to make maneuvering difficult. Could a Sabertooth swing around and bring down the intruders with plasma fire? That had worked in Fort Monkey . . . but there had been room to move there. The jungle canopy would make it hard to track the aircraft, too . . . though it might also give the Legion vehicles some cover.

Cut down the odds . . .

"Tell Sabertooth One to circle to the east side of the column and give us some cover fire," he ordered. "And get some more Fafnirs up, for God's sake!"

Russo shot him a worried look. Fraser took a deep breath, fighting for calm. He knew there was a panicky edge to his voice, and he had to get it under control. The unit needed a leader.

The unit needed *him*.

*Zeeraij* Kyindhee yanked hard on the control stick and the agile *Aghyiir* fighter-bomber climbed and banked, its overstrained engine screeching in protest. Kyindhee blinked as a brilliant flare of light engulfed squadron-leader Wyjlin's aircraft. Turbulence from the explosion made the *Aghyiir* buck like a maddened *zymlat.*

Kyindhee steadied the aircraft and adjusted course. Glancing up to the top of the cockpit canopy, ky took note of the digital readout on the face of the tiny black box fastened there in a hastily improvised mounting. The alien devices had only been installed a few days before as part of the *Asjyai's* program for driving out the demon Terrans. Rumor in the barracks claimed that the devices had been smuggled into Dryienjaiyeel by the Ancients themselves.

Kyindhee could well believe it. The device was like some kind of magic, able to locate a target from a great distance and guide kys plane toward it even when jungle obscured the view. And it would, so kys superiors said, gauge the aircraft's speed, range, and bearing precisely to tell the pilot the exact moment to release the bomb load slung on each wing.

A magical device, like having a co-pilot or a bombardier on board . . . but without the extra weight and loss of maneuverability larger crews entailed.

The instructions called for the pilot to lock out signals from other, extraneous targets before commencing the final bomb run, to keep the device from becoming confused. Kyindhee reached up and touched the stud at the bottom of the box and watched the numbers flash in a brilliant shade of amber.

Ky pushed the stick all the way forward, and the fighter-bomber dipped low toward the jungle below. Kyindhee's left hand hovered over the bomb release as the pilot watched the countdown.

Four . . . three . . . two . . . one . . .

Kys finger jabbed the button, and twin 48-*yiiz* bombs tumbled from the bomb rack.

A plasma flare consumed Kyindhee's aircraft three seconds later.

"Bomb release! Get clear! They targeted us!"

Fraser barely had time to react to Hamilton's shout before the first blast rocked the command van. The shock threw him against the rear wall, knocking the wind out of him. He staggered, bracing himself against the door leading back into the troop compartment.

Hamilton and Russo were on their feet now, struggling to maintain their balance as the uneven motion of the APC continued. The C³ technician pushed Fraser through the door as the second explosion went off.

This time the hit was much closer, tearing through the armor of the front left side of the vehicle. Fraser had a confused impression of screams from the driver's cab.

Hamilton lurched against him, his mouth wide in mingled pain and astonishment. A trickle of blood ran down his chin as the warrant officer sagged to the metal floor plates.

A shard of metal the size of a regulation bayonet protruded from Hamilton's back just above his heart.

Fraser stared numbly at the dying man until Russo took him by the arm and hurried him through the rear ramp door.

Legionnaire Karatsolis heard the servo-motors whine in protest as the Sabertooth's turret spun in search of a new target. "I've lost the feed from command!" he shouted.

"Yeah." Bashar's voice sounded calm, almost flat, in his headphones. "Looks like they took a hit. Switch to onboard sensors."

"What'd'ya think I'm doing, man?" Karatsolis squinted at his targeting screen, trying not to think of what would happen if Lt. Fraser was dead. The lieutenant hadn't been much of a replacement for Captain LaSalle so far, but the alternative wasn't pleasant—three subalterns or a Navy combat engineer.

Demi-Battalion Alice needed a leader with some kind of experience . . . even if he was still learning, like the lieutenant. At least Fraser had started to understand his job.

This deep in hostile territory, they couldn't afford to start breaking in a new commander. Not again.

"Look alive, Spear!" Legionnaire Ignaczak's voice was static-crusted. "Multiple targets headin' your way!"

He noted the blips at almost the same moment and

smiled grimly as one faded out, smashed by plasma cannon fire from Ignaczak's FSV-2. "Hammer 'em, Zak!"

He swiveled the turret again, letting off a string of rapid-fire bursts from his own gun. Each shot filled the turret with noise, the metal-on-metal clang as the solid steel round slammed into the chamber, counterpointing the raw noise of the ammo being superheated and then flung from the barrel by intense gauss fields, so hot it made the very air screech with its passage. Another hannie plane vanished from the screen. In his mind's eye, Karatsolis could visualize the plasma fireball engulfing a fragile native aircraft.

A cluster of smaller blips detached themselves from the main targets at the same instant. The plasma cannon thundered twice more as he tried to center on the arcing bombs, but though another enemy plane vanished the deadly ordnance escaped his fire.

"Rev us up, Basher!" he yelled. "Let's get the hell out of here!"

He fired again, the noise of the shot drowning out the whining fans as Bashar banked the FSV and accelerated. Karatsolis braced himself against the motion and stabbed the button controlling the turret motors again.

Then the Sabertooth rocked and swayed with a sickening lurch. Karatsolis was slammed back into his seat by the force of the motion.

"Hang on to your lunch, Spear!" Bashar called.

The legionnaire was about to shout a properly wisecracking reply when another blast caught the fast-moving vehicle from behind, slewing the FSV sideways. His head cracked hard against a projecting bit of hardware. Dazed, Karatsolis tried to clear his blurred vision. A warm trickle of blood ran down behind his left ear.

The pitch of the fans changed again just as a third explosion shook the Sabertooth.

"I can't hold her!" Bashar yelled, all trace of his earlier calm gone. "We'll—"

The FSV rammed into something hard and came to a shuddering halt. Even from the turret Karatsolis could tell that the Sabertooth had lost a magrep module in the crash. The front of the vehicle was tilting crazily to the right where the magnetic suspension had collapsed.

The *Angel of Death* was listing like a boat taking on water from a hole in the bow.

"Basher?" He felt groggy, disoriented.

Silence . . . then a groan from the driver's cab.

And a crackle of shorting electrical systems, a tang of ozone in the stale air of the vehicle.

Hurriedly he punched the release on his seat harness and dropped through the hatch from the turret into the cramped center section of the chassis. His head was throbbing where he'd hit it, but Karatsolis ignored the pain and forced his eyes to focus as he squeezed past the heavy machinery that drove the turret and into the driver's cab.

Sparks leapt from a half-dozen places on the control panel. He wrestled a portable extinguisher from the rack behind Bashar and sprayed fire-retardant foam on the damaged panels, then unsnapped the driver's harness. Bashar groaned again, but didn't move. There was a gash over his eye.

Karatsolis jabbed at the hatch release button, but the clash of grinding gears told him the mechanism was damaged. With a savage curse he reached up for the manual control lever. It took every ounce of strength to free it, and the effort made his head spin. Somewhere in the back of his mind a tiny voice was screaming, urging him to get clear before the hannies dropped more bombs on the helpless Sabertooth.

But he wasn't going to abandon Bashar.

All at once the lever unlocked and the hatch beside Bashar's seat sprang open a few centimeters. Karatsolis braced against it and pushed, and it reluctant swung up and back. Breathing hard, the legionnaire pushed the Turk through the hatch, then followed. A choking cloud of smoke made him gag.

Then he was clear of the wrecked FSV, inhaling deep breaths of hot, humid, but blessedly clean air. Bashar groaned again and tried to sit up.

"What the hell . . . ?" the corporal asked groggily.

Karatsolis knelt beside him. "I always knew you slept through MOS school," he said, trying to maintain the traditional banter. "Look what you did to the *Angel,* city boy!"

The FSV's front and right side were burnt and pitted

where the first near-miss had caught it. With the magrep module out, the vehicle was canted steeply, the rear still floating on magnetic suspension, but half the front smashed up against an embankment.

"Medic!" A legionnaire was shouting as he appeared beside the two FSV crewmen. "Hey, Watts! Two wounded over here!"

Karatsolis raised a cautious hand to the side of his head. It came away sticky with blood. He stared at it for a long moment.

Somehow the loss of the *Angel of Death* was the worst wound by far.

Fraser waved away Dr. Ramirez impatiently. "I'm all right, Doctor," he snapped. "See to the ones who really need your help."

Ramirez gave a reluctant nod and turned away. The Padre trailed after him with a mournful look that spoke volumes. Father Fitzpatrick would be administering the last rites many more times this day.

"What's the damage, Gunny?" Fraser asked Trent. The sergeant had arrived as if from nowhere moments after Russo, Fraser, and the other survivors from the command van had staggered out through the rear ramp door. Even Trent looked shaken.

"Three vehicles out, L-T," Trent said. "The command van, of course. One of the FSV's . . . and one of the vans carrying the wounded took a direct hit, too." A spasm of pain crossed the sergeant's face.

"Damn . . ." Fraser looked away. "How many casualties?"

"We're still checking, L-T. Except for the wounded, not too many. Bashar and Karatsolis got out of the *Angel* after she was hit, and luckily the weapons squad had already dismounted before the hannies hit us."

"How the devil did the bastards hit us that hard?" Fraser demanded, more to himself than to Trent. "That primmie junk shouldn't have done this much damage!"

"Probably some kind of simple targeting computer," Trent replied. "The planes that released their bombs knew exactly when to turn 'em loose."

"But they didn't get their licks in cheap," Kelly Winters added from behind the sergeant. "The other Sabertooth knocked out the rest of their planes before they could make another pass or cut and run.''

''Yeah.'' Trent spat expressively. ''I'll bet we killed every plane they had that was rigged with those damn computers.''

''Let's hope so, Gunny,'' Fraser replied wearily. ''Because another attack like that one could finish us off for sure.''

# Chapter 16

Their graves mark the sites of each night's halt.
—Captain Roulet
writing of the Madagascar campaign
French Foreign Legion, 1895

"Yea, though I walk through the valley of the shadow of death, I will fear no evil: for thou art with me; thy rod and thy staff they comfort me."

Lieutenant Colin Fraser shifted uncomfortably as the Padre read the psalm. The assembled legionnaires filled the clearing, but the silence was broken only by Fitzpatrick's soft, lilting voice as they paid their last respects to the comrades who had lost their lives in the hannie bomb strike.

Fraser stole a glance at the shrouded forms lined up at the edge of the mass grave the company had prepared. Fifteen men had died in the attack. He had hardly known any of them, and the realization made him feel guilty.

Donald Hamilton, for instance . . . the young warrant officer had probably saved Fraser himself from the metal shard that killed him. It was only afterwards that Fraser had heard Hamilton's friend, Vandergraff, telling Fitzpatrick about the man's hopes and dreams. Hamilton had volunteered for duty with the Legion right out of college, planning to get a tour on the frontiers under his belt before trading in his Specialist's Warrant for a regular officer's commission. Apparently the man had been regarded as a prime candidate for rapid promotion within the Commonwealth Army intelligence staff, the same department Fraser himself had once been assigned to.

Or Platoon Sergeant Persson, who had been in the command van's forward compartment alongside the driver, Hengist, when the explosion tore through the front of the vehicle. "Swede" Persson's confidential records showed that the had volunteered for the Legion as an alternative to being sent to a penal battalion after killing three civilians in a drunken brawl in a Triton Systerm dive. Persson had been disagreeable, unpopular . . . but a good soldier. A good legionnaire.

One man looking to the future, the other fleeing from the past. The Legion had been a home to both. And the rest of the dead were just as much of a mixed bag: the sentry who had been stabbed half a dozen times in the throat and chest during the first native attack on Fort Monkey . . . the legionnaire from Charlie Company who lost an arm in the fighting around Shelton's Head . . . the Navy man injured in the *Ganymede* crash. Death had claimed them all here on this remote world.

Fitzpatrick had closed his Bible now, but the burial service was still going on. Fraser wondered how many more times he would have to witness funerals like this one before Demi-Battalion Alice reached safety at last. Ten percent casualties from this one bomb attack . . .

And close to a thousand kilometers to go before they reached the frontier.

He felt the weight of his burden as the unit's commander like a tangible thing pressing on his shoulders. Those men had died, and as their leader he bore the responsibility for their deaths.

*What could I have done differently?* he asked himself bitterly. *What can I do differently the next time, to keep these men alive?*

They had a long march ahead of them, and Fraser knew there was sure to be a next time.

What he didn't know was whether he would be able to see this journey through to the end.

Slick felt the tension in the crowd as the Padre sketched out the Cross and signed for the assembly to bow their heads in prayer. He went through the motions of the ceremony, but inside he was wishing they would finish the funeral quickly.

The sight of those bodies in the pit brought back too many memories of battle and fear.

Unlike the weapons lances, Slick's unit had not been ordered to dismount during the attack. The lance had been rotated aboard the FSV crewed by Ignaczak and Sergeant Mason for a rest shift just an hour before the attack. They had ridden out the entire action in the cramped confines, deafened by the screeching plasma gun. For Slick, it had been the most terrifying combat of all, trapped in a metallic coffin and unable to take any active role in his own defense.

Somehow, *somehow* he had come through it all without breaking down. But the memory haunted him now as he thought of all those men killed when their vehicles had taken direct hits.

"In the name of the Father, and the Son, and the Holy Spirit, Amen," the Padre intoned at last with another quick sketching of the Cross.

Gunnery Sergeant Trent was stepping forward almost immediately. "Listen up! Pay your respects however you have to, but then get back to your details! I want you apes ready to mag out by 1800 hours." There was a rumble from the ranks. Trent scanned them with weary eyes. "That's 1800 hours *standard,* for those of you who were planning to make any excuses. Dismissed!"

The sergeant turned away to talk with the lieutenant and his staff as legionnaires began to disperse. Slick started to turn away, then checked the motion as Dmitri Rostov pushed past him toward the pit. The older legionnaire joined a queue, bending to pick up a handful of dirt. Curious, Slick followed him.

The line was a long one, filing slowly past the mass grave. As each man passed, he threw some dirt on the bodies. But they were mostly keeping some, too, tucking it in pockets or pouches. Near the head of the column, Corporal Strauss was opening a small vial already half full of varicolored soil and adding a little more from his hand.

"What're they doing, Rostov?" Slick asked softly. "What's with the dirt?"

Rostov looked at him with a surprised expression. "You never—?" Then he nodded. "Oh, yeah, you're still a nube. Look, kid, don't ask dumb questions if you don't like people thinking you're dumb, right?"

The line moved forward a meter or so in silence before Rostov spoke again. "It's tradition, kid. You help to bury the guys you can't take back, and you keep some of the

dirt. It's how we help our buddies on their way to the
Last March, y'know? Brings good luck.''

"Ah, come on, Rostov," Slick said. "Don't tell me
you believe in good luck charms! What kind of jerkwater
planet do you come from, anyhow?"

Rostov flared. "Watch your mouth, nube!" He paused,
visibly calming down. "Look, like I said, it's tradition.
Legion tradition, not something from Novy Krimski. Call
it what you want, but a lot of people believe in it. And
it's not for some damned nube to say whether or not it's
right. You get my signal, kid?"

"Yeah, sure, Rostov . . . sure." Slick looked away.
"It just seems kind of funny, that's all. It's not like any
of those guys were part of our platoon. Or was one of
them some kinda buddy of yours?"

"They're *all* my 'buddies', nube. And yours, except
you don't seem to understand it." He spat. "The Legion
looks after its own. Doesn't matter if a guy's a total
stranger or your tentmate for the last ten years. He's your
buddy . . . your comrade. And a part of the only family
you've got!"

Slick had a sudden image of Billy's face as he'd seen
it last, but pushed it out of his mind. How could Rostov
compare some dead legionnaire with his own flesh and
blood?

But he'd already angered Rostov enough. He wouldn't
argue it further.

Behind them a guttural voice rumbled. "You should
listen, nube."

It was Ghirghik, the Ubrenfar sergeant from Charlie
Company. The huge, scaled saurian still made Slick nervous. How could you trust an Ubrenfar to be a Terran
soldier?

Rostov didn't seem to share his feelings. "He's just a
nube, Sarge," he said with a grin. "You should know
by now that nubes don't listen."

"If they did, you Terrans would be better Warriors,"
Ghirghik replied. "Your Legion almost understands . . .
but fools like this one weaken your spirit." The Ubrenfar
rounded on Slick again. "Honor your comrades, young
one. The Warrior who fights without the respect of his
own fights a lost battle from the beginning."

"Is that something your people teach?" Rostov asked.

The Ubrenfar showed a menacing number of teeth and gave a rumbling chuckle. "Actually, one of your lance-mates shared it with me, though not in quite those words. Vrurrth. But it is very close to what our Warriors would say, if they were given to philosophy."

Rostov laughed. "I guess Warriors are a lot alike everywhere, Sarge."

"It is not something for laughter, Rostov." The Ubrenfar bent down to pick up a clod of dirt. "My people do not believe in this 'luck' you Terrans hold so dear, Rostov. But I hope none here will mind if I honor these men as you do." He shot an angry glare at Slick. "Even if some of their own kind will not."

Slick turned away before Rostov could reply.

Kelly Winters touched the center of the small disk clinging just behind Myaighee's ear. It came away on her finger, and the alien blinked several times.

"The . . . magic is so strange," Myaighee said slowly in Terranglic. "Like a dream . . ."

She smiled. "It isn't magic, Myaighee. Just technology. Do you feel all right?"

The native gave a tentative nod, Terran-style. Ky was progressing well with the adchip lessons, learning Terranglic and some of the more basic Terran customs. Kelly had borrowed the chips from Father Fitzpatrick soon after Myaighee's release from the medical unit. If the native was going to travel with the Legion, it only made sense to teach ky the language. Even the rare legionnaire who bothered to study the language didn't always remember—or particularly care—that the locals wouldn't automatically understand Terranglic.

Besides, it gave Myaighee a purpose, something to keep the native from brooding about the things ky had lost.

The hannie looked longingly at the chip in Kelly's hand. She frowned and returned it to its carrying case. "That's it for today," she told ky. "I think you've had enough."

Most sentient lifeforms encountered by the Commonwealth could use adchips with remarkably little adaptation; only a radically alien intelligence was incapable of taking the direct subconscious feed and translating it into symbols the brain could comprehend. But adchip addiction was a problem in many species, and from what she had seen so far Kelly was fairly sure the *kyendyp* were particularly susceptible. An adchip could be a useful learning tool, or it could be programmed to deliver many kinds of entertainment, from role-playing games to sports to the kind of pornographic experiences most people on Terra thought of when they talked about "the adchip problem." But in any form the chip's induced dreams were a powerful lure, offering an escape from reality. Back on Earth, adchip addiction was a major social problem, exacerbated by the essentially idle welfare society that high technology and virtually unlimited resources had spawned among Terra's billions.

Kelly wasn't about to let Myaighee fall into the adchip trap. Ky had problems enough without getting lost in Dreamland.

The native was recovering from kys wounds well enough, but there were psychological scars ky might never get over. Myaighee had given up everything—home, family, kys very culture—to help Kelly escape. The native had fastened on her as kys only real friend, and she could not ignore kys need. She owed the alien her life.

But it couldn't go on like this much longer. Even though she didn't have any real job she could perform on the march, it wasn't a good idea for her to spend every waking moment helping Myaighee cope. It wasn't fair to the native to make ky so dependent upon her and her alone.

The alien had to be given something more, something to hold on to.

She had taken the matter up with Lieutenant Fraser a few days back. If he could find useful work for Myaighee to do . . .

"Lieutenant Winters? I hope we're not interrupting anything?"

She looked up to find Fraser behind her, with Sergeant Trent and Legionnaire Garcia. Kelly smiled. "Not at all, Lieutenant. I was just wrapping up with Myaighee here."

Fraser nodded vaguely at the native. *"Zhyinin as-wai nyijyiik?"*

Myaighee replied in Terranglic. "Yes, Honored . . .

sir. The doctor says . . . full recovery." Ky looked at Kelly. "Is that right?"

She nodded, hiding a smile at Fraser's ill-concealed surprise. "Something wrong, Lieutenant?"

"No. The other way around, in fact. I've been thinking about the suggestion you made the other day about finding our . . . guest here something to do. Sergeant Trent had some suggestions I thought we should talk over."

She glanced at Trent. He met her gaze with shuttered eyes. He probably had talked Fraser out of it, and the lieutenant was just looking for an easy way to let her down.

"I was skeptical when you first brought it up," Fraser went on. "But the sergeant here thinks now that Myaighee here can help us more than I thought."

It took several seconds for the words to sink in. Trent actually *agreed* with the suggestion?

Before she could react, Myaighee was already speaking. "Help, Honored?" ky asked.

"That's right," Fraser said. "You see, one of the men we lost in the attack this morning was an expert advisor on your people. He gave me advice about the technical abilities of your army, about the people and politics we have to deal with. I'd like you to do the same."

"Honored . . . sir, I know little about . . . military. Only what I know from militia training. Very little. And technology . . ." The alien crossed kys arms, the hannie *no*.

"Maybe not," Trent said. "But you must know something about politics. Even if all you have is gossip, what you know could help us."

"And we need every edge we can get," Fraser said. He glanced at Kelly. "Maybe we're asking too much, though. If you'd feel like you were betraying your people . . ."

The alien crossed arms again. "It was the *Asjyai* who betrayed us," ky said bitterly. "Ky killed the *yzyeel*. Attacked the Terrans who had come in friendship."

"Then you'll help us?" Kelly asked.

Myaighee looked at her with grim, determined eyes. "Yes. Yes . . . I will help." Ky hesitated, studying Fraser with the same bleak expression. "And I thank you, Honored. Lieutenant Fraser. I do not know if my help

will be of value, but at least it will let me *fight back.*
Thank you.''

"Legionnaire Garcia will take you in hand," Fraser
said. "I will want to talk with you some more later."

Garcia gestured to the native. With a single glance back
at Kelly, Myaighee followed.

"Thank you, Lieutenant," Kelly said, interrupting his
reverie. "And you, Sergeant. Myaighee needs this."

Fraser nodded absently. "We've got to use *all* our resources, Lieutenant." He gave Trent an odd glance and
paused, apparently thinking about something completely
unrelated. Finally he looked back up at her and continued. "How are you getting along, Lieutenant?"

She shrugged and gave a rueful grin. "Bored to tears,
Lieutenant. And now I guess I don't even have social
work to keep me busy."

"Well, I'm not sure what I can give you to do. Not
much call for combat engineers out here . . . not unless
we can get some building supplies."

"I understand that, Lieutenant," she said. Inwardly,
though, she felt empty, useless. Even Myaighee had more
to contribute then she did. It surprised her to find out just
how much she *wanted* to be able to help the legionnaires.

"I'm sure Miss Winters could be very useful helping Doc
and the Padre with the wounded," Trent said blandly.

Fraser nodded vaguely. "Anything you can do is ap-
preciated, Lieutenant. Meanwhile, just stick with it.
We'll get clear yet."

She bit back an angry comment about nursing and
women's work. It was true. Her skills weren't that useful
out here. She was an outsider, not part of the Legion,
and there wasn't much she could contribute apart from
menial work.

At least it was *something.* "Maybe I should see if they
need any help getting ready now," she said slowly. "The
Padre said they lost a lot of medical supplies when the
APC was hit." She stood up. "Unless you need me for
something else, Lieutenant?"

"Not right now, Lieutenant," Fraser said.

She turned away, more unsure of her feelings than ever.

Fraser watched the Navy officer leave without really
seeing her. The bomber attack had unsettled him, sapped

what little confidence he had left, and it was hard to focus on anything beyond the certainty that the Legion's luck was sure to run out sooner or later. At each turn they had escaped total disaster . . . but the costs were mounting, and so were the odds against them.

Hamilton's death couldn't have come at a worse time. As they drew closer to the hannie garrison town of Zhair-hee, his insights on the capabilities of the enemy would have been invaluable. Now he was dead. What kind of replacement would Kelly's alien make?

It was hard to see what good ky could really do. Certainly Myaighee lacked Hamilton's training and experience, his day-to-day study of Hanuman's cultures, technology, and politics. This palace servant . . . what could ky do?

But Trent seemed to think it was a good idea. "First rule of dealin' with the natives, L-T," he had said when he came to present the idea right after the funeral. "A local always understands local conditions best. Why else do you think Battalion keeps a dozen natives on *their* intel staff?"

Fraser still wasn't sure . . . but if Trent liked the idea, it was probably a good one. More and more Fraser was coming to realize that he needed to lean on a veteran like Trent if he was going to pull off the rest of the long march out of Dryienjaiyeel. If Trent said a native would make a good advisor, that was good enough for Colin Fraser.

Alone with Trent now, Fraser sat on a log and gestured for the sergeant to join him. "Are you sure about pushing out of here so fast, Gunny?" he asked quietly.

"Aren't you, L-T?" Trent looked surprised.

"Just . . . having some second thoughts, that's all." He leaned forward. "Shouldn't we be salvaging what we can from the three wrecks? We did before."

"L-T, those bombers hurt us bad. If the hannies have any more of those things, we're in deep shit and no mistake."

"You said they didn't."

"I said they *probably* didn't," Trent corrected him. " 'Probably' doesn't cut it in the field. The only thing you can be sure about is what you see and hear for yourself, L-T. If we have a chance to find out I'm wrong, it'll be too damned late for all of us.''

Fraser nodded slowly. ''I see your point. But if they've got more planes, they can still catch us on the march.''

''Right now, sir, the only thing we can do is to *keep moving*. No matter what, we've got to keep ahead of their troops. That means we don't hold back for bombers, or patrols, or whole regiments. 'Cause if we let them catch us, we can kiss our chances of seeing home again goodbye.''

''There's still Zhairhee,'' Fraser pointed out. ''Hamilton said they were building up their forces around there.''

Trent looked grim. ''I know. We're just going to have to count on speed and surprise to get us past them.''

''Look, Gunny . . . I don't want to milk a dead sharv, but wouldn't it be a good idea to strip what we can off the command van? Try to get it running again, even? The recon drones would sure help us later on. And if we leave the van, we leave the sat link. Last time I talked to Battalion, Commandant Isayev said they were trying to bring in some extra troops. If we could wait it out, they might get a ship in here to lift us out. But only if they know where we are, what we're doing. I don't like being out of touch with HQ.''

''It's your decision, L-T,'' Trent told him. ''But do you really think the resident-general's going to risk another ship for us? We've got to proceed as if we're not getting any help. And I think every minute we're not on the march increases our risk of being caught about ten times over.''

Fraser shrugged. ''You're the expert, Gunny,'' he said at last. ''Hell, you're running this show anyway.''

Trent drew back. ''Hang on, L-T! This is still your decision to make. If you want to strip the vehicles . . .''

''Calm down, Gunny.'' Fraser spread his hands. ''They told me in OCS to listen to what my top sergeant had to say. So . . . I'm listening. We keep to the schedule.''

Trent seemed to want to say more, so Fraser forestalled him. ''Better make sure everybody *else* is sticking to it, too, Gunny. Report to me at 1700 hours.''

''Yessir,'' Trent responded reluctantly.

As the sergeant left, Fraser leaned back, feeling better than he had since the bombing raid had started . . . was it only this morning? As long as Trent was by his side, the burden of running the unit wouldn't push him under. Sergeant Trent was the man who could get them to safety.

If anyone could.

# Chapter 17

If hell falls on him, the legionnaire keeps marching.
— Lt. Colonel Magrin-Verneret
French Foreign Legion, 1940

The terrain in the Zhairhee valley seemed to leap toward him as Fraser switched his helmet controls to the image intensification setting. With his left hand, he carefully dialed the magnification knob on the side of his faceplate until the digital setting of the unit's HUD read *x500*.

"Not much of a city," he said quietly.

Trent stirred beside him. "It's enough, L-T. Believe me, it's enough."

They were pressed flat against a steep rocky outcropping on a hilltop ledge overlooking the valley from the south. The little native, Myaighee, was crouched beside Trent, examining the scene through a pair of native-made binoculars they'd captured in a skirmish three days before. Four legionnaires from Pascali's recon lance provided unobtrusive security around the hilltop, their camouflage suits blending into the grey-orange background. Out of sight almost five kilometers away, back where the jungle cover was still thick enough to provide concealment from prying eyes, the rest of the survivors of Demi-Battalion Alice awaited their return in the unit's latest temporary camp.

Fraser studied the terrain spread out below the position. The valley was broad and level, fed by two rivers which wound down from the Raizhee mountains and joined together just under the low rise which held the hannie city.

Much of the plain was inundated here. Myaighee had told them that this area was noted for *ylyn* farming, and

Fraser could see hannies wading through the knee-deep water tending the *ylyn* paddies. A few of the large, shaggy beasts of burden the natives called *zymlats* were visible as well.

The paddies were crisscrossed by an elaborate pattern of dikes and causeways, some little more than makeshift barricades, but others supporting multi-lane highways that connected Zhairhee to the outside world. The city rose above it all like an island in the midst of a shallow sea.

Beyond the valley, no more than seventy kilometers away, the jagged peaks of the Raizhee Mountains formed a spectacular backdrop to the scene. They were steep and forbidding, higher and more treacherous than Terra's Alps. But high above Zhairhee the narrow notch of a pass was visible. Beyond lay friendly Vyujiid . . . and Fwynzei, the Commonwealth enclave.

Safety . . .

But only if the legionnaires could get past the daunting obstacle that was Zhairhee.

It had taken nearly three weeks for the unit to reach this milestone after the bombing attack, a long time for a trip of a thousand kilometers as measured on their maps. But every step of that long march had been through rugged, untamed terrain, jungles and foothills and, most recently, the wide expanse of the Jyeindyein swamp. Fraser reckoned they had covered more than two thousand klicks all told as they dodged enemy units and skirted impassable terrain in search of a reasonably safe route north.

Through it all their pursuers had never been far behind. Skirmishes with patrols had become an almost daily affair for a time, and reconnaissance planes dogged every twist and turn of their route. By taking to the swamp route they had finally left the hannie army behind; primitive tracked and wheeled vehicles simply couldn't follow magrep APCs through such terrain. By overloading the Sandrays and improvising harnesses so some of the men could strap themselves to the hulls of the carriers they'd managed to move everyone in one jump, but the extra weight made the APCs sluggish and unmaneuverable . . . and the legionnaires couldn't travel far in such an awkward position.

At least no further bombing attacks had been attempted during the passage of the marshes. Fraser still shuddered at the thought of the casualties they could have taken if the overloaded Sandrays had received the same kind of treatment as the lost command van.

Still, it hadn't been easy. Battle, fatigue, and mishaps on the march had reduced the unit to no more than 110 effectives, with thirty-three more too seriously wounded to march or fight. Four more vehicles had gone as well, two of them engineering vans that had just given up the ghost, the third a fabrication van taken out of action by a hannie tank in one of the running skirmishes before they had reached the swamp. The fourth, one of the precious troop carriers, had been damaged in the marsh itself after a clinging vine-like plant had fouled the fans and burned out the main rotor bearings. They were still using the APC to carry supplies. Since its magnetic suspension system was still functioning, it could be towed . . . but, again, it slowed the pace.

Had it not been for the knowledge that friendly territory was so close now, the survivors probably couldn't have kept on marching at all.

But there was still Zhairhee, and the disquieting reports from the first scouting party that had led Fraser and Trent to reconnoiter the valley in person.

"Take a look over there, L-T," Trent said, touching his arm. "Bearing 354. Just beyond the airfield."

Fraser shifted his view until the HUD gave the right bearing. There was a small prop-driven aircraft touching down on one of the runways, but that wasn't what Trent had been drawing attention to. What was it . . . ?

*There.* Fraser's intake of breath was sharp, audible.

Just coming into view on the largest of the roads leading northward from Zhairhee a column of vehicles was rumbling slowly out of town. They were boxy, slow, mounted on wide tracks and painted a uniform greyish-orange. Fraser started counting but quickly gave up.

All-terrain transports of the Dryien army . . . at least enough to be carrying a full regiment. And making their way north, toward the pass. Toward the border.

"Corporal Braxton was right, then," Fraser said softly. He was sweating, and it wasn't all from the humid 30° C noontime heat.

Trent nodded. "He said three regiments went out of there yesterday . . . one of them armor. One more now. Good God, L-T, how many of the bastards are they sending up there, anyway?"

"More than we can break through, Gunny," he said. "Could they really be piling that many troops up there just to keep us hemmed in?"

"Doesn't make much sense, L-T," Trent replied. "I've been reading the survey reports on that pass. It's too narrow for that many troops to be used effectively. Hell, a couple of companies could hold that sucker against an army for a day or two. Four regiments would just get in each others way."

"Hmmm. Unless . . ." Fraser trailed off, watching the creeping vehicles on his II viewer.

"What is it, L-T?"

Fraser raised his faceplate and looked at the sergeant. "I'm just spinning this off the top of my head, Gunny, so bear with me. The hannies in these parts suddenly got the urge to throw out all the foreign demons, right? Killed the captain and all the diplomats they could lay their hands on, then went after us."

"Yeah." Trent lifted his own faceplate and spat expressively.

"Now we know the hannies have been getting some high-tech help, like info on our sensors and some kind of targeting gizmo. Probably Semti help, if that missile launcher Ghirghik brought in means anything."

Trent gave a slow nod. "Looks like some of our Semti buddies aren't so happy with us after all."

"Well, those ghouls would know that kicking us out of Dryienjaiyeel would just be temporary. Even if they'd wiped us out, you can bet a couple regiments will be heading south to let our monkey friends know that you don't just turn down a Commonwealth trading deal . . . or kill off legionnaires. Hell, Isayev'd be leading a punitive expedition this way now if the resident-general would let him off his leash!"

"So you think . . . what? That the Dryiens have something bigger in mind?" Trent frowned for a moment. Then his face went white. "Not an attack on Fwynzei, L-T?"

"Why not? It's not that far north of the pass. Push

through fast enough, and the hannies just might roll over the city before the garrison could react. The commandant's got less than half a battalion of legionnaires and a regiment or two of native troops. Everything else is spread out in local garrisons. Hit hard and fast and the hannies could at least lay siege to the port, keep out anything short of an assault ship.''

"Yeah, but they couldn't keep our boys out forever, L-T. And the Semti would know it.''

"Mounting punitive raids to punish Zyzyiig for his little massacre is one thing. But if we have to fight the whole goddamned planet . . . it'd throw a murphy into our plans for this entire sector, Gunny.'' Fraser stabbed his finger at the enemy column. "That's an invasion force, and they're headed for Fwynzei. I'd bet my life on it.''

Trent grunted. "Not a bet I'd take right now, L-T.''

Myaighee shifted uneasily. "Lieutenant,'' ky put in softly. The native's English had improved with further language lessons, and ky wore the rank insignia of a legionnaire third class on the improvised torso armor Sergeant Forbes had assembled in the unit's surviving fabrication van. "I do not know if this information means anything, but I have been studying the unit crests on those tracks.''

"They mean something special?'' Trent asked.

"My . . . father? Yes, my father's sibling served in that unit many years ago. It is the Regiment Miststalkers. A very good unit, Lieutenant Fraser.''

"Yes? So?'' Fraser couldn't mask the impatience he felt.

"The unit has always been stationed at the town of Ghynjyik near the head of the Jyikeezh delta, Lieutenant. On the eastern coast. The Miststalkers are light infantry, trained to operate in the jungles and marshes against the primitives of the inland regions.'' The alien trailed off, looking at Trent. "I don't know all the English words yet, Sergeant Trent. But they are very highly skilled soldiers, trained in rapid strikes, raids, operations against superior numbers . . .''

"Commandos,'' Trent said.

"That is one of the words I wanted!'' Myaighee

agreed. "Commandos. But the very best commandos. One of the most respected units in the army!"

"Elite troops, L-T," Trent said. "And way the hell off their regular stomping grounds. Would they bring in a unit like that to hunt for us, do you think?"

"If they were desperate enough, maybe," Fraser said without conviction. "But I think it clinches the invasion theory."

"Yeah." Trent flipped down the faceplate again and adjusted his image intensifier. "Yeah, a major mobilization on the frontier. Elite light infantry would be damned useful trying to overrun Fwynzei's defences. I think you're right on this one, L-T. Question is, what the hell do we do about it?"

"Damned if I know, Gunny," Fraser said. "But whatever we do, we've got to do it fast. Otherwise there might not be a way out even if we do get across the border."

The roar of the props diminished to a sigh as the aircraft rolled to a halt. *Asjyai* Zyzyiig unstrapped kyself awkwardly, waving away an eager staff officer who tried to help with the unfamiliar harness. Near the rear of the plane the crew chief was already unclamping the hatch.

With kys staff trailing behind, Zyzyiig stalked slowly to the opening. The wind blowing into the aircraft was uncomfortably cool, not at all like the pleasant climate of the capital. Of course Zhairhee was far more pleasant than the uplands north of the mountains, where the army was marching. It still made a distasteful contrast to the comforts of the Fortress of Heaven, though.

But with the final stages of the campaign against the offworlders beginning, it was essential for Zyzyiig to be close at hand to exercise personal control over kys troops. Otherwise, some local field commander might be in a position to claim more than kys share of the credit and threaten the fragile structure of Dryienjaiyeel's new government.

Workers were wheeling a ladder into place below the hatch. As ky had ordered, there was no ceremony being attached to the *Asjyai's* arrival. The invasion schedule must not be needlessly disrupted . . . and the Terrans, now that they were getting their first reports of the assault across the pass, must not have their attention drawn to unusual visits by VIPs.

Anyway, the last reports had placed the refugees from the demon Foreign Legion only a few days' march to the south, in the Jyeindyein region. Best not to tempt fate. After the ill-fated bombing raid, ky had a healthy respect for what those legionnaires could do against air power.

Zyzyiig suppressed a shudder at the sight of the tall figure swathed in black robes standing near the ladder. So Shavvataaars was back from his mysterious errands.

The *Asjyai* hoped that this time the Semti would have something more concrete to give than vague warnings and obscure philosophy. Ky knew the alien would have something to say about the continued survival of the Legion. Not that they mattered now. They could never reach their friends with the Army Demonslayer between them and their compatriots at Fwynzei. Once the demons had been swept away there, the legionnaires would fall into kys hands like *ylyn* at a harvest.

Ky descended the ladder slowly, with all the dignity ky could muster. *Indjyeek* Dwyiiel, the commander of the Zhairhee garrison, stepped forward to greet Zyzyiig. From the set of the general's neck ruff, it was plain ky was agitated.

"*Asjyai* . . . welcome to—"

Zyzyiig cut the officer off with crossed arms. "Never mind the pleasantries, Dwyiiel. I want a full staff meeting in one hour. And why in the name of the Eternal Mists was Regiment Blooddrinkers turned back to the south?"

"We . . . we had reports of the demons moving through the marshes, Honored," the luckless commander stammered. "I thought—"

"You are not equipped to think, Dwyiiel. There are other units moving up from the capital who are tasked to deal with the demons. Regiment Blooddrinkers is needed beyond the mountains to exploit success in the attack on Fwynzei, but for that they must *cross the mountains*. Your bungling may have delayed our attack, and that could cost us this campaign." Ky looked around the ranks of junior officers around Dwyiiel. "You. You are Executive Officer of this base?"

"Yes, Honored."

"Wrong. You are commander of this base. Make sure Blooddrinkers return as soon as possible. And assign this fool to them. Ky will make an excellent scout, since ky is so good at thinking and planning."

"Yes, Honored."

Ky turned away to meet Shavvataaars as he approached. "Welcome, my Companion," the Semti whispered. As they talked, they walked together away from the cluster of officers. It would not do to have junior staffers know too much about the deeper layers of the campaign against the Terrans. "I see you are truly taking command of the situation here."

Zyzyiig studied the hooded face suspiciously. "If you are about to voice your disapproval, save your breath. I will brook no interference in my handling of my troops *this* time."

"On the contrary, Honored *Asjyai,*" Shavvataaars demurred. "I am in complete agreement. The final phase of the Cleansing is at hand, and if we are to finish our burrow and set out traps, we must act swiftly and with decision."

"Then everything is prepared?"

"Everything. You will have had the reports on our agents' efforts at the pass, I believe. The traitors made sure the Vyujiid garrison offered no resistance to your lead column. There is a strong blockhouse near the head of the pass which was easily secured."

Zyzyiig made an impatient gesture. "Speak of the future, not the past, Honored."

"Very well, my Companion. Events in Vyujiid have proceeded satisfactorily. The merchants, the farmers, many of the common people are ready to throw off the demon yoke. By trying to circumvent the traditional trade routes, the demons proved the lie in their words of prosperity and social equality."

"Can we expect support in Vyujiid, then?"

"Perhaps not immediately," Shavvataaars admitted. "The demons are still regarded with great awe by the superstitious. When it is seen that they are not invincible, that they can be wounded and killed like any common mortal, then you will see support. The fall of Fwynzei will surely trigger a mass rising against the demons and their lackeys in the Imperial Government."

"If Fwynzei falls," Zyzyiig said, letting kys fears show through for a moment. "Much depends on overwhelming their garrison. Surely they have had time to detect our muster, to prepare for our attack?"

"Time they have had, my Companion, but not enough. Their garrison was not that strong to begin with—a mere battalion of their Foreign Legion, and a few regiments of native auxiliaries. Many of their units have been assigned to serve elsewhere, away from Fwynzei."

"And have these not been summoned to return?"

Shavvataaars gave a breathy, satisfied sigh. "Our sympathizers have caused many problems in the outlying garrison towns. Sabotage. Agitation. Bombings and threats of bombings. In most cases, the Terrans have not dared withdraw their garrisons, for fear it would turn the Imperial government against them. It was on their pledge of supporting the old order that the demons won the aid of Vyujiid's aristocracy, after all."

"Then perhaps we have time to prepare things further, draw off more of their strength?"

Shavvataaars replied with crossed arms. "I fear not, my Companion. Three transports carrying reinforcements are en route to the planet as we speak. I am afraid that this was one moment when fortune did not favor our plans. Their resident-general managed to divert these troops from a carriership that happened to be passing through the systerm on the way to Enkidu. Three battalions of assault troops . . . a dangerous opponent. We must act before they arrive. It is a matter of days."

"Then we have to call it off!" Zyzyiig said. Ky lowered kys voice as ky realized the staff officers were looking at them curiously. "There is no margin for error . . . no way to keep them from counterattacking, whatever we do at Fwynzei!"

"Now is the time of decision, *Asjyai,*" Shavvataaars whispered coldly. "We must move quickly, yes, though haste is not normally wise. But the rewards if we are successful . . ."

"And do you have a plan to keep them from counterattacking as soon as they arrive?"

"More than one plan, my impatient Companion. More than one." Shavvataaars drew close enough for Zyzyiig to feel his foul breath on kys face. "First, these troops were not equipped to mount unsupported assaults. They are unlikely to attempt a landing in the face of opposition, remembering what your army did to the transport that tried to evacuate the demons from their enclave in the south. If they lose Fwynzei as a base, they are likely to wait in orbit until fresh ships, assault ships, can arrive. That will take many cycles, many long cycles, in which we may consolidate our hold here.''

"It still sounds like a dangerous gamble . . .''

"Second, and far more important, you will soon have an ally with nearly the power of the Terrans and their Commonwealth. You have heard of the Ubrenfars?''

"Yes . . . yes, I remember some Terran boasting over a banquet once. The Terrans outbluffed the Ubrenfars in a dispute some years ago and prevented them from encroaching into this region.'' Zyzyiig's neck ruff bristled. "Are these the allies you offer me? They have lost to the demons once already.''

"I have been in touch with . . . contacts among the Ubrenfars, my Companion. There are two of their warships in this system now. They will not act unless this world can speak with a single voice to plead for their protection, but once they hear such a voice, their government is prepared to support you here. The Terrans are unlikely to risk a war over this one planet. This time they will be the ones who will back down.''

"And we exchange one set of masters for another?''

"I think not. The Ubrenfars seek only to humiliate the Terrans, to resume their rightful place as a Great Power in this region. Your independence will be protected, no more . . . unless your people want more.''

"So if we take Fwynzei . . .''

"The risings will begin in Vyujiid. And your nation in combination with the Empire can call upon Ubrenfar support. The Terran transports might never reach orbit, if our attack is swift enough. And decisive enough.''

"So it all comes down to a single throw of the dice, eh?''

"The Great Journey has been that since the first moments of the coup, my Companion. Any mistake could cost all. But success . . . success will spell the end of the demons on your world, and the effects could spread outward to bring down their entire Commonwealth. But we cannot have that success without making your gambler's throw."

Zyzyiig didn't answer the Semti. Instead, ky turned abruptly back to face the staff officers. "Where is my car? I need to get to headquarters now. Now! We must finish the preparations and launch the attack immediately!"

Behind Zyzyiig, Shavvataaars felt a cold flush of satisfaction. The Great Journey was rushing toward completion. Twilight Prowler would soon be in motion.

He thought of what he had told the alien. It was the truth—as far as it went.

But of course Zyzyiig did not need to know that success or failure on Hanuman mattered very little to the overall plan. Once Fwynzei fell and the rebellion began in Vyujiid, it mattered little whether the Terrans abandoned the planet and suffered humiliation, or invested vast time and energy reconquering the planet and exterminating the *Asjyai* and all kys followers. Either result would set back the Commonwealth and bring the return of the Semti to power one step closer.

Just let Fwynzei fall, and Twilight Prowler would be a complete success, no matter what came afterwards.

# Chapter 18

With or without helmet, death knows when it is
your turn.

        —Lt. Colonel Dmitri Amilakvari
      French Foreign Legion, June, 1942

"This is it, people, so make sure everyone's set. All
platoons, report readiness."

Fraser looked around the cramped interior of the engineering van that was now serving as the unit's command vehicle. It was much more cramped than the old
one, with lower overheads and more massive bracing
throughout. These rigs were meant for brute force construction work, not headquarters duties.

Beside him Legionnaire Garcia balanced her unfolded
C³ unit on her knees, with Russo on the other side of her
helping as well as he could. Across the dim compartment
WO/4 Vandergraff and Kelly Winters looked on help-
lessly. Myaighee, kys eyes wide, was crouched in one
corner. Excited or afraid? Fraser didn't know the little
alien well enough to be sure.

"First Platoon, ready," Fairfax's clipped, precise voice
was the first to reply over his headphones.

"Second Platoon, set," Watanabe chimed in. The
young Pacifican subaltern sounded calm and in control.
He had been a tower of strength throughout the march.

"Fourth Platoon is ready." That was Sergeant Baker,
nominally second in command of the provisional unit
formed around the survivors of Charlie Company. Sergeant Ghirghik, along with Gunny Trent, had been assigned a special role in this operation, leaving Baker to
run the platoon. Fraser didn't know much about the man,
but he had decided to keep a familiar NCO in charge of
the outfit.

"Third Platoon. Wait one." That was Sergeant Qazi, acting platoon leader since Subaltern Bartlow had stepped on a hannie land mine near the edge of the swamp. Bartlow was in a regen unit aboard the medical van. If they could get him to a civilized hospital facility, he might be able to walk again some day. "Third Platoon ready, Lieutenant. We've cut loose the damaged Sandray."

"Guardian ready, Alice One," Trent's voice added a moment later.

"All units," Fraser said. "Move out on my signal. Guardian, switch to channel two-nine."

"Two-niner, confirmed."

He nodded to Garcia, and there was a crackle in his headphones as she tuned in the private channel reserved for contact with the senior NCO. "Last chance for recommendations, Gunny," he said. "After this we don't get any time for new plans."

"Can't recommend anything when I don't know what we're up against, L-T. This is one where all we can do is wing it." Trent sounded tired. Fraser tried to imagine what it was like for the Gunnery Sergeant. He was strapped onto the outside of the unit's remaining FSV, his armor clipped to a ring hastily welded into the vehicle's hull the night before. It would be crowded on the back of the Sabertooth, with ten soldiers riding with him. But Trent had insisted that he needed to be outside, where he could see what was going on for himself.

"We could still send out a recon unit. Try to scout out the lay of the land, maybe knock out some of the bad guys before we make our move."

"It would be damned risky, L-T, like I said before. One slip-up and we've lost the only chance we've got."

Twenty hours had passed since Fraser and Trent had watched the column of hannie soldiers winding out of Zhairhee. Now, hidden in darkness, the Legion unit was poised near the edge of the jungle ten kilometers northeast of the city, as close to the road through the pass as they could get without breaking cover. The move had been carried out cautiously so as not to reveal the offworld presence to the patrols that were thick in the valley. Luckily, most of the Dryien attention was directed north, through the pass.

But that would change soon enough. Watanabe had

gone out on patrol with one section of his platoon earlier in the evening and brought back word that there were fresh hannie troops skirting the edge of the swamp south of their last camp. The pursuers were beginning to catch up at last.

Trent had come up with this last-ditch escape plan, of course. They had already overloaded the vehicles once before, for the passage of the marshes. They could do it again tonight, counting on surprise, speed, and superior maneuverability to get them past the hannies in Zhairhee before the enemy had a chance to react.

That would probably work, Fraser conceded. It was what would happen later that worried him.

There were surely hannie troops higher up, in the pass itself . . . and a whole army on the other side of the mountains. Could the legionnaires break through to safety against those odds? Or could they reach a defensible spot and hold out until help arrived.

If there was any help available. Fwynzei might be a burned-out ruin by now.

"Understood, Gunny," he said at last. "But it still sounds like the cafarde to me."

"The bug's not biting me, L-T," Trent replied with a chuckle. *Le cafarde*—literally "the cockroach"—had been a part of Legion life since the pre-starflight days when the Foreign Legion was still French. Legionnaires went mad from *le cafarde*, deserting, running wild, committing suicide. "Anyway, we have to try. There are legionnaires in Fwynzei, and we can't let them down."

"Then it's settled. Switching frequencies." Fraser waited as Garcia adjusted the commlink. "All units, ready to move out."

He saw Russo speaking into another microphone, and seconds later the van was filled with the hum of the fans beginning to rev up. As the magrep fields built, the vehicle swayed slightly.

Adrenaline pumped through his veins. *This is it!*

The Sabertooth rose slowly on balanced magnetic fields, its fans roaring as the FSV gathered speed. Gunnery Sergeant Trent double-checked his harness one last time.

Beside him Legionnaire Karatsolis nudged Corporal

Bashar. "Never saw the view from the outside of one of these babies," he said. "Makes a change, doesn't it, Basher?"

Bashar spat over the side. "Just so Zak remembers we're out here. You cannon jockeys like to play with the turret controls too much."

Some of the other legionnaires clinging to the hull laughed, but Trent saw a few of them looking up nervously at the looming bulk of the turret.

"Hey, Corp," someone said. "Is it too late to tear up those reenlistment papers I signed last month?"

Corporal Pascali chuckled. "All you gotta do is get to Fwynzei, Reuss. They probably lost your papers down in Personnel and are just waiting to get you in to fill out a new set."

Trent tuned out the chatter and tried to scan the terrain ahead. He knew a lot of noncoms, especially from the Commonwealth Regulars, who wouldn't tolerate talking in the ranks under conditions like these. But it kept up morale and helped the others keep their minds off what might happen in the next few hours . . . the next few minutes, even.

Anyway, these were legionnaires. Regular Army standards hardly applied to *them*.

The streamlined bulk of APC Number Two flashed past the FSV. Trent squinted at it through light intensifiers. Ghirghik, the Ubrenfar platoon sergeant, was crouched just behind the vehicle's CEK turret. A mix of legionnaires from recon and heavy weapons lances were clustered around him.

These two vehicles and forty-one soldiers were the vanguard of the column, the all-important strike force that would smash through the enemy defenses so the rest of the company could pass. They had been deliberately overloaded, but the troops they were carrying were the best equipped for the kind of fighting they'd be doing. It had to be hit-and-run tactics this time around: smash through anything in the way and keep going, no matter what. These two lead vehicles were a little slower than the rest, but they'd taken a good head start. As they cleared the way, the rest of the column would catch up and push on.

Or so everyone hoped. It wouldn't take much to derail

the plan entirely, and once the legionnaires were bogged down the game would be over.

Almost side by side now, the two Legion vehicles raced over the dark, misty surface of the *ylyn* paddies. That was one advantage they had, at least. Any native transportation fast enough to keep up with them would be limited to the network of causeways and roads, while the legionnaires could cross the waterlogged fields at will.

But the rising ground on the upper end of the valley funnelled everything into the one north-south road that wound up toward the pass above. That was critical. They could reach the road by way of the relatively safe paddies, but once they were on that road they'd be almost as badly hemmed in by the rugged terrain as the natives.

That was why surprise was so essential. They couldn't allow the hannies to prepare.

He spared a glance over his shoulder. The rest of the Legion APCs were breaking from the cover of the jungle now. Ten left, aside from the two in the vanguard, and three of those probably wouldn't make it all the way to the top of the pass. They'd lost half their strength over the course of the march, and the men and machines that were left were near the breaking point.

Trent hoped Lieutenant Fraser wouldn't hesitate when the battle started. If Trent's men ran into trouble, the lieutenant's natural instinct would be to try to support them. That would be fatal.

*The Legion looks after its own.* Maybe Fraser had learned the lesson too well. But there were more legionnaires on the other side of those mountains, and it was just possible Bravo Company could still help *them*—provided Fraser kept his priorities straight.

He looked ahead again. The main road was much closer now. They might make it all the way out of the valley undetected . . .

As if to mock the hopeful thought, a piercing wail lifted from the direction of Zhairhee, shattering the night. An alarm siren.

They'd been spotted.

The shriek of the alarm siren interrupted *Asjyai* Zyzyiig as ky was debriefing the pilots who had been flying reconnaissance beyond the pass throughout the previous afternoon. The noise made kys ruff bristle. What could be happening at this late hour that would make the guards sound the alarm?

Fear gripped kys bowels. Could it be a demon attack? Had Shavvataaars been wrong in his estimate of when their reinforcements would arrive?

An aide rushed into the conference room ky had appropriated for planning. *"Asjyai!* The sentries on the northern perimeter report demon vehicles crossing the farmlands!''

It was true! Ky slammed a fist against the table. "Why weren't they spotted sooner?"

"They . . . they were hidden, *Asjyai,"* the junior officer stammered. "In the jungle. They must have approached under cover."

"What about our air defences? Do you mean they can move at will over the mountains and not be seen?''

The aide stared at Zyzyiig uncomprehending. "But . . . but *Asjyai* . . . these did not cross the mountains! They are the demons from the south, the ones who escaped."

*The legionnaires!* Zyzyiig turned a baleful stare on kys subordinate. "Am I one of the Ancients, to know your mind without speech? Never mind. Are you sure of this?"

"Y-yes, *Asjyai,* the officer replied. "One of their vehicles was recognized. It has the markings of the unit from the Demon Plateau. There is one less vehicle than our last intelligence report estimated, but . . .''

"Enough! I will join you in the command center shortly. Meantime, order the Regiment Blooddrinkers to resume march immediately, and turn out the garrison." Ky could barely suppress the fury building within. *Their damned Foreign Legion again! What would it take to stop them?* "And pass the word to all checkpoints to be ready. I want them stopped—stopped, do you understand me?— no matter what it costs! Before they escape again!''

Spiro Karatsolis hefted the bulk of the FE-MEK and checked his magazine. It felt strange to be strapped to the hull of the speeding Sabertooth instead of cocooned within the armored security of the turret.

At least he'd acquired a decent weapon. The MEK had

belonged to Legionnaire Verdura, but he had been stung by a spineleech crossing the marshes. Before he'd died he'd given his weapon to Karatsolis and his armor to Bashar, who shared his short, squat built. Verdura had been a magger once, before getting busted and transferred to an infantry outfit. He'd understood how Karatsolis and Bashar felt.

The Sabertooth's fans changed in pitch as the FSV nosed over the embankment onto the broad causeway that carried the north-south road over the *ylyn* paddies. Up ahead there were brilliant points of light strobing in the darkness marking hannie gunners. A bullet *pinged* against the front of the turret.

Bashar returned fire with a short burst from his FEK. Then the Turk switched from needle rounds to his grenade launcher, and a ripple of explosions lit up the ragged line of natives ahead.

"Easy on the grenades, Bashar," Corporal Howell admonished. "Make 'em last."

They had plenty of ammo for their gauss weaponry; it was easy enough to fabricate the metallic slivers in the workshop van. But grenades were running short after the weeks of skirmishing.

"Fireball!" Sergeant Trent shouted.

Karatsolis reacted quickly, cutting in the polarizer in his helmet display. A moment later, Trent fired his rocket pistol into the air. The projectile rose quickly and burst, briefly turning night into day. For the legionnaires, prepared by his warning, the flare was a momentary inconvenience. Hopefully the hannies would find it much more of a handicap.

The Sabertooth's plasma cannon pulsed with an ear-tearing shriek of searing air and another blinding flash of light. Karatsolis, crouched on the other side of the turret, could still feel the heat of the shot washing past him. A hannie machine-gun nest up ahead vanished in flame and smoke.

"Pour it on!" Trent called.

Legionnaires braced against hull and harnesses and began to fire as the FSV raced toward the hannies. Karatsolis swung the MEK in a wide arc, the trigger held down to fire continuously. The flare was beginning to fade now, but he could still see the natives running, twisting, falling under the onslaught. One hannie with a bulky weapon, possibly one of their blunderbuss rocket launchers, was lifted from the ground and hurled backward five meters by the MEK fire. Ky toppled over the edge of the causeway with a splash.

For the first time since losing the *Angel* Karatsolis felt alive. After the long days of marching and evading and hiding, the pure rush of adrenaline was a welcome relief from the boredom that so often bred *le cafarde*. A legionnaire lived for battle.

Now they were rushing past the enemy troops, hurtling toward the rising ground of the pass. He had a confused glimpse of scattering hannie infantry being mowed down by the withering fire from the two vanguard vehicles, of a native tracked APC with smoke boiling from a hole where an onager had sliced through its armor. Then there were no more targets to fire at.

Karatsolis heard a complaining *click-click-click* sound that stopped as he released the trigger. Only then did he realize that he had burned up the entire five-hundred-round drum.

It had taken less than half a minute from the time Trent had fired the flare.

As he replaced the spent drum, he saw the Sandray carrying Sergeant Ghirghik's part of the vanguard pull past the Sabertooth. A couple of legionnaires waved nonchalantly. Bashar was waving back, and some of the men were cheering.

Karatsolis peered over the top of the turret and felt the enthusiasm of the first, easy victory ebbing. Up ahead, the hannies were preparing a more elaborate welcome.

The last of a double line of squat tracked vehicles was slowly taking up position blocking the road. He scanned the terrain with a sinking feeling. The hannie who had arranged this roadblock knew kys stuff, all right. On either side of the road fast-rising slopes would hamper the Terran APCs as much as any of the local vehicles. They would have to go through that barrier . . . and Karatsolis wasn't sure they could break through this time.

Slick clung to his harness straps and tried to keep his head down as the APC gathered more speed. Around him his lancemates and some of the other soldiers clinging to the manta shape of the vehicle were keeping up a desultory fire against the hannies behind the barricade, but Slick's rifle remained unused at his side.

The Ubrenfar sergeant was scanning the barricade through his LI display. "Full revs, Singh!" he called to the Sandray's driver. "We have to get through those tracks!"

Nearby, Legionnaire DuPont raised his head for a quick look. "Come on, Sarge! You don't think we can make it in one piece, do you? Those carriers look *heavy.*"

"Ve haf to try," Strauss said heavily.

"All right, listen up!" Ghirghik said harshly. "I do not know if the Sandray can take it or not, but we are going to break that barricade no matter what! It is the only way the others will have a chance to reach the pass!"

A blinding flare of light seared past them as the Sabertooth opened fire on the barricade from behind and to the left. Slick glanced back. Beyond the FSV the other vehicles were beginning to climb onto the causeway.

"Remember," Ghirghik continued. "If the APC cannot go on, dismount. Try to get aboard the other vehicles as they break through. You will have only one chance. The column will not stop if you are left behind."

"And meanwhile, keep those hannie bastards from forming up," Corporal Braxton, the leader of the Third Platoon's recon lance, added sharply. "We've got a lot of buddies counting on us this time."

Slick closed his eyes. They all sounded so cold-blooded. How could they talk about it so calmly?

There was a distant hammer of machine-gun fire, the terrifying sound of bullets rattling off the hull. DuPont rose to take a shot with his laser rifle but never finished the motion. He jerked back against the harness with half his face torn away below the visor of his helmet. The rifle spun lazily end over end, hitting the pavement far behind the speeding vehicle. Sickened, Slick turned his head.

The Sandray slammed into the barricade with a bone-wrenching force that stunned Slick. He was only vaguely aware of the sounds of gunfire, of screams and shouted orders and the jibbering calls of the enemy.

"Come on, nube! Cut yourself loose!" That was Rostov, shaking him. "Move it or you'll miss the shuttle, kid!"

His hands fumbled at the harness snaps as he tried to clear his head. The strap came free and Slick half jumped, half slid to the pavement. The APC had smashed all the way through, pushing two bulky native carriers out of line. Now it hung in the air, bow down, one fan still whining as it pushed the vehicle uselessly against one of the enemy tracks. The rear ramp was down, and members of Dmowski's weapons lance were already scrambling out even as the rear magrep modules failed and the Sandray collapsed to the ground with a crash.

Another enemy vehicle erupted in fire as the Sabertooth's plasma cannon pulsed. Then the FSV brushed past the burning hulk, widening the gap. Hands reached down to help legionnaires scramble aboard. Slick saw Corporal Braxton make it up, shouting encouragement to the others as the FSV plowed ahead.

A hannie appeared from out of nowhere, kys rifle blazing. Bullets slammed into Slick's chest armor, and he staggered back. He brought his FEK up and squeezed the trigger. The native's scream seemed to go on and on.

Rostov dropped to one knee beside him and fired a three-round grenade burst into the open rear door of the nearest hannie track. Flame shot from the hatch, and Slick could hear Rostov's satisfied grunt over his headphones. Then the demo expert fired again, and again.

The fourth time he pointed the weapon, nothing happened. Rostov cursed at the empty magazine and shifted back to needle ammo.

"Here comes the lieutenant!" someone shouted. Slick looked up in time to see the line of fast-moving Sandrays racing toward the breach in the barricade. He started forward to join the cluster of legionnaires. Something soft caught his foot and he tripped. For an agonizing long moment he spun around, desperately trying to keep his balance. A shooting pain in his right leg made him twist again. Then he fell, sprawling painfully on the road.

The first vehicle barely slowed as it came through, but several legionnaires managed to scramble aboard. The wind from its roaring fans was hot as it went past Slick. Groaning, he got to his knees. There was blood all over one leg, and his foot and ankle hurt, but the blood was thinner, lighter in color than it should have been. It took long seconds for Slick to realize that the blood had come from the body of the hannie soldier he'd tripped over. His own leg throbbed but seemed intact. Meanwhile, two more vehicles shot past.

He got up carefully, trying not to put any weight on the injured limb, then limped toward the breach awkwardly. Slick saw Rostov and Strauss clinging to the side of the medical van as it passed him. Rostov shouted something he couldn't make out. Only a few more APCs to go . . .

He tried to hurry, and that sent him sprawling again. Suddenly strong arms were lifting him, holding him, urging him forward while supporting his weight. The rough, dry, scaly hide, almost black with glistening highlights in this darkness, could only be Ghirghik's.

"Help him!" the Ubrenfar shouted. Slick felt himself being half-pushed, half-thrown. More hands closed around his dangling harness straps and his outstretched hands, hauling him aboard the engineering van. Legionnaire Vrurrth held on to him while someone else hooked his harness to a nearby ring.

"Ghirghik!" Slick gasped. "Where—?"

"He didn't make it," a legionnaire said quietly.

Slick looked back. There were no more vehicles behind this one . . . only a single dinosaurian figure towering above a swarm of hannie soldiers, wielding his broad-bladed knife as he howled a discordant battle song.

# Chapter 19

The mountain barred our way. The order was given
to pass, nevertheless. The Legion carried it out.
          —Inscription at the Foum-Zabel tunnel
          Morocco, French Foreign Legion, 1928

Two kilometers below the crest of the Zhairhee Pass, the
Legion APCs clustered under the sheer rock face of a
hundred-meter cliff. Legionnaires unstrapped their harnesses and dismounted to stretch weary muscles but kept
their weapons close at hand and their senses alert for
danger.

Inside Fraser's improvised command van, worried
faces studied a holographic map of the pass.

"I don't see any other way, L-T," Trent was saying.
"We can't just bull our way through, the way we did
down below."

"I agree," Fraser answered, studying the glowing image. "With the blockhouse sitting there at the very nar-
rowest point, and that sharp jog just beyond, we'd be
dead meat. As soon as a Sandray slowed down to take
the curve those bastards could nail it."

"Right," Trent said, nodding. "And don't forget they
could have more of those missile launchers like Ghirghik
found. Or tanks. I'm afraid the only way we're getting
through is to try a fast sneak. Over the cliffs and down
with the recon lances. Grab the blockhouse and we've
got a fighting chance of getting through."

"Timing'll be damned tight, though," Fraser pointed
out. "You know they'll be ordering troops up from
Zhairhee soon enough. If they catch us here before you
have the blockhouse secured . . ."

Kelly Winters spoke up from the other side of the compartment. "You could try to slow them down, Lieuten-

ant. Some demo charges on the cliff would bring down enough debris to block the pass for days.''

Trent scowled. "No way," he said bluntly.

"Why not, Sergeant?" she asked stubbornly. "Look, I may not know much about infantry tactics, but I'm a trained sapper. I know what a good dose of PX-90 up on that cliff will do.''

"I'm not disputing it, ma'am," Trent said patiently. "But we don't have time to do that kind of demo work. Their lead elements will be knocking on our door here in an hour or two.''

"Can you pull off your op that fast, Gunny?" Fraser asked.

Trent shrugged. "I'd better. Just to make sure, though, set the Sabertooth at the rear of the column and have Zak take a few potshots down the road. I guarantee those monkeys'll think twice before they push too hard.''

Kelly seemed about to say something, then stopped. Fraser glanced at her. "If the blockhouse can't be taken, we might have to try the lieutenant's idea.''

"Better hope you don't have to, L-T," Trent answered sourly. " 'Cause if we get trapped up here we're in a hell of a lot of trouble.''

"Sarge, if a couple of Sandrays tried to get past the blockhouse about the time you were ready to make your move, wouldn't that help the odds a little?" Sergeant Mason, senior NCO of the transport section since the death of Swede Persson, leaned forward and spoke for the first time. "Maybe that would give you the edge you need to take 'em.''

Trent looked at him. "Yeah, but it would be suicide for whoever was aboard them. We don't have time for the kind of remote-control games Garcia and I pulled back at Fort Monkey.''

"You won't find no shortage of volunteers, Sarge. Just say the word.''

"Wait a minute," Fraser said, holding up his hand. "I'm not asking anybody to run that kind of risk . . .''

"Let's face it, L-T," Trent replied. "Right now we're *all* running a risk here. And Mason's right about getting an edge out of it. Our hannie friends up there will be expecting somebody to try to break past 'em. I kind of like to give an enemy just what he's expecting . . . only not quite the way he's expecting it. That way the bad guys usually get to die happy.''

There were chuckles around the map. Fraser looked away for a long moment.

''All right,'' he said at last. ''If you think it's worth the risk, Gunny.'' He turned to Mason. ''Pick the two Sandrays least likely to make it out of the mountains. Volunteer drivers for each. *Volunteers,* though, got it? None of this 'you just volunteered for the job' crap.''

''Yessir,'' Mason said.

''All right, gentlemen,'' Fraser went on. ''Let's get this thing into orbit, shall we?''

Slick winced as the doctor's fingers probed around the swelling over his injured ankle. Ramirez gave a satisfied nod.

''A sprain, nothing worse,'' he said. ''It will clear up in a day or two if you keep this on it.''

''This'' was a tube 12 centimeters long which the doctor was clamping over Slick's leg as he continued. ''Keep the regen cast on until the diagnostic light turns green,'' he said. ''It will give you the support you need for limited movement, and it will stimulate the healing process. Don't try running or anything really strenuous for a while, though.''

Slick nodded, gritting his teeth a little as Ramirez adjusted the fit. The regen cast began to hum, and Slick could feel a warm, tingling feeling spreading over his ankle and foot.

''Here's a light duty chit,'' Ramirez finished, handing him a small chip-reader. The doctor straightened up. ''See me if there's any problem with the cast.''

As the doctor left, Corporal Strauss advanced on Slick. ''So, nube. Light duty, eh? You vill not be making the raid with us, then. Just as good.''

Before Slick could react the corporal had turned his back, dismissing him entirely.

The lance was gathered around the supply van, working in the illumination thrown by a single red-glowing battle lantern. Since Gunnery Sergeant Trent had passed the order to get ready for an attack on the blockhouse further up the pass, the three recon units had been kitting up with climbing gear and extra weaponry. Slick had watched it all with a sense of detachment, unreality. The events at the hannie roadblock still filled his thoughts.

Rostov paused near him, a climbing rope and a field pack loaded with pitons slung over his shoulders. The demo expert looked keyed up, as nervous as Slick had ever seen him.

"Looks like you're well out of it, kid," he said. "Wish I'd been smart enough to trip over a corpse or something."

"I thought you liked all the commando stuff, Rostov," Slick said.

"Yeah, well . . . climbing cliffs and launching suicide attacks aren't my idea of soft duty, kid. Vrurrth's, maybe, but not mine."

Someone from Braxton's lance laughed. "Come on, Rostov, don't go soft on us now!"

The laughter fell silent as Gunnery Sergeant Trent approached. "All right, you goldbricks, time to get moving. Pascali, you got my stuff?"

"Right here, Sarge," the corporal responded. She passed Trent a harness and a coil of line.

"Let's move out. First man at the top gets a bottle of Novykrim vodka at the Fwynzei Rec Room on me."

"Oh, great," Rostov said. "So now we gotta make sure we make it to Fwynzei *and* get you there in one piece, too!"

"I didn't just drop out of FTL yesterday, Rostov," Trent replied with a grin. "Now move out!"

Slick watched them moving away, his emotions a jumble of uncertainty and confusion.

*I should have died back there,* he thought. *I would have died, if Ghirghik hadn't saved me.*

Why had the Ubrenfar sacrificed himself to get Slick aboard the last APC? Ghirghik had been openly contemptuous of Slick the last time they'd talked, back at the funeral service. *He wasn't even human, but he died saving me . . .*

*The Legion looks after its own. Doesn't matter if a guy's a total stranger or your tentmate for the last ten years. He's your buddy . . . your comrade. And a part of the only family you've got!* Rostov had said that, back at the funeral. For the first time Slick was beginning to understand it . . . to believe it. The way Rostov did. And Ghirghik.

His eyes focused through his light intensifiers on the recon lances as they started their ascent. He glanced down at his foot, feeling frustrated.

He should have been up there with them . . . with the rest of the team . . .

Gunnery Sergeant Trent pulled himself over the edge of the cliff and rose to a half-crouch, scanning his surroundings through the LI setting of his helmet display. The top of the ridge was stark and rugged. Nothing grew there. This high in Hanuman's mountains, the high energy output from Morrison's Star was lethal to all but the hardiest life forms. Travelers could pass through the region in relative safety, but a long stay at high elevations was definitely not advisable.

That was the reason the Imperial Army of Vyujiid had built most of their frontier post in the Zhairhee Pass underground, in a network of caverns extending far back into the cliff walls that closed in around the pass itself. The blockhouse that barred the Legion's path was only the tip of the iceberg; the caves held storehouses, barracks, and armories that could support an entire regiment of hannie troops for a month or more without resupply.

Somehow the Dryiens had overrun the strongpoint. If they were still there in strength, the three recon lances would have to hold them in place long enough to squeeze the rest of the Legion through the pass. More likely, though, the garrison would be fairly small. The enemy would need every soldier for the drive on Fwynzei.

Trent dropped behind a boulder overlooking the central valley and turned on his image intensifiers. The scene leapt toward him.

There was a lot of activity down there. Soldiers were erecting barricades and maneuvering heavy anti-tank weapons into position to guard the south end of the pass. Raising his wristpiece, Trent ordered a quick tactical evaluation. In seconds, the computer fed the information straight to his visor HUD. The valley was a little less than five kilometers from end to end. There was roughly a company deploying to defend the position, with no sign of additional troops lurking in the caves. About what he'd figured. Rough, but not impossible . . . as long as the legionnaires held onto surprise.

Three depleted lances against a company . . . ten men taking on over a hundred. *Typical Legion odds,* Trent thought grimly.

Corporal Pascali dropped beside him and studied the pass. She pointed to the cliff, then held up a coil of line.

He nodded wearily. *I'm getting too damned old to be playing these games,* he told himself as he checked the valley one last time. It had been ten years since he'd last served as part of a recon lance.

But he still had a few moves these youngsters wouldn't expect.

Trent touched the communicator control, two light taps. He wasn't taking any risks with making noise, not now. But the drivers Mason had selected would know what the signal meant.

The countdown had started. In five more minutes the battle would begin.

Corporal Frank Weston watched the seconds ticking away on the countdown clock and smiled coldly. *Not long now . . .*

It seemed like more than six years since a man named Franklin West had come home to find his family dead after the quake that virtually destroyed the colony on far-off New Paradise. If he'd only been *home* instead of out drinking that night, maybe Kathy and Caroline wouldn't have been killed. Or at least he might have died with them, instead of having to live with the memory of what he'd lost that night.

But he'd been drunk, and his wife and daughter had died, and with the colony in ruins and every cent he'd ever saved lost with the farm, Franklin West had decided he was better off dead.

The Foreign Legion had sent him where he could die.

Most of his pay—what he didn't lose drinking or gambling—went to Kathy's family, anonymously. It wouldn't bring back the daughter he'd taken from them, or the granddaughter, but it was the only way he could face himself in the mirror every morning. Some day his fate would finally catch up with him, and his Legion benefits would go to Kathy's family as well. And Franklin West, now Frank Weston, would be at peace.

The countdown clock reached zero and Weston switched on the turbofans. He'd drawn the unarmed supply van, which had been running on good thoughts and makeshift repairs for days now. Singh had an engineering van, with a laser that no longer worked and a bow magrep module that was on the verge of complete failure.

He wondered idly what had made Singh volunteer for the mission. No one asked another legionnaire why he joined, but everyone wondered. Singh was tough and wiry, a natural with a knife. Speculation in the platoon put him down as a murderer hiding in the Legion to escape his crimes.

In a way that was a lot like Weston.

"All right, Decoy," Sergeant Mason's voice crackled in Weston's ears. "Mag out!"

The supply van seemed reluctant to lift, as if it knew what awaited it at the top of the pass. A work detail had hastily unloaded the battered vehicle while the recon lances made their climb. It had been almost empty anyway, except for a lot of plundered hannie food and a few spare parts that wouldn't be that useful, anyway. With Fwynzei less than a hundred kilometers away there wasn't much need for large supply stockpiles any more.

Weston urged the throttle forward and the APC gathered speed. Singh's vehicle fell in behind, and the two decoys began to climb the pass.

Faster . . . faster . . . Sergeant Mason had made it clear that he wanted the decoys to draw maximum attention. Weston grinned to himself. The way the fans were acting up, the supply van could probably simulate a whole regiment.

Then the van swept around a rocky outcropping and over the crest of the rise. Searchlights stabbed down at the hurtling Sandray from a dozen places, and the familiar rattle of monkey machine-gun fire shattered the night.

Seconds seemed to drag out like long minutes as the Sandray hurtled across the floor of the valley. Weston had time to note the defenses, to see the barricade and the blockhouse and the looming bulk of a tank. From the cliffside above the blockhouse, he made out the subdued flicker of a laser firing into the hannies, its beam revealed by the dust that had been kicked up by the heavy equipment moving on the valley floor. The attack was starting, right on schedule.

The tank gun fired. The shell narrowly missed, and the explosion rained rocks and dirt on Singh's APC as it followed Weston into the enclosed valley.

He smiled again. That tank could spell trouble even if Trent's attack went down smoothly. There was one last thing he could do . . .

Weston steered straight for the tank. He didn't see the hannie soldier at the door of the blockhouse who wrestled a weapon far too large for kys small body into line, or the missile that swooped across the pass.

It hit the APC squarely above the driver's cab, on the left side, killing Frank Weston instantly. But it was too late to completely stop the hurtling juggernaut, and moments later the native tank was engulfed in flame.

Franklin West had found his peace in the middle of fire and fury.

"Nail the little bastards!" Trent shouted, spraying FEK fire across the nearest cluster of hannie soldiers.

The surprise had been perfect, with the legionnaires moving into position on the floor of the valley just as the two decoy vehicles stirred up the natives at their barricade. In the confusion, the first few bursts from the three recon lances had gone largely unnoticed.

The collision between the lead APC and the native tank had sent a pillar of fire into the night sky, blinding the defenders. The legionnaires, their vision protected by the polarization on their helmet feeds, had been able to take maximum advantage.

But by the time the second Sandray was destroyed by three offworld missiles, the hannies were beginning to realize their danger.

A native swung a bulky heavy-caliber machine gun toward Trent. Bullets tracked across the rock wall of the cliff, and Trent ducked and rolled under the firing line. In the seconds it took the gunner to shift the weapon back again, Trent switched to grenades and fired a single round. It was dead on target. The machine gun fell silent.

Close by, Corporal Braxton was maintaining a steady stream of fire at the barricade, pinning at least ten monkeys. Suddenly Braxton turned, but not soon enough. A hannie with a blunderbuss opened fire, and the primitive rocket caught the lance leader squarely in the stomach. Trent returned fire and the native went down. He swung the FEK back to catch the hannies Braxton had been keeping pinned as they tried to take advantage of the distraction. Most of them fell. A pair sprinted for the nearest cave mouth, only to go down as two bright streaks of coherent light flashed in rapid succession through the dust and smoke. Legionnaire Doug Rydell gave Trent a quick thumb's up and turned his laser rifle on another target.

Another hannie vehicle clanked slowly around the bend from the north end of the pass, a tracked APC this time with an HMG in a cupola mount on the top of the passenger compartment. The hannie gunner looked up in surprise as Legionnaire Vrurrth leapt onto the hull from the rocks above. The massive Gwyrran hands closed on the soldier's windpipe, lifting the luckless alien right out of the cupola and tossing ky aside like an unwanted rag. Then Vrurrth pointed his FEK into open hatch and pumped several grenades into the vehicle. He jumped clear as the opening belched flame and the track ground to a halt.

Down by the blockhouse, Rostov and Cunningham slapped demo charges on either side of the door, ducked back, and triggered them. Firing through roiling smoke, they quickly cleared the building of native troops.

Then the fighting was over, with the remaining hannies streaming north out of the pass.

Trent slung his FEK and crossed the road to the blockhouse. Rostov met him beside the ruined door. "All secure inside, Sarge."

"Good. Signal the L-T."

Trent surveyed the battleground with a frown. They'd cleared the pass easily enough—perhaps too easily. He only hoped the column could win clear of the pass before the jaws of the trap sprang shut around them.

Fraser leaned over the driver's seat of the engineering van and squinted at the forward video display. The Sandray was at the head of the column, picking its way through the ruined native barricade. Somewhere toward the rear of the line the Sabertooth spoke, hurtling another plasma round into the hannie troops advancing from Zhairhee. The onager cannon had already torn up the road enough to block vehicles for a while, and there weren't many monkeys back there willing to brave the demonic weapon.

He saw Trent waving as the APC moved slowly toward the bend. The sergeant looked tired but cocky.

Trent had a right to be cocky. With ten legionnaires he had taken on over a hundred. Two dead and one wounded wasn't a bad price to pay for a victory like that.

Minutes passed as the column started down the Vyujiid side of the pass. They wouldn't have to keep on facing overwhelming odds on their own much longer . . .

"Holy shit . . .!" Legionnaire DiMarco, the driver, cut the fans. The vehicle floated at the crest of the hill overlooking the northern end of the pass. Vyujiid . . . the end of the long march.

Except that the valley was filled with soldiers and vehicles. It was a huge camp, stretching as far as the video cameras could scan.

The hannie army hadn't moved on for Fwynzei. It was right here, squarely across their only escape route.

The legionnaires were trapped.

# Chapter 20

If they're going to let the Legion die, then it will
die bravely.

—Colonel Joseph Conrad
French Foreign Legion, 1837

"Lancelot, Lancelot, this is Alice One. Do you copy?"
Fraser had to fight hard to keep from betraying his fears.
"Lancelot, please respond. Over."

The legionnaires had deployed around the top of the
pass, occupying the blockhouse and many of the positions the hannies had given up to Trent. That had been
almost two hours ago. Fortunately, the Dryien reaction
had been sluggish. The forces on the south side of the
frontier were still cowed by the pounding they'd taken
from the Sabertooth's plasma cannon; the regiments to
the north seemed to be in disarray, perhaps because they
were out of touch with their leadership in Zhairhee, or
possibly due to the exaggerated accounts the refugees
from the pass battle had no doubt been giving of Legion
strength and intentions.

How much longer the legionnaires could count on being left alone was anybody's guess.

"Lancelot, this is Alice One. Respond, please. Over."
Fraser bit off a curse. They *had* to raise the garrison at
Fwynzei.

While Trent and the platoon leaders took charge of
organizing some kind of defense, Legionnaires Russo and
Garcia had climbed the cliffs to rig up a directional relay
unit that would put them back in contact with Fwynzei.
So far, though, they weren't having much luck.

"Alice, this is Lancelot." The voice on the commlink
was ragged with static, but Fraser could also hear the

suspicion in those cold, impersonal tones. "Transmit authentication codes."

He keyed in the computer and let out a sigh. Finally! He'd been on the verge of giving up.

The computers on each end of the line compared electronic notes, verifying that each transmitter was genuine and setting up a coded, scrambled circuit. A few seconds later, the radio operator from Fwynzei spoke again.

"Alice, Lancelot. Hold for Commandant Isayev."

Minutes went by this time before the commandant's gruff voice took over. "Fraser? Good God, man, we thought you'd bought it. Where the hell are you?"

Fraser swallowed once and tried to sound calm, professional. "Sir, the demi-battalion has reached the top of the Zhairhee Pass. We have driven back a force approximately one company in strength and now hold the blockhouse and the rest of the central valley. We have encountered elements of the Dryien Army, approximately two divisions, blocking the north end of the pass between the mountains and Fwynzei."

"We know about 'em," Isayev replied. "They had sympathizers in the Imperial Army who helped them take the pass in the first place. They drove back the Seventh Imperial Division yesterday and engaged a battalion of our native auxiliaries."

"It is our belief, Commandant, that they are making an attempt on Fwynzei as part of the anti-Terran movement that started with the coup and the attack on Monkeyville."

Isayev chuckled. "Well, it's nice to see that our junior officers have a better grasp on things than the Colonial Office. The resident-general spent most of the last two days trying to set up a meeting to, uh, 'mediate the dispute between two sovereign nations.' It wasn't until a couple of batteries of monkey artillery started shelling Government House that he finally got it through his thick head that they were after *us.*"

Fraser looked up as Garcia came into the blockhouse, and gave her a thumb's up. "Commandant, we're stuck up here. We've got hannies on each side of the pass, and I'm down to under a hundred effectives. What's the chance of getting an evac from up here?"

"Wait one." There was a long pause before Isayev

came back on. "Alice One, if you can hold out up there for forty-eight hours I think we'll be able to get you some relief."

"Forty-eight hours?" Fraser couldn't hold back his pent-up emotions any longer. "Do you have any idea what you're asking?"

"I know it's rough, Fraser," Isayev said, ignoring the outburst. "But in two days we should be able to deploy three battalions of Commonwealth Marines to the surface. They're en route from the systerm now, off *Seneca*. And if you're holding the pass, some of them can ground right there and take over for you."

"Sir—"

"As long as there is a unit up there, Fraser, the Dryiens on this side of the mountains are cut off. No supplies . . . damned little contact with their HQ, unless they use aircraft to relay orders. The longer you hold out up there, the better our chances of keeping them out of Fwynzei. And if we can put the Marines down to take over from you, so much the better. I wouldn't want to try to retake that pass with unarmed transport lighters, and that's all we've got for now."

Fraser didn't reply for several seconds. Could they really hold out for two days? Or would the Marines arrive to find the legionnaires dead, overwhelmed by superior numbers?

But unless they could keep the pass blocked, Fwynzei was in danger.

*The Legion looks out for its own.* Zhairhee Pass could keep the hannies from getting at the rest of the battalion.

"Lancelot, instructions understood. Forty-eight hours until pickup."

Isayev let out a sigh on the other end of the commlink. "We're counting on you, Colin. If anybody has the guts to pull this off, it's your boys. You marched this far . . . all you have to do now is sit still and shoot, eh?"

"Just don't be late, Commandant," Fraser said softly. "Just don't be late."

Karatsolis cursed as the MEK ran dry again. Ducking behind the shelter of a wrecked Legion Sandray, he slapped the release switch and fitted another drum over the receiver. After this one, there were only two more magazines for the weapon, unless someone brought him a fresh supply soon.

It had been a grueling test of endurance, this past forty hours, far worse than anything the legionnaires had faced on the march. Holding on to the precarious positions at either end of the pass had stretched the survivors of demibattalion Alice to the limit and beyond. But they were still holding fast, and it was only eight hours now until the promised relief was supposed to arrive.

Karatsolis glanced over at Corporal Bashar. The Turk had a bloodstained bandage wrapped around his left arm where shrapnel from a hannie fragmentation grenade had scored a hit, but he was still fighting. A lot of the legionnaires had picked up light wounds in the course of six successive hannie attacks, although Karatsolis was still unmarked. Sergeant Baker, acting leader of the battered Fourth Platoon, was in charge of this part of the northern end of the pass despite the fact that he'd lost the use of both legs. Legionnaire Delandry had propped him up behind a boulder and applied regen casts to both legs, and Baker remained at his post.

That had been two assaults back. Luckily, the hannie regiments on the north side of the pass were still having trouble organizing their attacks efficiently, or the legionnaires wouldn't have held them this long. They seemed to be running low on supplies, and even lower on effective leadership. Word passed from Battalion HQ in Fwynzei suggested that a lot of hannie units had been purged of their old officers, with politically reliable coup supporters placed in charge of some of the units only days before the attack.

The monkeys were fighting well enough, but their morale was low. Stand up to them, and they broke despite their tremendous advantage in numbers.

Karatsolis had heard that things were different on the south side of the pass, nearly five kilometers away, where First and Second Platoons were trying to hold back troops out of Zhairhee. The assaults had taken time to get rolling down there because of the damage done to the causeway by Ignaczak's plasma cannon on the night of the first battle. Engineering vehicles had cleared the rubble by late afternoon of the next day, however, and since then the attacks had been mounting in frequency and determination. They had the leadership they needed down there . . . but most of the troops were poor-quality garrison units.

The Legion had been lucky. They could last the few remaining hours until pickup . . . but it would be close. Damned close. Casualties were starting to mount, and not just wounds. Two guys from Fourth Platoon had bought it only an hour ago when a hannie aircraft strafed the road, and Subaltern Fairfax had been killed by a mortar round during a native assault on the south end of the pass.

"Hey, Spear," Bashar called, firing an FEK burst to discourage a cluster of hannie soldiers a few hundred meters down the road. "What'd'ya think? These hannies any better than those buggers we were up against back on Loki?"

Karatsolis braced the MEK and sprayed needle rounds at another enemy squad as it tried to work its way past the remains of a burning hannie track. "Hell, no! Those bastards had decent weapons. Not like that crap the monkeys are using."

Bashar held his fire for a moment, searching for targets. "Yeah, but these guys are persistent, you gotta give 'em that. On Loki, you only had to knock the buggers silly once or twice. These hannies don't ever seem to learn!" As if to emphasize the point, he produced a native hand grenade and tossed it down the pass with a nonchalant flourish. The legionnaires had found plenty of native weapons in the underground armories, and most of the legionnaires were carrying grenades again. Not as good as an FEK's rocket grenades, perhaps, but very effective at discouraging unwanted visitors.

Even better, they'd recovered a number of heavier weapons, including ten of the high-tech missile launchers like the ones that had taken out the two decoy vehicles during the first attack. Those had been very useful in keeping the enemy tanks and tracks at bay.

Karatsolis stopped firing and peered cautiously over the smoke-blackened wreck. The enemy was pulling back again.

Another victory . . . for the moment.

"Called off? The assault was *called off?*" Asjyai Zyzyiig hit the map table hard enough to knock over a stack of markers. An aide hastened to clean up the loose counters and try to put the map right again.

Zyzyiig ignored ky. "What in the name of the Eternal Mists does that fool think ky is doing? There are two divisions on the north side . . . the Terran demons have less than a company! Far less!"

"But, *Asjyai*," an officer quavered. "The demons have all the advantages of position. And their magic weapons. And our forces are in disorder, out of supply, and out of contact for most of the time. It is very hard—"

"Demons take you!" Zyzyiig shouted, kys neck ruff going stiff. "Demons take all cretins who can't show a little initiative!"

"Perhaps, my Companion, you have not considered the benefits of drawing back and truly organizing a single assault," Shavvataaars offered from the back of the map room. "Instead of throwing forces in piecemeal, a single coordinated thrust launched from both your forces simultaneously would certainly break the resistance of your enemies at the top of the pass."

Zyzyiig glared at the Semti, breathing hard. That cold whisper, so calm and calculating . . . ky was beginning to hate the very sight and sound of the Ancient One.

But this time the advice was good. So far, the attacks had been organized hastily, with the assumption that a handful of demons couldn't possibly hold against the overwhelming numbers they faced. Yet time and time again their weapons knocked the assaults back.

What was needed was a final, all-out effort. That would break the legionnaires. Then the army could push on for Fwynzei and a final reckoning with the offworld interlopers.

Slowly, anger ebbed as ky turned the beginnings of a plan over in kys mind. "Yes . . . yes, that is the answer," ky said at last. The softly spoken words seemed to make the officers more nervous than kys earlier shouts. "Get a squadron in the air," ky ordered one of the officers. "Enough aircraft to be *sure* of getting across the mountains." Demon missiles out of Fwynzei had been taking a high toll against Dryien aircraft, making it even harder to stay in touch with the invading army.

"Yes, Honored," the staff officer responded.

"Order an assault for . . . call it two hours after dawn. Miststalkers to lead the advance."

"Yes, Honored," ky repeated.

Zyzyiig turned to another officer. "Pass the word to Blooddrinkers to be ready to resume the attack at the same time," ky ordered. Zyzyiig paused. "No, wait . . . I will go myself. Order me a staff car. I will *personally* make sure Blooddrinkers do their job right this time!"

"*Asjyai* . . . is that wise?" someone asked.

"Are you questioning my judgement?" ky thundered back. "This attack is too important to entrust to these time-servers and nay-sayers! I will command the attack! Submit final plans to me by dawn! Meeting dismissed!"

As the officers hurried to leave the room, Zyzyiig turned to Shavvataaars. "Do you wish to join me?"

Shavvataaars crossed arms. "I do not think my presence would be particularly useful, my Companion. I will remain here until you have broken through."

Zyzyiig showed kys teeth. "You do that, my Companion," ky said mockingly. "And I shall open the road to Fwynzei! No matter what it costs!"

Kelly Winters felt useless as she sat in the corner of the blockhouse. Outside the distant *crump* of artillery was louder and more frequent. The others in the building—Fraser, Trent, Garcia, and Russo—were staying busy, monitoring communications, fielding reports, and trying to decide on the best employment for a limited number of troops. Since dawn, it had become obvious that the hannies were gearing up for a major new attack. The question now was whether it would come before or after the Marines could deploy to take over the defense of the pass.

She had offered help to Ramirez, but the doctor and the Padre had things under control in the tunnel where the wounded had been shifted the day before. The medical van had been pressed into service as a regular APC . . . until a hannie missile had taken it out on the south road overnight. Hannie artillery and air attacks had left only three vehicles in working order. One, the Sabertooth, was still deployed on the south end of the line, suppressing enemy movements. The other two were parked near the blockhouse now. Members of the three recon lances, Fraser's only remaining reserve, were busy loading them up with supplies and fresh needle ammo. Two wounded legionnaires were using gear cannibalized from the fabrication van to crank out ammunition, but it was being used up almost as fast as they could produce it.

There was no place for her in the desperate work of defense. All she could do was sit and wait, hoping that the Marines would arrive soon to put an end to the nightmare. The Marines! How often she'd wished they would swoop in to the rescue as the Legion column straggled northward.

They couldn't be any tougher than these legionnaires, but at least they'd be fresh. How the legionnaires kept fighting was beyond her.

Even little Myaighee had gone out there, equipped with hannie weapons from the armory. Ky had volunteered to carry messages along the Legion positions on the north side of the pass. Myaighee's small build made the alien an ideal runner. The soldiers on the line had adopted ky as a sort of mascot.

She'd considered volunteering to take a rifle and go out there herself, but she knew what Trent would say. She was no combat soldier.

"Lieutenant?" Garcia held up a handset for Fraser. "Subaltern Watanabe on the line."

Fraser hardly look up from the holomap over Russo's C³ pack. "On speakers, Garcia."

Watanabe's voice, usually so calm and placid, was edged with something close to panic. "HQ, they've taken out the Sabertooth! The hannies're coming up the road and we don't have anything to hold them!"

Trent jumped in before Fraser could reply. "Are you sure the FSV's out of action? Not just damaged?"

"God, Sarge, they put a missile right into the turret while she was firing! The gauss field collapsed while the round was still in the barrel, man! Half the front end's melted to slag!"

"*Madre de Dios,*" Garcia muttered. Fraser and Trent were both looking sick. Mason and Ignaczak couldn't have lived through something like that.

"Come in, HQ? What the hell are your orders?"

Trent and Fraser exchanged looks, and the sergeant

killed the audio channel. "L-T, we've gotta reinforce them. Maybe send a couple of missile launchers down there. It won't make up for the Sabertooth . . ."

"We're stretched goddamned thin already, Gunny," Fraser said. He jerked a thumb toward the soldiers loading ammo outside. "You sure it's time to send in the last reserves?"

"No . . . we need to get that ammo up to the front. Damn it, if only we had a few more people." Trent glanced around the room. His eyes lit on Kelly. "You," he said curtly. "You can handle a commlink, can't you?"

Kelly nodded, ignoring the sergeant's abrupt manner.

"Russo and Garcia can handle launchers, L-T. If we put her on the radio, we can free these two up to do some fighting."

Fraser looked uncertain. "Putting technicians on the line . . ."

"They're legionnaires first, L-T, and every legionnaire's an infantryman before anything else. I'll take charge down there, if you want . . ."

"Watanabe can handle it, Gunny," Fraser said sharply. "I need you here. Garcia, Russo, draw some launchers and get down to the south barricade. Take Braxton's lance off the loading detail . . . and any stragglers you meet on your way down. Miss Winters . . ." He gestured at the C³ equipment.

Trent already had the circuit to Watanabe open again as she reached the table.

"Watanabe, hold on," Fraser was saying. "I'm sending you a couple of rocket launchers. Hold the bastards as long as you can before you give up any ground."

The subaltern seemed calmer when he responded. "Affirmative, HQ. We'll do what we can."

Kelly put on a set of headphones to monitor communications as Fraser and Trent returned to the holomap.

"Way I see it, L-T, if the transports don't get here soon, we're going to have to start thinking about last ditch schemes." Trent stabbed a finger at the map. "These caves could be a real godsend if we could just find a way to camouflage them a little better . . ."

A voice on the headphones made Kelly straighten up. "I see them!" someone was yelling.

"It's the friggin' Navy!" someone else shouted.

"Damn, I never thought I'd be glad to see those truck drivers!"

"Lieutenant!" Kelly called out. "We've got a visual on transports."

"About time," Trent said. "Have they requested landing info?"

Kelly cocked her head, listening as she ran the commlink through a channel search. "Nothing, sergeant. Nothing . . ."

"What the hell are they doing?" she heard on the radio.

Legionnaire Donovan appeared at the shattered door, supporting Warrant Officer Vandergraff. Kelly gasped as she saw the science specialist. He'd lost his helmet, and his face was a mask of blood. Donovan stopped, staring at the sky. "Hey, Lieutenant, the Navy transport's not stopping! It's magging out!"

Fraser and Trent rushed outside. Kelly could see them through the blasted door, heard Trent's curse. "Goddamned Navy bastards. They're heading too far south."

"Lieutenant," Fraser said, swinging around to look inside at Kelly. "Raise those transports. Now!"

She switched to the standard ground-to-ship channel. "Navy transports, this is Alice One. Transports, do you copy? Over."

"Alice One. *Tuyen Quang*. We copy five by five."

Fraser was beside her, his face flushed with anger. He took the handset. "*Tuyen Quang*, this is Fraser, commanding Alice One. What the devil are you people playing at up there? I was told you'd be landing here to relieve my people."

There was a crackle of static. Then another voice answered. "Fraser, this is Colonel Reginald Smythe-Henderson, commanding the Provisional Marine Assault Regiment. Your orders are to hold as long as possible. Relief will arrive if and when it can be spared."

"With respect, Colonel," Fraser came back angrily. "With respect, my people can't hold on much longer. Commandant Isayev assured me—"

"Commandant Isayev is not in command of this operation, Fraser," the colonel broke in. "*I* am. Under the authority of the resident-general. We are launching an assault on the enemy supply depot at Zhairhee to relieve the threat to Fwynzei once and for all. Your unit forms a key part of this operation. Once we've secured an LZ and have the enemy on the run, we'll be able to spare ships to evac you. Until then, carry out your orders. Smythe-Henderson out!''

The silence in the blockhouse was broken only by the sound of hannie field guns. They were getting closer.

Lieutenant Commander Charles Wingate looked across the bridge of the lighter *Tuyen Quang* at the stiff, rigid figure of Colonel Smythe-Henderson. The Marine officer was studying a terrain map. He seemed to have put the radio exchange with Alice One entirely out of his thoughts.

As CO of the lighter, Wingate had participated in the planning sessions where the colonel and his staff decided on the attack on Zhairhee. It had sounded like a good scheme, using the legionnaires to draw the enemy's attention away from the critical area so the Marines could hit them hard and fast around their key supply nexus.

At the time, Wingate had admired the courage of the legionnaires who had volunteered to hold the pass in the face of such overwhelming odds. Now he was beginning to realize the truth.

''Colonel?'' Wingate asked tentatively. ''Colonel, shouldn't we do something to help those men down there?''

''What men, Wingate?'' Sykes-Hamilton seemed genuinely confused. ''What, you mean those Legion people?''

''Yes, sir. It sounds like they were expecting us to support them directly.''

''We're not doing things by half-measures, Wingate,'' the colonel replied gruffly. ''This op'll smash most of the Dryien army in one blow. That's better than Isayev's damned-fool relief mission!''

''I know, sir, but aren't you expecting too much of them?''

''They're dead men already, Wingate. You saw the recon views—the hannies are hitting them with everything this time. I'm not throwing away a chance to knock out the whole damned monkey army for dead men. While the hannies are busy with them, I'm winning this campaign.''

The colonel looked back at the scrolling map. ''Anyway,'' he said quietly, dismissively. ''It's not like we're losing real soldiers. They're only legionnaires.''

# Chapter 21

These are not men, but devils!
—Colonel Francisco de Paula-Milan, Mexican Army
Speaking of the defenders at Camerone
French Foreign Legion, 30 April 1863

Kelly stared at the C³ unit in disbelief. How could the Navy just abandon them?

Beside her, Fraser was clenching his fists, his face white. "He lied to me," he said softly, as if to himself. "Isayev lied to me!"

"Or someone lied to him," Trent said. He seemed to be handling it better. "Let's face it, L-T, the Legion's always been considered expendable. Put all the malcontents and bad apples in one unit, then give 'em the jobs you wouldn't give anybody else. That's the way it's been done for as long as there's been a Legion!"

Fraser stared down at the holomap. Behind them, Vandergraff moaned as Legionnaire Donovan headed for the barracks tunnel Ramirez was using as a hospital.

"Hold on, uh .. Donovan," Fraser said suddenly. "Vandergraff . . . how is he?"

"Shell sent a cloud of rock chips into his face, Lieutenant," Donovan replied. "I've given him a dose of analoke for the pain."

"Vandergraff . . . did you find out anything before you were hit?" Fraser asked. The science specialist had been sent with a lance to scout out the top of the cliff face overlooking the southern side of the pass. Kelly glanced over at Trent. It had been her idea to bring it down originally, but it hadn't been until Trent reminded him of it that Fraser had consented to check it out.

"I'm . . . I'm not sure, sir," Vandergraff said weakly.

"Looked . . . possible, but I didn't have much time . . . not much of a geologist, anyway. Or explosives man."

"All right, Vandergraff," Fraser said. "You did your best. Donovan, get him to Doc."

Trent was looking at the work party around the two APCs. "I'll take Rostov to check it out, L-T," he said. "Should've done it that way in the first place." He looked angry. "Cunningham's our only other demo man, and he's with Braxton's lance. No time to get him back now. Damn!"

Fraser rubbed the bridge of his nose. "Take everyone who can be spared from getting those supplies forward, Gunny," he said at last. "Bringing down that rockslide's our only chance now."

"Let me come, too," Kelly put in. "Since you don't have Cunningham."

Trent shook his head. "You should stay here. You can help best by running C-cubed."

"Damn it, Sergeant," she exploded, angry at his patronizing tone. "I'm an engineer, not a commtech. I know explosives . . . and I know stress points. Digging techniques. This is what I was trained for. Let me do my job, for God's sake!"

Trent took a step back, assessing her with a long steady gaze. "I'm sorry, Lieutenant," he said in a subdued tone. "I didn't mean any insult."

"Take her, Gunny," Fraser said. He hesitated. "Perhaps I should go too . . ."

"No, sir," Trent said firmly. "There's no sense in a commander taking foolish risks. Your place is here, giving orders. Not screwing around on the front lines and letting the rest of the battle go to hell."

He looked at Trent. "My decisions haven't been much good without your advice, Gunny," he said softly.

"Nonsense, L-T . . . with all due respect." Trent grinned. "You've got everything you need . . . inside. All you need is the confidence to use it." He turned to Kelly. "Come on, Miss Winters. We've got some fireworks to set off."

Kelly followed him out of the blockhouse, listening to him shout for Strauss and Pascali.

She found herself wondering how anyone could cast aside men like these.

* * *

Slick looked up as Sergeant Trent and the Navy lieutenant crossed the paved expanse between the blockhouse and the mouth of the main tunnel.

"Looks like trouble," Rostov said quietly beside him. "Any time the Sarge starts looking for a recon lance . . ."

Slick hid a smile. Whenever Trent wanted something hard done, it was the recon lances who got the job. And Trent was usually right among them.

The regen cast was still on his leg, but there was very little pain now. He'd joined in the work detail when the recon units were pulled off the lines at dawn, and no one had said anything. It felt good to be contributing . . . like he really was part of the team now.

"All right, you goldbricks," Trent said loudly. "Time you got back into the war. Pascali, Strauss, I want your lances with me. Lieutenant Winters thinks she can bring down part of that damned cliff over there and block the monkey advance."

Slick bit his lip, worried. Warrant Officer Vandergraff and Dmowski's weapons lance had gone up there soon after dawn with the same idea. He'd seen Vandergraff and the medic. It sounded like a dangerous mission.

"Want me to take my bag of tricks along, Sarge?" Rostov asked cheerfully.

"No, Rostov," Trent said sarcastically. "I was figuring you'd bring down the rocks by showing them your ugly face!"

There was laughter. Trent held up his hand and went on. "Every man draw a pack of PX-90 in addition to regular kit. You won't need climbing gear this time. Vandergraff found a tunnel that comes out near where we're heading. Corporal Johnson, your lance stays here. Finish loading and get this ammo to the front lines ASAP. Then come back here. You're still in reserve until the L-T says different. Got it?"

"Yeah, Sarge," Johnson said.

"Oh, yeah. Don't forget to use the chameleon tarps on the Sandrays this time. Might make 'em a little harder to spot." Trent paused. "All right, get moving!"

"You vill stay here, nube," Strauss said. "Help load. Light duty gets you off of another mission, eh?"

Slick turned to face the stocky corporal. "If it's all the

same to you, Corp,'' he said evenly, ''I'll stay with the lance. The foot's not bothering me much now. I can fight.''

The corporal started to say something, then stopped and gave him a curt nod. ''Good. Draw your gear.''

For a long moment, Slick stared at him. It had almost seemed like there was a note of pride in Strauss's voice.

Rostov slapped him on the back. ''Come on, Grant. Let's get you kitted up.''

Slick followed him, his surprise and confusion stronger than ever.

It was the first time anyone in the lance had called him by name.

Fraser sat in the blockhouse staring at the holomap, alone with his fears.

Trent's unit had started for the top of the ridge a half an hour before, and the two APCs had finished loading and headed for the front a few minutes later. Now, except for the chatter on the commlink from the two ends of the pass, it was as if he'd been isolated from everyone, friend and enemy alike.

*We can't hold out without relief,* he thought bitterly. *Damn the Navy . . . damn Isayev. How could they let these men die?*

It would take a miracle to save the legionnaires now. Even if Trent managed to blast enough rock to block the south pass, it was only a matter of time until the inevitable breakthrough.

The legionnaires would die . . . and for what? Would they really buy enough time for the Marines to mop up Zhairhee? He'd seen the city, its defenses. The Marines would need more than a few hours to win a victory there.

And the legionnaires didn't have hours.

''HQ . . . HQ, this is Leader Four.'' The voice on the commlink sounded strained. A man at the breaking point. Fraser remembered the voice. Sergeant Baker had been wounded, but he refused to leave his post in command of Fourth Platoon. All he would say about his choice was ''I owe it to Sergeant Ghirghik.''

''Fraser here,'' he said, keying in the channel. ''Go ahead.''

''HQ . . . we've got another wave heading out your

way. Light infantry. Our hannie says they're the Mist-stalkers, whatever the hell that means.''

He remembered the conversation during the recon of Zhairhee. The Miststalkers were the elite commandos. They wouldn't be turned aside as easily as past attackers.

From things Myaighee had said later, after the recon, he suspected the Miststalkers were likely to use the same sort of tactics Trent had used to grab the pass in the first place. Once the hannies stopped focusing on the pass and started climbing the ridges, the legionnaires would be finished for sure.

''Any estimates on their speed, Sergeant Baker?'' he asked, surprised at how calm his voice stayed.

''They're moving cautiously, sir. Maybe an hour before they hit our lines . . . unless they can't take the firepower and turn back.''

''Don't count on it, Sergeant,'' Fraser said. ''I'll see what I can do. Keep me posted. Fraser out.''

*I'll see what I can do.* The phrase was empty. There was nothing he *could* do. The hannies were finally going to break through. They could expect to have their two forces united in another hour or two.

They could expect it . . .

He remembered Trent's words the night they'd come up the pass. ''I kind of like to give an enemy just what he's expecting . . . only not quite the way he's expecting it.''

Was there a way to use their advantage, to take them by surprise?

Before the transports had gone over, Trent had been talking about a last-ditch plan. Something about the tunnels. They could withdraw into the tunnels, of course, but that would only delay the inevitable. And once they pulled back, there'd be nothing to keep the hannies from using the pass to stop the Marine landing . . . or to renew the drive on Fwynzei.

What would Trent do? *If only I had him here to help me plan . . .*

But Trent was busy with his own problems now. It was up to Fraser to come up with the answer this time.

They had to find a way to draw the enemy into a trap . . . to keep the legionnaires out of harm's way long enough to get the Miststalkers onto a decent killing ground. If the commandos met no resistance, they probably wouldn't deploy on the ridgetops.

The tunnels would be useful only if they could be blocked or camouflaged.

Fans whirred outside as one of the APCs touched down. Corporal Johnson scrambled out and started toward the blockhouse. His uniform was a dusty grey-brown, to match the rocky cliffs around him.

Like the tarp that half-covered the APC.

Fraser stood up slowly, the idea finally jelling in his mind. There might be a way to stop the hannies after all . . . at least for a little while longer.


*"Asjyai!* We have spotted more demons on the ridge. Up there!"

Zyzyiig followed the soldier's gesture. Far up on the cliff, a few tall figures moved. Ky couldn't tell what they were doing.

"If they have any of their magic weapons, they could fire on us from there," the commander of the Blood-drinkers observed. "Perhaps we should pull back . . ."

"No withdrawal!" Zyzyiig screamed. "Not until we've destroyed them! Order the regiment to attack again. Once we are past the shoulder of the ridge, their weapons cannot touch us! Attack!"

The officer nodded to an aide. "What shall we do about them in the meantime, Honored?" ky asked carefully.

"Artillery will discourage them," Zyzyiig said, regaining control. "Turn the clifftop into dust if you have to."

"Yes, Honored."

The enemy lines were weakening now that their lone tank had been silenced. Soon the demons would give way, and the pass would be clear.

Soon . . .


Alarm sirens shattered the air. Shavvataaars crossed to a window of the headquarters building and trained a pocket-sized image intensifier on the moving dots circling slowly over the valley. The image swam into clear view. A Terran transport lighter . . . two . . . three. The Commonwealth reinforcements had arrived.

There was still a chance of victory, but it was growing

more slender with each passing moment. Shavvataaars tucked the magnifier into a pocket of his black robes and pondered for long minutes. Then, slowly, he turned from the window and crossed the room, his decision made.

It was time to leave the Dryiens to the hands of Fate. All he needed to do now was see that they mounted one last attack, to cover his escape from this wretched planet.

"Officer," he whispered as he opened the door. A Dryien staff officer looked up, hastily made a gesture of respect to the Ancient. "Officer, three demon skyships are approaching. If you have a stock of portable missile launchers available, you may yet drive them off. But you must act quickly."

The Dryien repeated the respectful salute and turned to kys radio equipment.

Shavvataaars felt the cold chill of satisfaction. This was one time that haste would pay off . . . at least for him.

Lieutenant Commander Wingate scanned the instrument readouts one last time and gave a nod to his Exec, Lieutenant Greene. "Make it 'Landing Stations,' Number One," he ordered crisply.

"Landing Stations, aye aye," Greene replied. The transport shuddered once and began to settle toward the water-covered surface of the *ylyn* paddy. Wingate glanced at Colonel Smythe-Henderson. The Marines would have a soggy time of it crossing that muck. *Glad I'm a Navy man, and not some miserable mudfoot,* he thought.

It was a daring move, grounding three light transports so close to an enemy garrison town. But the bulk of their fighting forces were concentrated around the pass. The hannies wouldn't catch him the way they'd caught *Ganymede.*

The ship shuddered again and the noise of the drives faded. "Down and safe," Greene reported. "Troop doors opening . . ."

"Targets! Targets!" a bridge crewman shouted. "Multiple missiles. They have a lock on us!"

"Countermeasures!" Wingate snapped.

"No good . . ." Greene looked up from his console. "No good, Skipper! I'm reading twelve missiles. They're going to—"

The Semti warheads tore through the bow of the transport, wrecking the bridge and spraying shrapnel through the forward troop bay. Over a hundred spacers and Marines died in the explosion, including Wingate and the Marine Colonel. It took Major Alvarez, the next in line of command, nearly an hour to restore order and reorganize the attack on Zhairhee.

Meanwhile, as the first column of smoke and fire coiled skyward from the stricken ship across the farmlands, the black-robed figure of the Semti agent watching from the edge of a causeway gave a cold, almost human nod.

"Incoming! Incoming!"

Kelly barely looked up as Corporal Pascali shouted the warning. They were so close to finishing. So close . . .

It had taken nearly an hour to get into position and get started setting the charges. The tunnel Vandergraff had found was part of the fortifications of the pass, leading from the valley floor not far from the still-smouldering wreck of the Sabertooth on the southern perimeter up to the very top of the south ridge. Stairs had been cut in the worst places, making it easy enough to haul the explosives up. They'd found some extra help near the top, Corporal Dmowski and three of the legionnaires from his weapons platoon. The two onagers in the unit were proving useful for carving holes in the rock where charges could be placed.

The first explosion was no more than fifty meters away, and Kelly worked faster. Two more detpacks to program and they'd be done.

"Come on, Lieutenant!" Trent shouted. "Get under cover, for God's sake!"

"Two more!" she shouted back.

Kelly sprinted to the next charge and dropped to one knee, checking the detpack carefully before she started to program it. Motion to her right made her glance up. It was Rostov, at the last of the PX-90 charges. He grinned and flashed her a thumb's up.

More shells shrieked overhead, a doomsday sound that made Kelly want to run. She forced herself to keep at it. A few last adjustments, and the ready light glowed.

Another blast, closer this time, showered her with dirt and splinters of rock. It made her think of Vandergraff.

She grabbed her pack and started to run for the tunnel mouth, crouching low.

A giant's fist slammed into her from behind, accompanied by an ear-shattering roar. She fell, banging her head. Her ears were ringing, and it took an effort of will just to focus on her surroundings and sit up.

Trent was shouting something, but she was having trouble hearing. Slowly she shook her head, trying to clear the fog, then winced as it throbbed in pain.

The sergeant ran toward her, as if in slow motion.

Then another explosion, barely ten meters from Trent. He was flung forward by the force of the blast, and lay still.

Rostov was beside her, lifting her up. "Can you move?" His voice was distant through the pain in her head. She gave a nod. "Then come on!"

He supported her, but she pushed him away. "Get the sergeant!" she shouted. "I can make it!"

Rostov nodded and ran to Trent's side. Somehow, she made it back to where the others were waiting, clustered near the mouth of the tunnel.

The legionnaire had to carry Trent back. Inside the cave, he lowered the sergeant to the floor. The other legionnaires pressed close, their faces sharing the same apprehension.

Feeling a little better, Kelly knelt beside Rostov to check Trent's pulse. It was thready, but strong enough. The sergeant's eyes opened, focusing slowly on Kelly.

"Glad . . . you made it . . ." he whispered weakly. "It's all . . . up to you now . . ."

He lost consciousness.

Outside, the shells were still falling, but they hardly registered. She held the sergeant's wrist in one hand, staring down at him.

He was right. It really was up to her now.

"They're falling back! The demons are falling back!"

The call swept through the ranks of the Regiment Blooddrinkers. Zyzyiig climbed to the top of a track and waved kys command baton in the air. "To the top!" ky shouted. "Forward to victory! Forward!"

Other voices took up his call, and soldiers surged up

the road eagerly. Engines roared as the armored vehicles lurched into motion.

It was an unstoppable tide. Success at last, despite hundreds of soldiers dead and wounded. The demons had fought like cornered beasts, but at last the Dryien army had broken their defenses. *Ky* had broken them.

"Honored! Honored, an urgent message from Zhairhee!"

"Forget Zhairhee," ky snapped at the aide who was waving from the ground.

"But Honored! They—"

"Forget them! Press on! We will take the demons!"

# Chapter 22

I have a rendezvous with Death
At some disputed barricade
                    —Legionnaire Alan Seeger
                    French Foreign Legion, 1916

Kelly Winters straightened up from beside Trent and gestured at the hulking Gwyrran near the tunnel mouth. "Bring the sergeant. We've got to get back from here so I can set off the charges." She picked up his rifle and slung it over one shoulder. He'd want it back.

"The hannies are breaking through down below!" Corporal Pascali called from further down the tunnel. "Watanabe's falling back on the blockhouse!"

"We'll be trapped up here!" one of Dmowski's men said.

"Just head for the other end and worry about it when we get there," Kelly ordered. "Rostov, you get the relay in place?"

"Yes, ma'am," the demo expert said. They needed a radio relay near the mouth of the tunnel so they could transmit the detonation signal. Rostov had left it to help finish wiring the detpacks. She hoped he hadn't missed something.

A glance at his determined features reassured her. Rostov came across as a joker with a wry sense of humor, but she could recognize competence when she saw it.

None of these legionnaires would miss anything important. Even the youngster, the one with the regen cast on one leg, looked ready for anything.

"Move out!" she ordered.

The climb down seemed even longer than the trip to the top. Finally, only a few meters from the lower entrance, she held up her hand to signal a stop. Pascali's lance was already lurking in the shadows by the mouth of the cave. Sounds of native gunfire were all too close. If the monkeys decided to lob a grenade in here now . . .

She pulled out a remote control and armed all the charges. "This is it," she said aloud and saw an answering nod from Rostov.

Her finger closed on the detonation switch. Thunder rolled endlessly from the ridgetop above them.

The track's gears ground as it steered past the rocky outcropping and started up the incline toward the crest of the pass. Zyzyiig was still on top of the vehicle, where the soldiers could see their *Asjyai*. Ky basked in the moment.

The demons couldn't hamper the Cleansing any more. Even Shavvataaars could not dispute kys victory this time.

Almost directly overhead there was a brilliant ripple of flashes and a thunder that seemed to echo on and on. The noise drowned out the sounds of the engines, the cheers of the soldiers. Heads swiveled upward, and terror seemed to spread over every face at once.

Zyzyiig followed their gaze and felt kys spines stiffen in fear.

No . . . it was not possible. Not at the very moment of victory!

With a rumble that grew stronger instead of weaker, tons of rock and dirt slid free of the cliff face.

Zyzyiig never felt the impact.

The ground shook until it seemed the tunnel was sure to collapse, and Slick dropped to his knees. Dust and loose earth showered the party. The rumble of the explosions and the falling rock outside lasted for a long time.

Then it was over. Slick could hear someone choking on the dust, and somehow the familiar sound was enough to make everything seem normal again.

Outside, the gunfire had stopped.

"The hannies are still out there," Pascali said. "A hell of a lot of them. But they seem to be confused. I think the blast must've done the job!"

Lieutenant Winters pushed past Slick and peered through the tunnel mouth. She was clutching Sergeant

Trent's FEK in one hand. "They won't stay surprised long. Another couple of minutes and they're going to start getting mad!" Her teeth gleamed bright in the darkness of the cavern. "Well, what are you apes waiting for? Let's show those little monkey bastards what the Legion can do!"

She sprang from the cave mouth, leveling the FEK and spraying fire at the nearest knot of hannie soldiers. In an instant the rest of the legionnaires were surging after her, Slick among them.

Natives whirled to face the sudden onslaught but died where they stood. Slick dropped to one knee behind a boulder and switched to full autofire, listing to the whine of the gauss fields as they hurled burst after burst of fléchette rounds. One hannie pointed an SMG straight at him, then toppled backward, torso shredding under the impact of dozens of needle rounds.

The surprise didn't last long. A hannie track made an awkward, clanking turn and rumbled toward the tunnel mouth, the cupola-mounted machine gun on top chattering death. Bullets slammed into the rock centimeters from Slick's head, making him duck back for cover. He rose up again to fire at the gunner.

The FEK whirred . . . out of ammo. His grenade magazine was empty, too.

Corporal Dmowski trotted past him, looking like a miniature tank himself in the head-to-foot plasteel armor he wore to protect himself from the heat of his onager. Dmowski's plasma rifle spoke twice in quick succession, and the plasma rounds punched through the cupola armor as if it was tissue paper. The hannie screamed and slumped sideways.

A native with one of their awkward-looking blunderbuss rocket launchers dived around the side of the track and fired. The rocket dipped low, skimming only centimeters from the ground. It caught Dmowski in the left leg. The corporal went down with blood spraying from the shattered stump of his leg.

For an instant, Slick had an image of Childers, the gunner who'd fallen the same way in the battle for the trenches outside Fort Monkey. He started forward . . .

Strauss pushed him aside and ran to Dmowski's side,

dropping his FEK as he ran and groping for the first aid kit at his belt.

The hannie with the blunderbuss raised kys weapon again, then pitched over as Kelly Winters fired from the far side of the tunnel. The other onager gunner, Chundra, hit the driver's compartment of the track.

Slick groped for a fresh magazine, but he was out. Cursing, he looked around again. Another armored vehicle was stopped dead in the road fifty meters past the wrecked track, but its turret was still working. The barrel of the big 138mm smoothbore cannon swung slowly across the battlefield, lining up with the tunnel mouth.

Chundra fired again, missed. Slick tried to scream a warning as a hatch banged open on the top of the track, but before the words came out a pair of monkeys had leapt on Chundra, slashing at him with knives. Despite his armor, Chundra was helpless. Slick saw blood where one of the hannies found a weakened joint.

Strauss started to drag Dmowski back toward the shelter of the rock. Slick leapt to help him.

A native rifle barked, seemingly right in his ear. Slick dived and rolled as the hannie soldier fired again from close range. The native must have used the cliff wall itself for cover.

The bullets passed so close Slick could feel their hot wind across his cheek. A second later, the hannie was down. Behind him Slick heard Rostov's yell. "Grant! The Corp's hit!"

He turned. Corporal Strauss was sprawled backward over Dmowski's body, unmoving. Slick crawled to him.

The corporal's eyes were wide, staring sightlessly at the sky. Red stained the front of his coverall, just above the chest armor. The bullet had caught him low in the neck. There was nothing Slick could do for him.

His probing fingers touched a broken length of chain around Strauss's neck. Slick drew it out. At the end dangled a small vial filled with dirt.

The dirt of all the dozens of worlds where Corporal Helmut Strauss had lost comrades fighting for the Legion mingled together in one small container.

Slick stared at the talisman, the battle suddenly far away.

\* \* \*

"Sir, Subaltern Watanabe on the line."

"Thanks, Griesch." Fraser plugged in the lead from the C³ pack to his helmet. "Alice One. Go ahead, Leader Two."

"HQ, we're falling back on the blockhouse," Watanabe said breathlessly. "There were just too damned many of them. I'm sorry, sir . . ."

Fraser looked around the cramped, darkened confines of the cave he shared with ten legionnaires. When the explosion down by the south pass had gone off, he'd thought the pressure would be off Watanabe. Apparently he'd assumed too much.

"Understood," he said grimly. "Are you in contact with Sergeant Trent's team?"

"Negative, HQ," Watanabe answered. There was a pause, the sound of gunfire over the radio. "The tunnel to the top of the cliff is cut off now, L-T. There's a hell of a lot of hannies between us and them. Even if they're alive, they're probably too heavily engaged to report."

Fraser didn't answer right away. Just as his plan was starting to look like it might work . . .

"Sir," Watanabe went on. "Sarge blocked the pass. There were just too many hannies already through for us to stop. I'm down to maybe twenty men here. If I just had some reinforcements, we could still break these bastards. They're shaky from being cut off."

At least Trent's party had cut the pass. *Damn! If Watanabe had only held a few minutes longer* . . .

The Miststalkers were still advancing carefully, but they'd be past the old perimeter positions in another five minutes if they continued at their present rate. All the legionnaires had withdrawn from the pass now, taking shelter in several tunnels and caves above the northern side of the pass. Everything was carefully prepared for the hannies. This could ruin the entire plan.

Or would it? If the troops facing Watanabe were as shaky as he claimed . . .

"Listen to me, Sub," he said slowly. "Stop trying to hold the hannies on your end. Pull back out of their way. Defend yourself if you have to, but give them an easy way through the pass."

"Sir? Won't that drop them in your laps?"

Fraser grinned. "That's precisely what I'm hoping,

Sub. When I give the word, close in behind them with everything you've got left.''

"Affirmative, HQ. We'll do our best."

"I know you will, Sub. Fraser clear."

He was already trying to hand the Miststalkers the appearance of an easy victory. What could clinch it better than to see their friends from the south already surging through the pass?

He bit his lip and looked at the handful of legionnaires around him. If he miscalculated, a few more hannies wouldn't make much difference, anyway.

The roar of an explosion yanked Slick back to reality. He dropped Strauss's vial and threw himself flat as the cliff wall above the tunnel erupted in a shower of rock and flying dirt. Over the sound of the battle he heard Rostov's voice shouting "Get clear! Get clear of the tunnel!"

The native tank rumbled closer, the barrel of its cannon depressing for another shot. With Dmowski dead and Chundra still trying to shake off the hannies slashing and stabbing at him, there was nothing left that could stop that armored beast.

Nothing left to save the unit . . .

Something bulky and angular prodded Slick's thigh. His hand closed around it. Dmowski's onager, still linked to the gunner by its ConRig targeting harness.

Slick looked up at the tank. Nothing left.

Fumbling with the unfamiliar fittings of the weapon, Slick unhooked the cable that tied the onager to Dmowski's helmet, then freed the harness clasps and raised the awkward plasma rifle. He remembered the lectures on onagers in training back on Devereaux.

They were designed to be used with an aiming system tied to the movement of the operator's eyes, but a plasma rifle could be used without the ConRig, especially against a target as big as a tank.

Of course, the heat buildup of the weapon was enough to badly burn an unarmed man, but the first few shots wouldn't be too bad . . .

And the legionnaires needed him now. Slick wasn't going to let the team down. Not this time.

He braced the weapon as well as he could and touched

the firing stud. Heat washed over his hands and arms, and the onager bucked wildly.

Without waiting to see the effect of the shot he fired again . . . and again.

Pain seared him, but Slick hardly noticed it. He squinted through the heat shimmer, saw the tank's turret leaking smoke. A machine gun flashed from the hull and he fired one more time.

Then the real pain hit, agony shooting up his arms. The onager fell, and Slick sagged to the ground.

Through a haze of shock Slick made out Rostov bending over him, heard the demo man's voice as if from kilometers away. "Don't worry, Grant. You got the bastards. The rest are running . . ."

"Not . . . not Grant," Slick whispered.

"Don't try to talk, Grant," someone else said.

"Not Grant . . ." he repeated. It was important . . . vital that he tell them. "Slick . . . call me Slick . . ."

He wanted his family to know his name.


Fraser lifted the edge of the tarp carefully and peered through. The vanguard of the native force was already well past the cave, close to the gap where the valley widened at the top of the pass. In another minute, the hannies would be at the blockhouse . . . and it would be time to spring the trap.

He only hoped he had set it right. The way Sergeant Trent would have.

The natives passing by now were drawn up in a close formation, like a column on a parade march. That much had gone well, at least. The vanguard had advanced in a loose skirmishing formation, moving from cover to cover, ready for the first sign of resistance. When none had materialized, though, their vigilance had started to relax.

No doubt the slackening sounds of battle from the south were giving them some confidence. They probably imagined that the demons had already been overcome by the troops from Zhairhee.

*Give them what they expect . . . but not the way they expect it.* He hoped he'd be able to tell Trent how he'd put those words into practice. If either of them was alive after today.

Even if they savaged the Miststalkers, there were still

a lot of hannies on the north side of the mountains, and after this battle Fraser knew his battered legionnaires wouldn't be able to fight again. But at least they'd bloody the enemy's elite before they went down.

Maybe the last stand of Bravo Company in the Zhairhee Pass would go down in the annals alongside such Legion hallmarks as Camerone and Ganymede and Devereaux . . . lost causes that still shed luster on the Legion.

These men deserved to be remembered in such company.

"Alice One, this is Lookout." That was Myaighee's voice in his headphones. The little alien had volunteered for the most hazardous job of all. Lying sprawled in an uncomfortable position near the final barricade, with gear scavenged from a dead Dryien soldier and kys hair matted with blood from a cut Legionnaire Donovan had made in kys scalp. Myaighee was pretending to be a casualty so that Fraser's men would have a spotter in position to watch the enemy's progress into the valley.

Ky would be in almost as much danger from friendly fire as from the Dryiens when the shooting started, but Myaighee hadn't flinched. "I am the only one who can be safe, Honored," ky had said. "One of your men might be bayoneted . . . just to be sure he was dead."

"Lookout, go ahead."

"A soldier is approaching the blockhouse . . . two of them now." There was a pause. Myaighee's voice crackled with excitement as ky spoke again. "I see more soldiers coming from the south! They are coming! Miststalkers have seen them!"

Through the heavy material of the tarp, Fraser could hear the unearthly cheering, the enthusiasm. He nodded to Corporal Johnson. "Now!"

Johnson stabbed at the remote control in his hand savagely.

Out in the valley, the last twenty Galahad antipersonnel mines in the company's arsenal went off almost as one—not just a single round at a time, but all the charges in quick succession.

Legionnaire Griesch ripped away the tarp and the rest poured out into the morning sunlight, their FEKs spitting death.

Fraser's weapon swung easily in his arms, tracking across the dense-packed mass of enemy troops. The confusion was complete. Some of them were still cheering, still trying to press forward in a rush to meet their friends from the south. Others, reacting faster, tried to find their assailants, but too late. From half a dozen tunnel mouths the legionnaires charged, the whine of their guns echoing in the pass like a swarm of enraged insects.

And hannies died from their deadly stings.

"Hammer them! Hammer them!" Fraser looked up to see the big Greek from New Cyprus, Karatsolis, wielding an MEK with the same glee he'd once reserved for his Sabertooth's plasma cannon. The man's crewmate, Corporal Bashar, waved a hand over his head and urged a handful of legionnaires to the attack.

They weren't just firing from cover this time. The legionnaires rushed forward, eager to get to grips with the enemy. And that compounded the confusion, as Fraser had hoped. The hannies were killing almost as many of their own soldiers as the legionnaires were bringing down with FEK fire.

Baker, the sergeant with the injured legs, shouted to two of his men. They dragged him forward and helped him set up behind a boulder. He tossed a native grenade into a cluster of hannies, then another. He yelled a harsh battle cry he could only have learned from the Ubrenfar, Ghirghik. A hannie bullet took him in the face, pitching him back, but another legionnaire killed the native and snatched up the grenades. The fighting went on.

And farther up the pass, beyond the killing field where the Galahads had torn through the front ranks of the hannies forces, more shouts announced the coming of Watanabe's men.

The hannies wavered. Good as they were, the Mist-stalkers weren't prepared for this onslaught. Some fought and died. Many more broke, throwing away weapons and equipment and running back down the pass.

Those who could escape the wrath of the Legion.

Terran figures topped the crest of the hill . . . Watanabe, slender and pale, grinning and flashing a "V-for-Victory" sign. Garcia, her helmet gone, her dark hair streaming in the breeze, carrying a native blunderbuss. Kelly Winters and a handful of the recon troops from

Trent's force. More legionnaires closed in behind them, even Ramirez and the Padre, unlikely soldiers with FEKs and grenades tucked into their pockets and dangling from their belts.

The Legion had held.

Johnson caught his arm. "Lieutenant! Listen!"

He pulled off his helmet to hear better. Sounds of gunfire rose from the bottom of the north pass, carried on the wind. Gunfire, heavy machinery, shouting . . . and something else . . .

"Goddamn!" Griesch said. "Not another monkey attack!"

"We can't hold them this time," Johnson said. "No ammo left."

"We've got our knives," Bashar put in grimly.

"Wait!" Fraser held up his hand. "Quiet!"

He strained his ears, and a smile spread over his face. "Don't you hear it? The music?"

Some of them were looking at him as if he'd lost his mind, but Karatsolis was smiling now too. He'd heard the mournful fanfare drifting on the breeze.

*"Le Boudin"* . . . the age-old marching song of the Foreign Legion.

Shavvataaars tightened his harness and slapped the automated launch sequence control on the courier ship's main console. Drives cycled, and the ship stirred with barely a whisper of sound.

The boat lifted off, out of the concealment of a *ylyn* paddy east of Zhairhee, and hurtled skyward.

Below, on the surface of the planet the Terrans called Hanuman, Twilight Prowler lay in disarray. The ephemerals had failed.

From the moment Zyzyiig allowed kyself to be killed, the Great Journey had gone wrong. Nothing could put it back together now. The rising in Vyujiid, the Ubrenfar intervention . . . lost now, with the failure to defeat the Terrans and their Foreign Legion.

At least Hanuman would tie up extra resources, troops the Commonwealth had wanted on Enkidu and elsewhere on the frontier. And Shavvataaars was free. He would leave this hellworld behind and take passage with the

Ubrenfar warships when their carriership returned for them.

Shavvataaars was patient as only a Semti could be. He would wait . . . and he would plan.

And some day he would see the Terrans defeated.

The command van grounded beside the blockhouse with a triumphant flourish of roaring fans and a swirl of dust. The rear door opened slowly, as if with a conscious sense of drama.

Fraser drew himself to attention and saluted Commandant Isayev as he stepped onto the ramp, holding the pose until the older officer returned it crisply.

The Fwynzei garrison had attacked the Dryiens in force, catching them off-guard at the height of the Miststalker assault. Already disorganized, with morale low from successive reverses at the pass, their supply situation worsening and their leadership out of touch with the headquarters in Zhairhee, the hannie army north of the mountains had fallen apart at the first touch of the Commonwealth counterthrust.

Now, an hour after that desperate last fight, Bravo Company was being relieved.

Isayev's eyes wandered over the valley, still littered with bodies and abandoned equipment. They came to rest on the shrunken ranks of Fraser's command, no more than fifty men and women still on their feet after the savage day's fighting. There were more alive, of course, the ones already being loaded aboard medical vans for the trip to Fwynzei. Like Gunnery Sergeant Trent, and Myaighee, the native.

But the unit had suffered over seventy percent casualties since the first attack on Fort Monkey. The survivors were ragged scarecrows, hardly able to walk.

Yet they stood in ranks proudly, soldiers of the Legion to the last.

"A good job, Fraser," Isayev said slowly. "A damned good job. You've done the Legion proud."

"Not me, Commandant," he said. He gestured at the others. "They're the ones who did it."

The commandant didn't seem to hear him. "That bastard Smythe-Henderson ordered us to sit tight, stay on the defensive. Said he'd relieve you. But we couldn't just sit still when we heard him changing the plans." His eyes locked with Fraser's. "I just wish we could have broken through sooner."

Fraser shook his head. "It didn't matter, Commandant. I think they all knew you'd come, somehow. They knew the Legion would take care of its own."

# Epilogue

It's our captain who remembers us, and counts his dead.
—Captain de Borelli, Tuyen Quang
French Foreign Legion, 1885

The streets of Fwynzei were a riot of color as the parade made its way down the streets toward the Commonwealth Spaceport. Hannies and humans mingled in an enthusiastic throng, shouting encouragement and tossing flowers.

At the rear of the long column of soldiers and Marines, marching to the slow beat of eighty-eight paces per minute, came the soldiers of the Third Battalion, First Light Infantry Regiment of the Fifth Foreign Legion. And leading the legionnaires, in the position of honor, marched Bravo Company.

Captain Colin Fraser stood next to Commandant Isayev on the review stand, watching the parade march past. His stiff dress uniform with black kepi and heavy epaulets felt heavy and uncomfortable; he would have preferred the issue battledress he'd worn through the long march from Fort Monkey. But the people of Fwynzei demanded a show from the soldiers setting out to restore order in Dryienjaiyeel.

In the three months since the Battle of Zhairhee Pass the Dryiens had fallen into virtual anarchy, with coups and countercoups and a state verging on civil war. With the arrival of fresh Colonial Army troops aboard the Carriership *Nestor*, the Commonwealth was ready at last to return to the war-torn country.

Fort Monkey would be reoccupied and expanded . . . and it was only proper that soldiers of the Foreign Legion—soldiers of Bravo Company—should be among those who led the return.

And Colin Fraser, still hardly daring to believe his promotion and confirmation as commander of the unit, would be leading them on this new campaign.

From the reviewing stand he could see their faces. Most were unfamiliar, fresh drafts from Devereaux to bring the unit back up to strength. But there were plenty he recognized, too.

Gunnery Sergeant Trent, for instance, recovered from a long battery of regen treatments and looking as stolid and unemotional as ever . . . and Subaltern Watanabe, who sported a ragged scar over one eye and a decoration for bravery on his breast.

He caught sight of Second Platoon's recon lance, the towering Gwyrran Vrurrth, the fresh-faced young legionnaire second class named Grant, and Dmitri Rostov, sporting corporal's stripes on his dun-colored uniform. And Myaighee, now a legionnaire third class in the same lance. Ky had enlisted even knowing that Dryienjaiyeel might be safe to return to as a civilian. The alien had adopted the Legion as a home.

As had Kelly Winters. After the battle, she had come to him for advice; the way the Navy had abandoned them at the pass had convinced her that it was no place for her. Now Kelly Ann Winters, CSN, was listed as dead in the fighting . . . but Ann Kelly, Warrant Officer Fourth Class, would be accompanying the Legion as an expert on combat engineering. It was a bit of deception Fraser—and Isayev—had been glad to connive in. The Legion looked after its own, and Kelly had proven herself as much a legionnaire as any of them.

The last of Bravo Company went by, followed by the rest of the newly-designated Demi-Battalion Beatrice. Fraser turned to the commandant and saluted sharply.

"Permission to join my unit, sir?"

"Permission granted, Captain Fraser," Isayev replied, returning the salute.

Fraser gestured to Legionnaire Garcia. "Let's go."

An open-topped floatcar hovered on magrep fields behind the stand, waiting for him. Legionnaire Karatsolis held the door open for Fraser and Garcia, then slid into the passenger seat next to Corporal Bashar. Their full dress uniforms were perfectly tailored, impeccably clean, but the men look just the same as ever.

They were legionnaires first . . . always.

And Captain Colin Fraser was one of them.

THE END

# Glossary

**adchip:** Short for "adhesive chip," any of the button-sized minicomputers designed to hook directly into the human nervous system for total sensory interaction. A cheap alternative to computer implants.

**ale:** Slang for "alien"; applied to any nonhuman.

*Asjyai:* Military title in Dryienjaiyeel; roughly translates as "chief of staff."

**Battalion:** Military formation which, in Commonwealth usage, fields 6–9 companies under the command of a commandant or major. Three or more battalions form a regiment.

**blunderbuss:** Bazooka-like rocket launcher employed by the hannies, so named for its bell-shaped muzzle.

**C³:** Command, control, and communication, used in referring to specialist technicians, to the computer/commo packs they carry and operate, or the larger control centers in bases or vehicles where these operations are performed. Also "C-cubed."

**Camerone-class lighters:** Standard unarmed battalion-level transports employed by the Fifth Foreign Legion. Names are based on famous Legion battles (Camerone, Ganymede, Devereaux, Tuyen Quang, Somme, Ankh-'Qwar, etc).

**cargomod:** "Cargo module," a standard shipping container used for transporting shipboard cargos. Also slang, the equivalent of "crate."

**carriership:** Generic term for the multi-million-ton FTL ships used by the Commonwealth and other interstellar cultures, so called because they are used to carry large numbers of interplanetary vessels from one system to another. Requiring the computing power of a full artificially intelligent computer to handle the intricacies of interstellar navigation, carrierships are imbued with distinctive computer personalities. These carry the names of famous philosophers or wise counselors from history and mythology. Breaking with usual navy traditions, the computers and the ships are both referred to by using masculine pronouns.

**CEK:** *(Cannon d'Énergie Kinetique)* vehicle mounted autocannon.

**Colonial Army:** The military arm of the Commonwealth employed to defend and extend the Colonies. Unlike the regular Terran Army, the Colonial Army is raised entirely from the Colonies, generally as part of each planet's own Planetary Armed Forces. A few designated regiments of each of these PAFs will then be assigned to Colonial Army service, seeing duty on worlds other than their home planet (usually in the Conclave Sphere or along the frontier of Commonwealth space).

**commandant:** Commonwealth military officer commanding a battalion; equivalent to the rank of major.

**commlink:** Radio with a range of roughly 250 km, mounted in combat helmets or on vehicles.

**company:** Smallest independently fielded fighting unit of the Terran Commonwealth. A standard Light Infantry company of the Fifth Foreign Legion comprises three platoons plus a command lance of five (CO, Exec, Company NCO, and two $C^3$ technicians), as well as any attached personnel such as warrant officers, transport units, sappers, etc. Typically a company will contain 109 officers and men.

**ConRig:** Control harness which governs onager-aiming in conjunction with helmet HUD sights.

**demi-battalion:** An ad hoc formation of two or more companies, usually commanded by the senior company commander present. Demi-battalions are frequently fielded for long-term detached operations where a full battalion may not be appropriate or available.

**detpack:** A programmable detonator system used with PX-90 explosives. The operator may select remote, timed, or conditional detonation; without programming, the detpack/explosive combination is completely safe.

**Devereaux:** Frontier world, attacked 2729 by a Semti invasion fleet. Site of the heroic Fourth Foreign Legion resistance to an eight-month siege, which saw the destruction of that Legion as an effective fighting force.

Now the homeworld of the Fifth Foreign Legion and site of its extensive training facilities.

**dwyk:** Unit of time on Hanuman. Ten dwyk is roughly fifteen minutes.

**Fabrique Europa:** Prominent Terran manufacturer of small arms, headquartered in Brussels. The company supplies such well-known weapons systems as the FE-FEK/27 kinetic energy rifle, the FE-MEK/15 kinetic energy assault gun, and the FE-PLF rocket pistol, all in use with the Fifth Foreign Legion.

**Fafnir:** Man-portable rocket launcher issued on a section level to the Fifth Foreign Legion. The Fafnir rocket is "smart" (able to discriminate various target silhouettes preprogrammed by the operator) and is equally proficient in antitank and air-defense roles.

**FE-FEK/27 (Fusil d'Énergie Kinetique Model 27):** Kinetic energy rifle manufactured by Fabrique Europa, standard longarm of the Fifth Foreign Legion.

**FE-MEK/15 (Mitrailleuse d'Énergie Kinetique Model 15):** Kinetic energy assault gun manufactured by Fabrique Europa, the standard lance-level support weapon used by the Fifth Foreign Legion.

**FE-PLF (Pistolet Lance-Fusée):** 10mm rocket pistol manufactured by Fabrique Europa, a popular sidearm with officers of the Fifth Foreign Legion.

**floatcar:** An open-topped magnetic suspension vehicle used in both civilian and military applications. A staff car or jeep.

**Fwynzei:** Island enclave ceded by Vyujiid to the Commonwealth. The enclave is garrisoned by a reinforced battalion of the Fifth Foreign Legion (two companies were later detached to develop the trading post at Monkeyville) plus native auxiliary regiments, and is home to the Commonwealth's resident-general, diplomatic and Colonial Administration personnel, and several large trading concerns.

**Galahad:** M46 anti-personnel mine. The open-topped tube contains ten separate egg-shaped bomblets loaded with shrapnel, and sensor gear that triggers the mine when a living creature comes within 10 meters—unless it is wearing a Legion helmet with working IFF gear. Galahads are safe to friendly personnel, but lethal to anyone else.

**Grendel:** Large vehicle-mounted missile found on the Sabertooth FSV.

**hannie:** Slang term for the natives of Hanuman, applied by Terrans. Considered derogatory, but by no means as bad as "monkey," the other popular label.

**Hanuman:** Fourth planet of Morrison's Star, a former Semti subject. Now a client of the Commonwealth.

**lance:** Designation of the Commonwealth's basic military unit, either five infantrymen or a single tank or aircraft.

**legionnaire:** Loosely, a member of the Fifth Foreign Legion (or any other "Legion" in the army, if there are such). Specifically, an enlisted soldier holding the rank of legionnaire first class, legionnaire second class, or legionnaire third class. Non-Legion units use the designation "soldier" instead of legionnaire.

**lighter:** Generic name applied to the small transports used for the bulk of ground-to-orbit transport. Lighters are grav-powered ships with a fair-sized cargo capacity, and generally run in the five to ten thousand ton displacement range. They are slower and less maneuverable than scramjet shuttles and other boats, but compensate for this by their superior loads. In Legion parlance, a "lighter" almost invariably refers to the 10,000-ton transports which can carry several companies of legionnaires and their equipment from ground to orbit or between any two ground bases. Lighters are usually unarmed, though this is not always true.

**loke:** Slang for "local"; applied to a native nonhuman.

**magger:** Anyone who operates an MSV; a tank or APC crewman.

**mag:** Slang derived from magnetic suspension technology, meaning "move." To "mag out" is to "move out" or "bug out"; a "mag-out" is a hasty departure.

**magrep module:** Small semicircular projection unit (linked to a generator) that produces a magnetic suspension cushion.

**magnetic suspension cushion:** Effect produced by the interplay of a magnetic repulsion generator and a planetary magnetic field. The cushion allows a vehicle to float up to a meter away from any semi-solid surface, providing a magnetic field is present to interact with the vehicle-mounted generator. The effect is much more powerful (and infinitely quieter) than an air-cushion, allowing really massive vehicles to be moved fairly easily by turbofans (or, occasionally, fusion airjets). However, the cushion does not function effectively over extremely rugged terrain or allow the vehicle to "fly."

**magnetic suspension vehicle (MSV):** Official designation of any vehicle operating on a magnetic suspension cushion.

**Mark 18 Mjollnir KEC:** A heavy kinetic energy weapon found in a vehicle mount aboard Sabertooth and Sandray class vehicles. It is the kinetic energy weapon equivalent of a contemporary Vulcan gatling cannon, with an extremely high rate of fire and muzzle velocities that will defeat almost any type of conventional armor.

**murphy:** Any unforeseen and potentially catastrophic occurrence.

**nube:** A newcomer or rookie.

**onager (fusil d'onage; storm rifle):** Plasma gun, originally invented during the French Imperial period (hence the French-derived name). The onager is one of the standard section-level heavy weapons used by the Fifth Foreign Legion (the other is the Fafnir rocket launcher). Onagers require soldiers to wear fairly cumbersome body armor to protect them from heat effects, but are devastatingly powerful on the battlefield. A larger version of the weapon, the onager cannon, is found in a turret mount on the Sabertooth FSV.

**platoon:** Basic tactical unit of the Commonwealth's ground forces, containing either six tanks, thirteen APCs, or two infantry sections plus a sublieutenant as platoon leader and a platoon sergeant as unit NCO (for a total of 34 men).

**platoon sergeant:** NCO rank equivalent to the contemporary USA rank of staff sergeant. Serves as platoon XO.

**primmie:** Commonwealth slang for "primitive."

**PX-90:** Explosive compound, packaged in 1-kg blocks. The explosive is a high-tech version of plastique used with a detpack programmable detonator. PX-90 has both military and engineering applications.

**ra-pack:** Ration pack; the twenty-ninth century equivalent to an MRE.

**regen therapy:** Advanced medical technique for regrowth of damaged tissue.

**resident-general:** Colonial Administration official appointed as administrative head of Terran interests on a Client World. Unlike governors, resident-generals have little direct influence over local governmental affairs; their job is to administer and look after the Terrans who live or work on the planet. In fact, though, the resident-general's control of Commonwealth trade and Colonial Army garrisons gives him a tremendous ability to influence native rulers.

**rezplex:** A residential complex.

**Sabertooth (M-980 FSV):** Company-level Fire Support Vehicle employed by the Fifth Foreign Legion, mounting 2 Grendel missiles, an onager cannon in a turret, and a fixed-forward kinetic energy cannon. It can carry up to 6 men plus a crew of two. Typically, a company mounted on 13 vehicles will include two Sabertooths.

**Sandray (M-786 series):** Generic name for an entire family of armored personnel carriers and specialty variants used by the Fifth Foreign Legion. Typical vehicles include an APC, a command van, an engineering vehicle, a supply carrier, a medical van, and so on. They carry six men plus a specialty compartment (except the APC, which carries twelve men). Many of them mount kinetic energy cannons in a remote-controlled turret; the engineering vehicle mounts a low-power laser cannon and various types of engineering hardware such as bulldozer blades or cranes.

**savkey:** A retreat, derived from French "sauve qui peut."

**section:** Designation for an infantry unit containing three lances, plus a sergeant as section leader. The section thus contains sixteen men.

**Semti:** An alien race, formerly rulers of the Semti Conclave but now subject (for the most part) to the Terran Commonwealth. Evolved from scavenger stock, they are bilaterally symmetrical, upright bipeds, basically humanoid in appearance but with dry, leathery skins and large eyes. They apparently evolved in desert conditions under a K or M class star, and frequently shroud themselves in dark robes when visiting planets around more energetic stars. Their voices are soft and whispery.

The Semti have been civilized for many thousands of years, and have a rich civilization full of tradition and high culture. Unfortunately, they also are rather disgusting to humans (thanks to a carrion stink on their breaths and their cold, clammy skin), frequently earning such appellations as "ghoul" or "zombie." Their ruthless pragmatism brought them into direct conflict with Terra during the Semti War, in which they lost control of the two hundred-world empire known as the Semti Conclave.

An aptitude for administration has made them an invaluable part of the post-war Commonwealth administrative system, despite their place as former enemies, and despite the distaste they generate on a personal level. Having a Semti mandarin on one's staff is considered to be the height of status within the Colonial Administration; they can do the work it would take a hundred human bureaucrats to accomplish.

Semti philosophy is extremely alien to human thought. They are very long-lived, and "taking the long view" can, for a Semti, involve many centuries. For example, the Semti showed no particular ill-feeling at the loss of their empire, and they work tirelessly at their jobs helping humans govern the same territory "because that is our function in life." Once humans could accept this attitude, they welcomed the Semti with open arms.

**Semti Conclave:** Interstellar state, now disbanded, lying to coreward of the Terran Commonwealth. The Semti Conclave was dominated by the Semti, who were able to administer approximately 200 planets and perhaps 125 separate races in a stable government which had survived almost unchanged over a span of several thousand years at least. Semti policy was to discourage technological or social change and maintain an iron grip over individual civilizations through the manipulation of local religions, rulers, and institutions. Though they had a reputation for excellent government, the Semti proved quite capable of taking whatever measures they deemed necessary—even genocide—to maintain control over members of the Conclave.

The Conclave collapsed after the destruction of the Semti capital at the hands of the Terran Commonwealth in 2744. Since that time the Conclave Sphere has been a wide-open colonial frontier over which the Commonwealth and other interstellar powers have extended their control.

**subaltern:** Lowest officer rank, commanding a platoon. Commonly "sub."

**systerm:** "System Terminal," the major port facilities used for carriership operations near the fringe of a star system.

**Terran Commonwealth:** The human interstellar state that fields the Fifth Foreign Legion. Following the Semti War, the Commonwealth acquired virtual control over most of the Conclave Sphere, and thus become a colonial power in the old (nineteenth century) sense of the term.

**Toeljuk:** Alien race, another of the colonial powers exploiting former Semti space. The Toeljuks are a squat, low-grav race with tentacles. They have a reputation for brutality and greed.

**Ubrenfars:** A saurian race with a growing empire along the fringe of the former Semti sphere. The Ubrenfars contributed to the downfall of the Conclave, which was engaged in a campaign to subdue them when the Terrans declared war. They are now widely considered to be the chief rivals for dominance in interstellar affairs. Heavily caste-oriented, the Ubrenfars field a dedicated and highly skilled military force.

**Vyujiid:** Nation dominating the northern hemisphere of Hanuman. Remnant of a former empire, Vyujiid is the most civilized of the nations on Hanuman and the main point of Commonwealth penetration on the world.

**warrant officer:** A specialist officer in the Colonial Army, not in the regular chain of command but with many of the privileges and responsibilities of regular officers. There are four grades (WO/1 through WO/4); a WO/4 is equivalent to a sublieutenant and is found on a company staff. Ability as a warrant officer frequently leads to a full officer's commission. Typical specialties include medical, chaplain, sciences, intel/alien technologies, combat engineering, and others. Note that other branches of the armed forces do not use this system.

**Whitney-Sykes HPLR-55 (High-Power Laser Rifle Mark 55):** A laser rifle manufactured by the Australian small-arms company Whitney-Sykes, commonly used as a sniper's rifle by the Fifth Foreign Legion.

**Wristpiece:** A computer terminal worn on the wrist and forearm. The wristpiece is now becoming largely obsolete on Terra (where computer implants are the cutting edge of technology), but are still quite common off Terra. They can perform a wide variety of functions, including calculation, data storage/retrieval, translation, and other jobs. Some are designed to link to implants or adchips worn by the operator, while others are voice-activated with a remote radio receiver worn behind the ear.

Commonly known as a "piece."

*yiiz:* Standard kyendyp unit of measurement, equal to about 1.76 kilograms.

*Yzyeel: Kyendyp* word, translated roughly as "king." The ruler of Dryienjaiyeel.

*zymlat:* Beast of burden used on Hanuman.

# SENSATIONAL SCIENCE FICTION

If you and/or a friend would like to receive the *ROC Advance*, a bimonthly newsletter featuring all the newest and hottest ROC books and authors, on a complimentary basis, please fill out this form and return it to:

**ROC Books/Penguin USA**
375 Hudson Street
New York, NY 10014


Your Address
Name _____
Street _____ Apt. # _____
City _____ State _____ Zip _____

Friend's Address
Name _____
Street _____ Apt. # _____
City _____ State _____ Zip _____